LOADED

B. E. BAKER

EASTON

For years, I've been the only person making decisions for Sacrifice Nothing. Every single major decision I made would keep me up at night. After I went public, I actually looked forward to having a board. What could be better than having a whole team of experts in the business world, all of them working with me to make Sacrifice Nothing the best luxury brand in America?

It was a dream, basically.

Or at least, that's what I thought, because I'm a moron.

"The profits from the Vicenzo Imbruglia line have held strong," Mr. Jimenez says. "And the men's watches are also outperforming the projections."

"The evening jackets have done very well," Mrs. Yaltzinger says. "But not by as much as the grooming kits."

"You're all saying good things," I say. "So why does it sound like you're complaining?"

"This company went public six months ago," Mr. Dressel says. "And you brought us in just after, along with one of the best pots of money from any IPO last year. You did all that so that Sacrifice Nothing could really take off." He frowns. "And yet, our profits have simply. . ." He shrugs. "Risen a little."

I blink. "I'm sorry—twenty-five percent in two quarters isn't meteoric, but it's a far cry from—"

Mrs. Yaltzinger runs a hand through her hair. "Sure. The market as a whole has declined, and we've turned a profit. No one's upset, but we still think, as we did when we first came in, that we need to launch a women's line."

I blink. "Vincenzo doesn't do women's shoes."

Sometimes I wonder why someone who clearly has no interest in fashion is sitting on our board, but Mrs. Yaltzinger is a professor at Harvard Business School, so I suppose that's something. "If you'd rather, we can start with watches, then, or professional wear. Our concern is that you've been ignoring half the population. Think what kind of gains we could have if we were also serving the other half of the professionals and wealthy socialites—"

Now it's my turn to be annoyed. "How do you think I've managed to create six separate lines of products that have all turned consistent profits with relatively minimal expenditures in the last six and a half years?"

"Celebrity support?" Mr. Dressel's borderline obsessed with celebrity attention, and I'm beginning to think my endorsements are the only reason he joined the board.

"Scarcity?" Mr. Jimenez is the only person on my board without a fancy degree. He has started and subsequently sold six very successful startups in different sectors, so his input is usually just a little different. "That's what makes your products consistently sell out.

People have to pay full price or they won't get them at all."

They're smart people, but they don't get it, not really. "Have you ever heard of *Undercover Billionaire?*"

The board blinks. A dozen of them, and no one has any idea what I'm talking about.

"It's a reality show that started in 2019 with a billionaire named Glenn Stearns. He was dropped into a small town with a hundred bucks, a car, and a tank of gas. He was tasked to turn that into a million-dollar business in under ninety days."

Mr. Jimenez frowns. Mrs. Yaltzinger arches one eyebrow. Mr. Dressel clears his throat. The others shift in their seats and grunt or scrunch their noses.

Clearly none of them would have taken that gamble.

They're smart people, but other than Mr. Jimenez, they aren't entrepreneurs. They don't *create*. They've been trained to *add value*.

"This particular man did do it—can you guess how?"

Still, blank stares.

"It was not in any way related to the way he turned his first million when he started out. That had, in fact, taken him quite a bit longer than ninety days, but he had learned something valuable in his years of business."

Still no one has input. My board is useless.

"What he did was start a barbecue joint that had live music. He knew nothing about barbecue, and that wasn't even his first venture. He turned the hundred bucks into seed money by selling used tires on the side of the road at first. But once he had startup capital, the barbecue joint is where he went next." I smile, because I'm about to connect the dots for them. "Why did Glenn Stearns start a barbecue? Because he kept his eyes open while selling used tires and he noticed something about the area. He didn't develop a product and then market it." I shake my head. "That's what almost every business person does, but it's really a fool's errand. No, Mr. Stearns identified a need, and once he had done that, he crafted the perfect solution for an existing problem. People there wanted live music, and they needed a good barbecue place. The last one had closed."

Mrs. Yaltzinger says, "You're saying that your men's line does well because you've identified needs and are filling them."

I nod slowly. "Do you know how I started? My first product was designer shoes that were also comfortable. I knew it was possible, because my first pair of designer shoes were so comfortable that I couldn't bring myself to replace them. In desperation, after the soles wore out, I took them to a cobbler."

Mr. Dressel's always the most impatient of the bunch. "We've humored the storytelling, but the point is—"

"The cobbler tried to kick me out of his shop." I lean closer, bracing my hands against the conference table. "He said to throw my shoes away."

"But you didn't?" Mrs. Yaltzinger's getting it, finally.

"I had just graduated from business school," I say. "I needed an *idea*, and I was flipping through them, casting off one bad idea after another. I mean, for designer shoes, you'd need a *designer,* right?" I smile. "My shoes—Vincenzo Imbruglia's—couldn't be replaced because after the poor man took his family on vacation, there was an accident in which all of them except for him *died*. After that, he stopped working. There *were* no more Vincenzo Imbruglia shoes in the world."

Their mouths dangle open. Every last one.

"It turned out that the cobbler I'd been arguing with

for almost half an hour before he replaced my soles *was* a broken, depressed shell of Vincenzo Imbruglia. What were the odds that he would turn up in my neighborhood, essentially disguised as a humble cobbler, just trying to make enough to pay his rent?"

The board is at least listening.

"The passion I had for his beautiful, comfortable product convinced him to try again, with my help this time." I shrug. "I knew there was a need, and that made it a snap to market."

"You didn't have the idea to create a designer shoe label in the beginning?" Mr. Jimenez looks floored.

"Nope. I knew that men's designer shoes, by and large, looked nice but felt like torture devices. When I realized that the person who had unlocked the code to providing both comfort and beauty was right in front of me, I spotted my first latency in the market."

"When you added jackets?" Mr. Jimenez asks.

"It was the same," I say. "Most designer coats were ruined by rain. *Rain.*" I shake my head. "Something so basic, so common, that in New York City, you're almost doomed to ruin your designer jackets within a month or two. A latency."

"But surely finding such latencies in the women's side of things should be even easier," Mrs. Yaltzinger says.

"Ah, ah." I shake my head. "You may not have noticed, but I'm a man."

Mrs. Yaltzinger frowns. "But surely your girlfriend—"

"It might be a boyfriend," Mr. Jimenez hisses.

I splutter. "I'm not in a relationship, but it would be with a *girl* if I were."

"Then you should find her," Mrs. Yaltzinger says. "She can help you identify latencies." Her brow furrows.

"I haven't had time to date," I say. "I built this business from the ground up."

"But now you have us," Mr. Dressel says. "We can, and really should, be picking up some of the slack of management. Let us do our jobs, so you can go do yours." He tosses his head. "Sniff out the latencies we can find solutions to, and then come back to us so we can actually expand."

"It's not that simple," I say. "You can't just *wish* me a girlfriend, believe me. I'd have one with silky hair and big, full lips, if that was possible."

Mrs. Yaltzinger's face is pinched as she whips out her phone, taps on a few buttons and holds it to her ear. "Yes, Ursula. I've got a new client for you. He'd like to start right away, and look for women with silky hair and big, full lips."

Oh, boy.

Turns out, I'm still a complete halfwit. Having a board is even worse than being stuck with my parents.

❧ 2 ☙

BEA

Most people hate their job—there's a reason you're paid to do it.

I know I'm not special.

And to be fair, when I started waiting tables, I didn't hate it. My first time working as a waitress was at Dave and Seren's inn, and it was small enough that there were never many people.

Thanks to Dave and Seren, it never felt like work.

But when I started college to study music, it never occurred to me that even after I graduated, I'd still be waiting tables. I'm working at the nicest place in Scarsdale, but that cuts both ways. My tips are so good that I haven't been able to quit. No music job I could find would come close to what I make working five nights a week at the Red Horse.

Well, that, and I haven't actually gotten a job I'd want.

"No, not like that," Mrs. Stevens says. "Lighter. Springier, like the notes are sassy."

I still take piano lessons, but it might be out of habit at this point.

I was a music theory major, and I've taken piano lessons since I was twelve, so you'd think that by now, I'd be teaching lessons instead. Or maybe I'm still taking lessons because my teacher has my dream job and she lets me help her most weeks.

After another twenty minutes of somewhat rewarding torture, my lesson's finally over. That's when the fun part starts. "I thought you might want to take a look at this one." Mrs. Stevens hands me a sheet of music.

"Who's it for?"

"The Honda dealership."

"And?"

"They want it to be fast, upbeat, and staccato."

I lift my eyebrows. "They said staccato?"

Mrs. Stevens laughs. "Of course not."

The world around me disappears as the notes on the page begin to play in my head. Her jingle isn't bad, but it's soggy in the middle. Right when it should really pop, it sinks. "This line is the one that needs work," I finally say. "You should bring it up a third, and maybe cut the weird chords here." I point.

"Like this?" Mrs. Stevens' fingers fly over the keys.

"More like this." I sit next to her and she shoves over. As I'm showing her what I meant, I have another idea. It's a good one.

"Oh, that's much better." She plays it twice, and then she tightens it up a bit more, condensing two measures into one to segue better than mine. The bridges are always the trickiest part. Almost an hour later, when I leave, it's *perfect*. She lets me sit in on the conference call when she plays it for the client.

To the car dealership, the melody is probably the least exciting part of their commercial, but Mrs. Stevens and I know that we're making the magic happen. The reason people will remember the commercial, the reason they'll think of Holdam Honda is because we did our job.

Of course, it's not really *my* job. It's hers.

But still.

One day, hopefully. I have applied for over a dozen jingle jobs in the last year, but they're hard to land. It's a job that can be done from home, and it's a job that most everyone who can play basic musical instruments is qualified to do. But you can *work from home*, and for an introvert, that sounds magical enough already.

Add in the bonus that you're able to take the notes I love so much and turn them into a limitless number of new songs that will stick with people, and it sounds like nirvana. Being paid to create music that people will hear, and I can do it in my pajamas in my own home?

Please and thank you.

Unfortunately, with as long as working on that jingle took, I barely have time to shower before my shift. My long hair takes forever to dry, so I always try to blow dry it before heading in. I'm going to wind up with water all down my back, but hopefully my hair will cover the damage itself. Sometimes I wish we had a more flexible dress code, but it's nice not to stress over what I'm wearing as I pull on the same boring black pants and white button-down shirt that I always wear.

Our uniform could turn a supermodel into a frump, but when you start out at barely five feet tall, and you already have almost nothing in the way of curves, it's a death knell. When I pass the mirror, it could be a teenage boy staring back.

Not that it matters. When I wait tables, I disappear. It's actually my favorite thing about the job. Yes, I have to interact with a never-ending stream of people all night long. And yes, the other wait staff and cooks are talking to me constantly, but it's not the kind of thing that requires thought or effort. It's, "table five needs this cooked longer." Or "they need water at table six." None of them care about me—the diners or the staff—and I like it that way. I'm a tool to them. I show up with a pleasant expression, bring their waters, their mojitos, and their whiskey neat when they ask for them. Their food is hot. Their drinks are cold.

And I get a decent tip.

They promptly forget me, exactly like I want.

There's actually one guy who literally comes in every single Friday night at eight p.m. He has eaten at Red Horse for more than three years, since a few weeks after I started working at the Westchester, and I'm pretty sure he doesn't even know I've been his waiter every single week. He's a pretty good tipper, so that's just fine by me.

Actually, I like it that way.

I don't have hard feelings about being invisible. In fact, it's the one thing in the world I've always been best at. Waiting tables is the kind of job where people noticing you and remembering you is a liability. The less they think about their waiter, the better you're doing your job. It means their drinks are never empty. Their check is never wrong. And their food is done *just right*.

The key to that, of course, is making sure the chef and other cooks like me best.

I'm not above bribing, but since I have almost no social life, I'm also available to cover shifts when the restaurant is down a waiter, and that makes them grateful. There's nothing worse than a bunch of customers who are mad because their food was cold, and that's what happens when we're short-staffed on wait crew. The chefs take the blame, but it's usually our fault.

When I walk through the door, I'm a little shocked when the head line cook points at me. Iggy isn't usually a pointer. "You—we called a sub for you."

I blink. "But I'm here—I'm not even late."

"Our pianist canceled again."

I suppress my groan and remind myself that this is just another way I can make sure that everyone loves me. On weekends, the fine dining at the Westchester always has live piano music. They usually want someone who can sing, but when the musician cancels, as flaky artists often do, well. Let's just say that when I offered to pinch hit once, I didn't realize it might happen once a *month*.

The tips aren't awful, and even though I'm asked to play *Piano Man* far too often, it's really not that bad.

Usually.

Most of the time the guests who come in are pretty busy with what they're doing. Usually they want to come in, eat some food, chat with their dinner companion, pay the check, and leave. That's the ideal, anyway. But sometimes you find people, especially when you play well, who stop eating, who don't bother chatting, and who just turn around in their seats and *stare*.

I swear, I can feel their eyes on me.

After spending a lifetime learning to make no impression on others, to attract no attention, it's disconcerting. There's a reason I wasn't a performance major. There's a reason I never considered trying to write and perform my own music. I have a terrible voice and shouldn't sing in public, for one, but for another, it makes me feel absolutely ill to have people staring at me. Talking about me. Paying attention to me.

I can usually muddle my way through, as long as it's sprung on me.

Instead of grumbling, or cursing Paul for flaking again, I just put my bag in my locker and head for the piano. At least at five in the afternoon, there's hardly anyone here. None of the few patrons we do have seem to care that I'm playing. There's an art to not playing *so* loudly that people can't chat, but playing loudly enough that it creates *ambiance*.

That's one thing I'm very good at gauging.

About three hours later, right as my arms are so exhausted from playing that I'm about to cry, Stacy shows up. They usually stack musicians on weekends. There's only so many songs you can bang out before you need a break. I get paid almost the same thing for a three-hour shift as I make waiting tables for six, which is pretty nice.

Unfortunately, before I can leave, Iggy catches my eye and shakes his head. "Lincoln puked in the sink. You're covering section 7."

I don't argue. I don't complain. I just nod and close my locker without touching my bag. It takes me almost half an hour to get caught up on his tables, who *cannot* be told their waiter just puked his guts up. They were not super happy to have a twenty-minute interruption in their service, but I've nearly gotten them all happy when I catch a new table.

It's only a two-top, but the client's a VIP, apparently.

I used to think all VIPs would tip huge, but I was wrong. It's honestly just as hit and miss with them as anyone else, but they're much more likely to throw tantrums, so they almost always give them to their top servers, either me or Ollie.

When I reach the table, our host Frank is handing

them menus. "Not that you'll need this," he says. "Not with Beatrice as your waitress."

"What does that mean?" The woman's lips are pumped so full of collagen that I'm shocked she can talk at all.

"She has a magical skill," Frank says.

I wave him off. "Stop with that."

"I mean it," he says. "It's uncanny. If you answer just three questions, she can order the perfect meal for you. Guaranteed."

"You're kidding," the man says.

"Not at all," Frank says. "You should let her work her magic. You won't regret it."

I was so distracted by the collagen-lipped, saline-chested woman that I hadn't even glanced at her date. When I finally do, I realize to my horror that I know him.

It's Easton Moorland.

His sister Elizabeth is married to my brother Emerson. We've met twice now—once at their friend's video game launch, where my brother Jake half-knocked him over when they arm-wrestled. Jake doesn't ever play fair, but it was pretty clear at Emerson's wedding that Easton hadn't let it go.

And now he's my VIP.

His company was doing well for years, or so I hear, but it exploded not that long ago, and I'm kind of sick of hearing about it. If I'm lucky, he won't even recognize me.

"Weren't you just playing piano?" Easton asks.

I blink—how could he have seen that?

"The idiot hosts didn't realize who he was." The collagen-woman pouts. "They made us *wait* for a table."

Easton, at least, has the decency to look embarrassed, but he doesn't appear to know who I am. Thank heavens for small blessings. "I didn't mind waiting—the music was incredible."

"Incredible?" The woman arches one eyebrow. "If you like elevator music."

"I do happen to like Chopin," Easton says.

"I actually prefer Beving," I say, "but they want straight classical here."

"It was boring, so they should let you branch out," she says. "Now, if you could play, like, the *Piano Man*, that would be something."

"I'll make note of it," I say with a smile that I hope doesn't look forced.

"How about it?" Easton asks. "Feel like working a little more magic tonight?"

"What?" Collagen asks.

"What questions do we have to answer to have you order for us?" He's smiling, but not at his date.

At me.

"It's probably easier if you just choose what you like from the menu," I say.

"Oh, come on, Bea," Easton says.

Apparently he knows exactly who I am, and that means he probably knew when I was playing, too. I hate when real life collides with work. I force another smile. "The first question is whether you have any allergies, Easton."

"Wait, do you two know each other? Or, like, did they say your name earlier?" Collagen's squinting as she stares at my very small chest. I'm assuming she's looking for a nonexistent nametag.

"Bea's brother Emerson married my sister," Easton says. "Though until I saw her playing earlier, I had no idea she worked here."

"It's not like people advertise when they have *this* kind of job," Collagen says.

Easton frowns. "I've spent the last few years chained to my desk at the office, but had I known you worked here, I'd have been here sooner. I've heard their pork chop is to die for."

I cluck. "I don't think that's the right choice for you," I say. "Once you answer the questions, I'll pick something better."

And I really, really want to get this one right.

EASTON

Over a year ago now, I made a complete fool of myself.

In my thirty years of life, I've never done anything else that was so completely embarrassing. In fact, when boys got into fights at school, I always kind of laughed. Sometimes I'd roll my eyes.

It's not that I never understood why they fought.

I get angry too.

But I always prefer to use my brains to sort things out. Only, when I met Bea for the first time, something in my brain broke. She was the most beautiful woman I had ever seen. She was so petite that I ached to wrap her up and protect her from the world. She had a gorgeous waterfall of shining, ebony hair. Her eyes were huge, almost anime-sized, and velvety brown. Her mouth distracted me so badly that I continuously found myself lost in the conversation.

And then her movie-star brother had flung his arm around her shoulders and something inside of me snarled. It wasn't a friendly arm. He was saying "mine" with the movement. It made me angry.

Which was insane. I barely knew her.

But when, a few moments later, he suggested that someone who spent all day in a board room instead of physically training for action movies would have no chance of beating him in an arm wrestle. . .I'm not sure what happened. I mean, looking back on it, *obviously* my hours of sitting at a desk hadn't prepared me to beat him.

I worked out.

Apparently not nearly enough.

I put up a decent fight, straining, heaving, puffing, and then he winked at me—*winked*—and slammed my hand down so hard it sent a bowl of popcorn, a whole bunch of water bottles, and a stack of papers flying off the table to scatter on the ground.

It was loud.

It was humiliating.

And while I fumed, that cretin slung his stupidly muscular arm around Bea and waltzed out of the party. To make everything even worse, he winked at me again as he strolled out.

With Bea.

In my entire life, I have never done something so shamefully embarrassing. But I did find someone online to show me how to arm wrestle after that, and I never skipped shoulders again.

Not that any of that matters.

After that infuriating and humiliating interchange, I spent the weeks leading up to Emerson and Elizabeth's wedding preparing to meet Bea again. I asked Elizabeth about her, but my sister was worse than useless. She giggled, she made jokes, and then she threatened to tell Emerson I had asked.

It was almost worse than the arm wrestling.

At the wedding, that horrible Jake Priest never left her side, not for a moment for the entire wedding. I swear, maybe it's because I know they're foster siblings, and not real siblings, but he acts like she's his girlfriend. No matter how many times I ducked around corners when I saw her head around one, Jake was already waiting there like a shield.

He didn't wink again, but it was almost worse than if he had.

And now, as if the *only* time I can possibly meet her is when I'm at my worst, I bump into her here, at her job, with the most plastic, ridiculous date I could ever imagine. The contrast between Bea's shining, natural beauty and this woman's purchased and polished face is appalling, frankly.

I have no idea how I'm supposed to somehow make any inroads with her tonight, while I'm on a date, but if I have to come back here every night for a month, I will.

I decide to start by telling her that I'm excited to be here. "I've spent the last few years chained to my desk at the office, but had I known you worked here, I'd have been here sooner. I've heard their pork chop is to die for."

"I don't think that's the right choice for you," she says with a shy smile. "Once you answer the questions, I'll pick something better."

"Allergies?" Chaliesah asks. "Wasn't that the first one?"

Bea nods politely.

Before I can say anything, Chaliesah continues. "Hmm, well. Citrus, sesame, and gluten, though I guess gluten's not really an allergy, but I can't eat it, or my face bloats. This face is worth a lot of money, so I can't have it bloating." She giggles.

I'm going to kill Mrs. Yaltzinger. *This* irritating woman is who their matchmaker came up with? They didn't even tell me her name before our date—they just said my match has over a million followers on social and is an up-and-coming influencer for women's cosmetics, like that matters more than her lack of a personality.

In spite of the fact that my last ten plus years were devoted almost entirely to either school or work, I'm not willing to marry anyone they point me at. I wonder what they'd say about Bea. For some reason, I doubt she even has social media. Although, who knows? Maybe she has a piano or music account. She looks exactly like a starving artist should, and not just because she's thin. She just has this air of, "I won't change who I am for you or anyone else, no matter what." I had no idea how attractive that was until they set me up with this chameleon who desperately wants me to like her.

I'm wishing I'd spent more time with my new brother-in-law Emerson right about now. Maybe I'd already have run into Bea under better circumstances.

"And you?" When Bea turns toward me, her bright eyes locked on mine, my churning brain goes blank.

Just like the first time we met. I swallow.

"No allergies?"

The only thing I'm allergic to is bee stings, but saying a tiny bug can do me in doesn't sound very manly, so I don't mention it. It's not like it impacts what I eat.

"Question two is, what was the best meal of your life?" She lifts her eyebrows. "Like, tell me what it was, how old you were when you ate it, and where you consumed it."

"That's like three questions," my braintrust date says with a frown that somehow inexplicably creates no wrinkles in either her forehead or the place between her eyebrows. . .probably thanks to an extra helping of Botox.

"I'll start with this one." Maybe I can redeem myself. "When I was twelve, my parents took us to London, and I had fish and chips from a food cart, and we ate it while sitting on a bench on the Thames."

"London sounds posh," Bea says, "but eating fish and chips on a bench? That doesn't fit the image of one of the youngest multi-millionaires in New York City."

"Who knows?" I ask. "I might surprise you."

Chaliesah's frown turns into a scowl, which is only apparent by the pursing of her lips and the daggers she's staring at Bea. "Why would you surprise her? She's the *waitress*."

"You're right," Bea says. "It's my job to surprise both of you. So tell me, what was your best meal?"

"Last week." Chaliesah straightens, glancing down at her immaculate manicure. "At *Per Se* in the City, I had the most epic chocolate mousse cake I've ever had." She shrugs.

"That's not a meal, though." Bea bites her lip. "Did you love the entree you had there?"

"Of course I did," Chaliesah says. "The lobster was amazing."

Bea's sigh is so slight I wouldn't have caught it if I wasn't watching her so closely. Her smile falters for the briefest of moments, like a computer screen that glitches.

It makes me laugh.

"What's so funny?" Chaliesah snaps, but then, as if she has remembered something, she laughs. It may be the most forced laugh I've ever heard. "Just kidding. That was funny."

Bea's expression, like she's seen someone urinating in

public and desperately wants to back away slowly, is even funnier than the glitching smile. "My last question is what was your *worst* meal, and why?"

"Mine was every single time my mom tried to cook," I joke. "Luckily it almost never happened."

Bea's laugh isn't forced. It's quick, sharp, and high. She tamps it down quickly, though, and that bums me out. "If you could be a little more specific—"

"He answered," Chaliesah says. "And mine was peanut butter sandwiches at a friend's house."

"You don't like peanut butter and jelly?" Bea's lips pucker. "A good PB&J is one of life's true indulgences, I think."

"No one asked what you think, though. Right?" Chaliesah turns toward me and widens her eyes like I should be horrified that our waitress has more than two brain cells, and they aren't fighting.

"Actually, I'm delighted to hear what she thinks, and like her, I love peanut butter and jelly, especially if the bread is soft and the jelly's grape."

"Grape?" Bea scrunches her nose. "Yeesh."

"Too boring?" I ask.

She shrugs. "Not nearly as fun as, say, orange marmalade."

Chaliesah tosses her napkin on the table and stands. "Why are we talking about peanut butter sandwiches?" She shakes her head. "We should go to a new place."

"I like this one," I say. "And I think that if you're set up with someone by a high-end matchmaker, even if you don't like them, you should grit your teeth and endure the meal, wherever you go, instead of making a scene." I lift my chin and look right at her. "At least, that's what I've been doing."

Her jaw drops, her bright red lips parted alarmingly

wide. "You've been. . ." Her mouth snaps closed and she frowns. "Wait, are you saying—"

"Get it faster," Bea mutters so softly that I almost miss it.

She shouldn't have to deal with this just because I am. "Bea, why don't you take your best stab at what you think we'll like," I say. "And then we'll let you know whether you were right."

Bea inclines her head, spins around, and darts off.

Chaliesah huffs. Twice. I think she's trying to decide whether she can bring herself to sit back down. The problem with her is that she's used to being adored, and people who are always catered to—all their whims and fits indulged—become incapable of polite interactions. I could tell that was her problem within two minutes of meeting her. It was a common affliction when I was growing up, surrounded as I was by spoiled rich kids.

Of course, the slit running from her ankle to her hip bone was another red flag that this woman was probably not the kind of girl I was hoping to meet. I could have done without seeing her electric blue thong peeking out at me with every step, but I'm ignoring the things about her that bother me. She could at least have the decency to do the same.

"Are you really not having fun?" She sticks her bottom lip out.

"Is that a shock?" Maybe she really is extremely stupid.

"You're not what I expected either." She narrows her eyes, as if she's trying to decide whether this can be salvaged.

"Yes, sticking around is a big waste of your time."

"What happened to gritting your teeth?" She snaps.

Maybe she has more insight than I gave her credit for. "I suppose I couldn't even take my own advice."

She grabs her purse and stomps off. About three steps later, though, she's shifted back into her sultry sway. I suppose it's not very gratifying to stomp in four-inch Jimmy Choos.

Not three minutes later, Bea breezes by, setting two square plates in front of me. "I brought lobster dumplings for Miss Collagen USA, and I brought the burrata cheese and prosciutto salad for you." She straightens and frowns. "Did she ask someone where the bathroom was?"

"No." I shake my head.

Bea winces. "I should check and make sure she found it."

"Is that something waitresses generally do?" I can't help teasing her a little.

"Well, not usually, no, but. . ." She leans closer and drops her voice. "I was told you're a VIP, and for VIPs, we'll do most anything."

"What if I told you my date ditched me, and I'm now terribly depressed?" I spread my hands across the top of the white linen tablecloth. "Would your boss let you eat with me to take some of the sting away?"

It's that same laugh again. Short, sharp, high.

I love it. "I'm not kidding." I hold her gaze.

"She really left?" She tilts her head. "I find that hard to believe, honestly. She seemed ready to challenge me to a duel when I—" Her mouth snaps shut.

What was she going to say? When she *what*? "When you. . .?" I raise both eyebrows.

She ducks her head. "Never mind."

When she *flirted* with me? Is that what she meant? I

hope that's what she's been doing. Is that really why Chaliesah stormed off? Can she tell I like Bea?

More importantly, is there a chance Bea likes *me?*

"I'm sure you're teasing, but I definitely can't eat with you," she says. "I'm working."

"Right," I say. "Of course. But maybe you could get that to go." I toss my head at the lobster dumplings. "Then you can take them home and pretend you were eating with me." Oh man, I'm corny. She's going to laugh and walk off.

But she doesn't.

She inhales and ducks her head again, like she's embarrassed.

That might be worse. Am I harassing my waitress? Am I *that* guy now? Before she has to say anything else, I reach across and grab the lobster puff things and shove them both in my mouth. "Wow. Those are good."

Bea straightens, her shoulders squaring. "That's not usually how people eat them."

I chew, chew, chew, and swallow. The bite is so big it hurts my throat going down, like it's dragging its hands down the inside of my esophagus. "No?" I cough. "You don't say."

There's the laugh, but at least she doesn't walk off, and she's laughing *at* me, not because I've made her nervous or uncomfortable. "I didn't bring those for you, though." She tosses her head at the prosciutto and cheese thing. "The burrata's what you're supposed to like."

"You thought Chaliesah would love the lobster dumplings?" I ask. "Why?" I mean, they were good, but they tasted pan fried, and I don't imagine she eats a lot of oil.

Bea narrows her eyes at me. "Just try yours."

I stare at her for a moment, wondering what she's thinking, and then I nod and look down at my food. I cut the cheese into a smaller piece and spear a slice of prosciutto, making sure to get some arugula and the balsamic. When I pop it in my mouth, I don't expect much. At the end of the day, prosciutto's really just ham in a tux.

But this is. . .*more*. The pickled onion, the hint of seared squash, and the tang of cider—together with the balsamic—the flavors are amplified in a way I didn't expect. I scoop up a second little blob more slowly, and when I pop it in my mouth, I savor it, closing my eyes, inhaling slowly.

When I finally open my eyes, Bea's smiling. "Told you."

"How did you—why'd you pick this?"

She shrugs. "I was right, though."

"It was phenomenal," I admit. "But now you have to tell me why you picked lobster for Miss Collagen USA." Which has to be the funniest nickname I've ever heard of someone giving a person they've barely met.

Bea purses her already full lips, and I want to reach out and brush my thumb against them.

Because apparently I'm insane around her.

She sighs, like she's decided something, and then she says, "I'm not proud of it, but I chose them because she said she liked seafood, and I know they're made with flour, so I thought she might still eat them in spite of that." Her lip's twitching. "I'm a jerk, but she said it wasn't an allergy, so I won't apologize for it."

This time, I'm the one laughing. "It's too bad she didn't get a chance to bloat," I say.

"Her face *is* worth a lot of money," Bea says. "I guess I'm kind of a bad person." She spins around on her heel and disappears.

I should probably pay and leave, but even the Hulk couldn't drag me out of this restaurant. I know it's not a date anymore, but it *feels* more like a date now than it did with my date sitting across from me.

Like a creeper, I pretend to be on my phone, but really I watch Bea take care of her other tables. She's so small that watching her carry big trays is, well, it's surprising somehow. She acts like a tray with four or five plates on it weighs nothing, setting it effortlessly on the small stand she whips out with her free hand.

It's not very long before Bea returns with two plates for me. "I'd already put in the order." She bites her lip.

I swear, if I wasn't sure she's not some crazy vixen, I'd assume she was pursing and biting her lips just to draw attention to them. They look like what Chaliesah clearly wanted hers to look when she had all that collagen put in.

Large. Plump. And currently? Being bitten by very white teeth.

One of which is just a tiny bit crooked. The one just to the left of her front two teeth is angled just a hair, and I love it.

"No?"

Shoot. She asked me something.

"No?" I repeat her question like a moron.

A tiny smile curves at the edge of her mouth. "You don't want freshly ground pepper? Right?"

Yes. The food. Because that's her job.

I glance down for the first time to see what she brought. "A burger?" I can't help my surprise.

"For your date, I brought the sweet Melissa Surf and Turf—crab leg, a six-ounce filet, butterflied, with chili butter. It's got a very subtle zing that only the most discerning palate will catch."

"So she'd be sure to miss it." I point at my burger. "But explain this."

"Try it first." She folds her arms across her chest.

I want to argue, but she's channeling a pretty impressive amount of third-grade teacher, so I duck my head, pick up the burger, and take a dutiful bite.

Like the prosciutto, this is an explosion of several flavors that I do not expect. Burgers at steakhouses usually have a thick, juicy patty, often flavored with a lot of salt and strange seasonings.

This is nothing like that.

Instead, it tastes like maybe two or three very thin, very crispy patties. They're almost *lacy* on the sides, and they're seasoned only by salt, unless I'm wrong. Anything more would fight with the strangely sharp gouda cheese that's not quite melted, the crisp red onions that were clearly marinated in something tangy, and some kind of sauce I can't place.

Maple?

"And?" She arches one eyebrow.

The bun's soft on top, crunchy underneath, and the sauce, the onions, and the cheese offset the patties perfectly. It's the best burger I've ever had, and I *love* burgers. I didn't tell her that. After what I did tell her, I expected seafood.

"It's really, really good. But if this burger costs a hundred bucks, I'm going to be annoyed."

"Will you really?" She drops one hand on her hip.

Nothing she does could annoy me. "Absolutely," I lie.

"You're in luck, then. It's the cheapest thing on the menu."

"Doesn't that cut into your tip?"

She shrugs. "I think happy customers tip better."

"But surely ten percent of a hundred bucks is better than twenty or thirty percent of twenty-five?"

Bea leans closer, her breath washing over the side of my face when she whispers, "People come here for an experience. As long as we deliver, we're doing our job."

An experience.

I turn so I can see her face, and I'm lost again. Her eyes are like nothing I've ever seen. So earnest, so sincere, and so doe-like. "Well, I appreciate your sensibility about my budget." I cringe as I say it. What's wrong with me? I haven't flirted in so long—have I forgotten how? That's embarrassing.

She straightens. "What should I do with hers?"

"Do you happen to like crab or filet?"

She scrunches her nose. "I prefer mine medium rare, but there's no way she'd eat that."

"So you ruined a perfectly good filet."

"It's butterflied." She shrugs. "So yeah, ruined."

I laugh again. "Better throw it to the dogs."

"Do you have a dog?"

I've never wanted to have a dog more in my entire life. "I should get one, now that I have a little more time." I smile. "I know someone who could help me with it." Gah, Easton, you idiot. I should have told her I needed her help in picking one.

"Elizabeth's very passionate about pets," she says.

"You're not?"

"I like animals," she says. "But I'm not really in a position to take care of one. I work long hours, and I'm not exactly ordering steaks and crab to toss to a dog." She winks.

I'm such an idiot. She's a waitress, and I'm just reminding her of that. "I feel you on not having the time." And now I'm just staring at her again.

"Well, I'll let you eat that burger." She shoots me a half-smile and then she's gone.

Like a buttercup at sunset, I slump over my burger. It's delicious, but I swear it tastes twice as good when she's smiling in my direction.

When she brings me a dessert—just one this time—I perk back up. "What's this?"

She's literally carrying a balloon suspended by what looks sort of like a sour straw, connected to a tray that's covered with chocolates and syrup.

"You seem like someone who appreciates presentation as much as flavor." She tilts her head. "Is that wrong?"

"You brought me a balloon? Do you think I'm five?" Oh, shoot. Does she?

Her smile's tentative. "It's an edible helium balloon. Our chef's best friend invented the idea with him in cooking school, and the restaurant Alinea in Chicago and this one are the only two places that serve them, as far as I know."

"Whoa, you're saying I can eat that?" I lean closer. "But it's floating." It's clear, shiny, and. . . "Is there helium in it?"

Now her smile widens. "There sure is. If Miss Collagen USA were here, you could serenade her in falsetto."

"Who will I serenade without my date?" I fake a frown. "I'm all alone, no one to sing to. Don't you feel sorry for me?"

"Not even a little bit." She shrugs.

"Heartless."

"I suppose."

I poke it and suck in the helium immediately, hoping to keep her around a little longer. But when I start to talk, I surprise even myself. I sound like Peewee Herman. "Bea—is it short for Beatrice?"

She nods.

"You know, I don't even know your last name. How can I serenade you without your last name?"

She's laughing now. "No serenading, please. It's frowned upon."

I inhale the last bit of helium and sing, "Bea, Bea, Bea, Be-a-trice Ann," to the old Beach Boys hit.

"The Beach Boys?" She waves me off. "How old are you?" But she's laughing.

"I discovered as a kid that if we put on the Beach Boys, my dad would drive faster on road trips."

"You're kidding."

I shake my head. "That one thing cut our trips down by like an hour, I swear."

But just then, the table behind us starts waving. "Check?"

In a blink, she's gone. I console myself by eating the sugary, sticky, almost taffy-like balloon, and mopping up the chocolate sauce with the sour-straw-esque string.

When Bea returns with the check, I'm ready. I throw my card down without even looking at it. Before she can dart away, I make my move. "So, Bea. You couldn't eat with me tonight, and that bummed me out. I'd love to take you out—anywhere you want—and actually eat at the same time as you."

Her brows draw together, and she ducks her head

again, but when she does look up, I can tell it's not good news for me. "I'm sorry, but I think that's a bad idea."

The really terrible news hits when another waiter brings the card back. "Bea's shift ended," he says.

Only, I'm pretty sure she ran—from me.

Now I have to find out why and fix it. She's good enough that I can't let her get away a third time.

$$\maltese \quad 4 \quad \maltese$$

BEA

When I started high school, Seren insisted that I try a sport. "You're the most talented pianist I've ever met," she said. "But that's all you do." She crouched down so we were eye-to-eye, and when someone who's five-foot-four has to crouch, you know you're short. "I worry that you're hiding in that music room." She pressed a kiss to my forehead.

Then she bought me a pair of running shoes.

The irony was not lost on me—instead of hiding, I should run?

But hiding was easy; I hated running.

In fact, there were very few things I liked *less* than going outside, tightening the laces on my shiny, new running shoes, and pounding the pavement. But it was a solitary sport—perhaps the most solitary, unless you include swimming where you're literally underwater the entire time so that you can't talk.

I liked solitary.

Within a few weeks, the agony in my chest wasn't quite as acute. The misery of my aching muscles eased, too. A month after Seren forced me to try track, I was actually *improving*.

At least, it felt like I was.

Until Jake breezed over to join the team as well. Like every single thing he ever tried, he was a true natural. The solitary nature of my runs, the one thing I liked about the activity, disappeared as I was plagued by Jake. . .and his accompanying fan club. It wasn't surprising, I suppose, that he was followed by at least half a dozen attractive girls everywhere he went, even then. He had the face of a Greek god and the body of a, well, a lean runner. He was also tall, which meant that running next to him made me look even more like a child than I already did.

Running, which I had tolerated because it provided a lot of time for me to think quietly, was now my least favorite part of every day. Physical misery and social torture were all rolled into one. I tried to complain to Jake, but as always, he persisted in misunderstanding my complaints. He yelled at his followers, telling them to leave us alone. They listened, and that worsened the rumors about us, making my non-Jake interactions even more fraught.

After years of those types of things happening, I've learned.

My dream guy is basically Jake's opposite.

Short.

Unattractive.

Socially awkward.

That's the kind of person who's likely to accept that I'm small, shy, and quiet without trying to change me. Since I work in a restaurant, which keeps me busy nearly every night of the week, it's been easy for me to avoid dating anyone like Jake.

Or really, I haven't been pursued by anyone at all.

Unless you count the sous chef, which I do not. She's one hundred percent not my type, her gender only one of many reasons I had no interest.

So when Easton asked me out, I was floored.

Why someone like him would be interested in me. . .it makes no sense. My brain rejected the idea before I could even consider it. Our first meeting was disastrous enough, what with the arm-wrestling challenge and Easton's subsequent embarrassment. I swear, it's the one consistent theme in my life.

If Jake can cause trouble, he does.

In his defense, I used Jake as a shield at the wedding.

I noticed right after the ceremony that Easton was heading my way. I figured he wanted to somehow smooth over the awkwardness between all of us, but I didn't want any part of that. There's no reason for us to see Easton in the future, just because Emerson married his sister. I decided it would be simpler to avoid him entirely. Jake's always been really good at social situations, so when I mentioned that I'd rather not talk to Easton after the nightmare of the arm wrestling, he stuck by my side for the entire reception.

I had to endure Jake's gaggles of admirers, but it was fine.

Only now, after spending a bit of time with Easton, I wonder. Was he trying to clear the air? Or could he have been interested in me, even then? What are his intentions?

In the split second I had to respond, all of that shot through my mind, and I decided that none of it mattered. Not really. Easton and I are like hummus and honeydew melon—we may share the same first letter, as in, we have a relation to one another, sort of. But we do *not* go together, and we never will.

He's tall, for one, while I am quite the opposite. If we dated, I'd need a stepstool just to kiss him. He's also rich as sin, whereas I sometimes check the couch cushions for gas money. Jake loses change more often than most people. But the worst problem is that the media is all over Easton, almost as bad as they are with Jake. If I search 'hot, young, and rich,' he's the third hit. Forbes basically painted a target on his back the second his company went public. Elizabeth said it was his life's dream, making a billion bucks, and he's well on his way. But there aren't many hot, rich men who are single and also not fat.

He's a unicorn.

A lot of girls want someone just like him, but that's basically the *opposite* of what I want. With money comes eyes. Scrutiny. The loss of any anonymity.

Hard pass.

I have no idea why I toss and turn for so long before I fall asleep after running home, but I finally drift off. And I do *not* dream of Easton.

I don't dream of him eating an ice cream cone—that would be odd.

I don't dream of him swimming, pushing up out of the pool, shoulder and chest muscles rippling.

I don't dream of him walking beside me on a city street, arms swinging, eyes sparkling.

I definitely don't dream of him sitting on the couch next to me, stuffing his face with popcorn and then offering me some, like he's my boyfriend.

Because I don't like Easton Moorland.

Not one bit.

But when I lace up my shoes and set the activity on

my watch to "run," his stupidly handsome face *does* flash through my mind. I smack the side of my head once to clear it, but all I get for that is a headache. I doggedly turn my playlist on and head for the door.

"Hey, wait."

I've barely made it six steps when Jake's plaintive voice penetrates the singing of Tim McGraw. I grit my teeth and stop, turning to look over my shoulder. "What?"

I must have spoken too loud, because he motions for me to take out my earphones.

I groan, but I do it. "What?"

"Wait two minutes and I'll come with. I just have to lace up my shoes."

I shove my earphones back in and take off.

I hear him swearing behind me, but that just widens my smile. It's hilarious, annoying Jake, one of my favorite things to do. I speed up a little.

By the time he catches up to me, he's really puffing. His shoelaces aren't tied, and he's scowling. Anyone else would have fallen on their face, but the sheen of sweat just amplifies his ridiculous good looks. It's obnoxious.

So of course I pretend that I don't see him.

"Bea," he shouts like I'm hard of hearing. "Slow up."

I speed up a little more, which is really silly, because my legs are short and his are long. There's no way I can outpace him once he's caught me, no matter how hard I try.

"What's going on with you?" Jake grabs my arm.

I shake him off.

The second time he grabs me, I spin around and glare. "You want me to mace you? I'll do it."

He rolls his eyes. "Who lit a fire under you?"

Who? Why's he asking *who*? "What did you hear?"

His jaw drops. "Wait, no way." He shakes his head. "Is there. . .a guy?"

I take off jogging again.

"You have got to tell me what happened."

"I do not," I mutter, bumping the volume on my music up a little higher. Long-term hearing loss is a problem for tomorrow-me.

Unfortunately, Jake's well equipped to outrun me. He runs way more, firstly, and also, he's six-foot-three, so his strides decimate mine. After we reach the park, I finally surrender, collapsing on a bench.

"Six miles." Jake whistles. "Whoever upset you *really* upset you."

The park is three point two miles from our apartment. He always calls it a six-mile run. To me, that's seven miles. I round up with physical activity, always. "No one upset me." I lean back and close my eyes, tucking my headphones in my pocket. "Except you."

"Oh, come on, Hornet. I haven't really upset you." He bumps me with his shoulder. "If I had, you'd have stung." He's always called me that—he thinks it's hilarious that my name, Be*a*, is so close to bee. But there's no way to highlight the connection because they sound the exact same.

Hence, hornet.

"Who was it? I've been doing a lot of boxing to get ready for the next Miller film. I'll go pay them a visit." He does that weird head toss thing guys do when they're saying hello to another male.

It makes me snort, at least. "Not necessary."

"I'll decide that, once you tell me who it is and what happened."

"Nothing at all," I say. "Happens to you a dozen times a day. Someone asked me out, and I said no."

He frowns. "Who asked you out?" He scratches his nose. "And why'd you say no?"

I put my headphones back in, hit play, and close my eyes.

"Oh, come on. You've told me the worst part. Just give me the details." He pulls a water bottle out of his little running belt and rips the top off.

"We're not in high school."

Suddenly, Jake's right in front of me, his hands gently taking my headphones out. "Softly, Hornet," he whispers. "You're yelling, and now everyone's looking."

I peer around his shoulder and notice a few people looking my way. He's blaming my volume, but that happens every single time I go anywhere with him. It's probably his fault, so I refuse to apologize.

"Now, who was it? Not the sous chef again?" He drops back onto the seat next to me. "Tomorrow, I'll show up at work, right after you get there, snog you good, and then you can tell everyone we're secretly dating."

That's an idea so ridiculous it makes me laugh.

"So that's a no to the semi-public make out?" He takes a huge swig of the water.

"That's a heck no," I say. "But it wasn't her. She's given up. I think she's dating the wine supplier, actually."

"Good for her," Jake says. "So who do I need to kiss you in front of, then?"

"Jake."

"What?" he asks. "You're not really my sister, you know. It would probably fix the problem, once I know where and in front of who to lay one on you."

"It was Easton Moorland," I say, expecting him to have no idea who I'm talking about. "That's Emerson's wife's brother, who we met at the video game launch party. You challenged him—"

"I know who it is." He downs the end of the water, crushes his water bottle, and tosses it into the trash can next to us. It goes right in, as always. Everything for Jake is like that. Effortless. Charmed. He stands up, tosses his head back and forth, and then starts to jog in place. "Let's go. Long way back."

Not for him, but to me? Three miles sounds like absolute torture.

"Are you okay?" Jake frowns, tilting his head. "I can jog back, grab my car and come get you."

That's why I let him get away with so much crap. At the end of the day, Jake really is a pretty good brother.

"It's fine." I drag myself to my feet. "I won't *die* of a little exercise." A few dozen strides in, and he still hasn't said a word about Easton. I find it strange. "What? You no longer care about fixing my problem?"

He shrugs. "Like you said, it's no big deal. You told him no."

It's not like Jake to let things go, but he does. It's. . .bizarre.

About a mile later, when my thighs are cursing me for my stupid burst of energy earlier, and my lungs are screaming that September's still too hot for running outside in New York, I need a distraction, so I poke the bear. "Tell me why you stopped badgering me when you found out it was Easton Moorland."

"I didn't." Unfortunately for him, I know Jake's practiced scoff.

"You're lying," I say. "I'm probably the only person who can tell."

"It's just that." He stops. "That guy's a jerk." His eyes are wide, his expression earnest. For him, that's rare.

"Whoa. Did you hear me? I told him no."

"But when did you even see him?" he asks. "Why'd he think you might say yes?"

I shake my head. "I don't think he did."

"Guys don't ask unless they think the girl will say yes." He narrows his eyes. "Where did he ask you?"

"He came into the restaurant last night."

Jake throws his hands into the air and jogs around me in an outraged circle. "See? That's my point. What kind of guy asks a girl out while he's on a date?"

"I didn't say he was," I hedge.

He blinks. "So, wait. He went into your restaurant on a Friday night for what? A business dinner?"

"It was a date," I admit, "but his date was a nightmare. They got set up by some kind of matchmaking thing, and she left in a huff."

Jake's shaking his head, but he starts jogging again, and I have to scramble to catch up.

"I mean it," I say. "It wasn't gross, okay?"

"Did he tip you a ton of money before he asked?"

I frown, wiping at a bead of sweat rolling down the side of my face. "No. I mean, he asked me out *before* he paid."

"But he did tip you well?"

"I'm not sure," I say. "I left early."

Jake huffs. "See? He's gross."

"He's not, though," I say.

"Well, if he's so great, then why did you say no?" Jake's voice is uncharacteristically soft.

"He's not the right guy for me."

He throws his hands up in the air. "That's what I said, but then you jumped in to defend him like he just won the Nobel Peace Prize." Jake's always so melodramatic.

"I just wanted to go for a run, because——"

"Because he was gross, and it upset you that he stalked you at your work to ask you out."

"He didn't even know I worked there. Seeing me once, months after the wedding, is hardly stalking me." I swear, one of these days, I'm going to punch him. Hard. "Just. Whatever." I wish I had longer legs. I'd *love* to leave him in a cloud of cartoon dust as I sped away. Maybe I should start carrying a rolled-up newspaper. Then I could bop him on the nose like a puppy peeing on the rug whenever he's out of line.

He'd probably throw a big fit about how the ink from the paper left a stain that would ruin his pre-film photo-shoot or something.

Jake thrives on drama.

He used to get his fill from Emerson. Those two clashed all the time. But now that Emerson's gone, he's been picking at me more. I'm usually hard to irritate, but apparently not today.

My feet are throbbing and my t-shirt's drenched when we finally get back to the apartment. "Look." Jake spins around in front of the door, blocking my entry. "If he calls or comes by again, you need to tell me."

"Why?" I lift my eyebrows. "So you can go practice your boxing on him? Or did you plan to challenge him to another arm wrestle?"

He rolls his eyes. "I mean it."

"Yes, sir." I salute, and then I duck under his arm and type in our door code—Emerson's birthday—and squeeze through the door. He's too fast for me to slam it on him, but I make a token effort before sprinting to my room. I take such a long shower that I'm shocked when I finally emerge to find Jake in a towel. He's drinking orange juice straight from the carton, standing in front of the fridge.

"You're not filming a commercial." I throw a hand towel at him. "Put some clothes on."

"You know, most girls would kill to be in this room right now." He bobs his head.

I groan and point. "Go get dressed. Now."

He listens, but he's never in a hurry about it, which is irritating. I'm a little sick of living in an apartment that feels even more like a frat house now that Emerson's gone, but Jake took over Emerson's portion of the rent and utilities when he left, and I can't afford to look any gift horses in the mouth.

Not until I find a more lucrative job, anyway.

Which is why, now that I'm clean, I work on my submission for the Jello Jingle competition that's due tonight at midnight. Most people probably think it sounds lame, but if I win, I'll have my first jingle credit —and also a paid job—to put in my portfolio, and I'll have my foot in the door at the agency that set it all up.

I've got the melody worked out; that's always a snap for me. Now I'm just agonizing over the words. In reality, someone else at the songwriting firms often handles lyrics, but for your first jobs, you have to do it all. It helps that the product's an easy one to work with. Jello rhymes with everything.

In some ways, that also makes it harder. Standing out is the key, but when any idiotic first-year musical studies major can bang out a rhyming verse for a product, the songs all start to blur.

Mine needs to shine.

I've just scribbled out the entire thing, balled it up, and chucked it at the trash when Jake's body gets in the way. My sad little paperball ricochets off his calf and rolls under the sofa.

"Easy there, Babe Ruth."

"I think you mean Nolan Ryan," I say. "Babe Ruth was a famous batter."

"Yeah, well, Nolan Ryan didn't get a candy bar." Jake plops on the sofa, popping his ankle up on his knee. "Angry about a text from Lover Boy?"

"As if." I sigh, my shoulders slumping. "I hate Jello."

"Not this again." Jake leans forward. "Just let me call my agent. I can get you some jingle work, and—"

I shake my head. "No thank you."

"You are so stubborn."

"They'd only be giving me a job to try and make you happy. I do *not* need my boss sucking up to me so you'll consider their movie or their commercial or whatever. I want my songs to be chosen—"

"Because they're good." He sighs. "Same song, different verse."

"No, same song, same verse." I let Jake call in a favor for me once. He sang a song I'd written on the one album he ever released, before he transitioned to doing blockbuster movies and was still sort of exploring the various options in the entertainment world. The album did fine, but my song was the worst seller on the album. . .until the media did an article about how he'd only included it for his poor, pathetic foster sister. It blew up, and those twice-yearly royalties still float me for most of the year.

I should be grateful.

But it was the most embarrassing month of my life. A few times, some crazy pop-culture weirdos actually recognized me. When they tried to take photos with me and wanted my signature, I wanted to die. The only reason that story disappeared is that my very angry grandfather made it go away. It didn't make him look good, that I had a 'foster brother.' Any way you look at it, the last thing I need is more strings connecting me to one of the hottest new actors in America.

When Jake won't let it go, I wave him over. "I don't want a referral, but I will take your input on my ideas." I play the melody for him.

"That's really good." I wish he didn't sound so surprised.

"Of course it is. That's like telling an ant he's good at carrying heavy things. A bright and clear melodic line is kind of my thing."

Jake nods. "Then show me your lyrics."

"Keep in mind, I'm jingling a jiggly dessert no one eats anymore."

"I'm aware, believe me. Go ahead."

"I'm not singing it." I point. "You."

"No way. The only reason I agreed to this was so I could hear you sing it." But he's smiling, so I know he's kidding. No one needs to hear me sing.

Not ever.

I'm not off key, not after years and years of music, but my voice is scratchy, always, probably from years of secondhand smoke from my mom. Who knows? "Okay. Start."

I play the lead in, and Jake comes in flawlessly. After spending more than five years in choir together, musical stuff is the one place where we always harmonize. Forty minutes later, when it's time for me to get ready for work, I've come up with a winner.

Or at least, I hope I have.

After another few moments of agonizing, I upload the file, and then I click submit.

"You'll win," Jake says.

I'm almost to my door, but I pivot and point. "You will *not* call anyone. Swear."

He rolls his eyes so hard that a preteen girl would be jealous. "You think I have connections to *Jello*? I'm not Bill Cosby."

"That's not a promise."

He leans against the wall, the set of his jaw so familiar I could draw it with my eyes closed. "I swear, Hornet, that I won't mention your submission to a soul, not even to Seren and Dave."

"Alright, then."

He's gone by the time I come out, ready for work. That's typical Jake, too. He's not big on hellos and good-byes. I think he's still broken from his dad. Eventually that guy will get out of prison again, and then things will get ugly, I'm sure.

But for now, I just have to accept that I'll never know where Jake is without microchipping him. Mom and Dad talked about doing it a lot. Seren and Dave, I mentally correct myself. Making a mistake in front of my birth mom or my grandfather always results in a *lot* of drama, so for years, I've tried my best not to call my real parents 'mom and dad' where anyone can hear.

As a bonus, it makes Jake feel easier that he's not the only one calling them by their first names. We all know they're Mom and Dad to him too, but some of us can't always say it. The great thing about Seren and Dave is they just take us as we are, damage and all. They always have, from the first time I split Seren's meaty lasagna with Dave.

I'm almost to work when Kiki-the-sous-chef calls.

"Hey," I say. "I'm almost there, but I'm not late. Is everything okay?"

"I forgot you do that," Kiki says.

"What?"

"You're always on the defensive. You're not late."

"Then what's up?"

"There's a super hot guy here waiting for you," she whispers. "He said not to tell you, but he asked if you're working."

My heart races. "What does he look like?"

"Tall. Dark hair. Striking blue eyes. I mean, he wouldn't turn me straight, but it would be a close call. You know those Jude Law lookalikes do it every time."

It's Easton. It has to be.

Until she said it, I didn't realize how much he looks like Jude Law. Why is he there?

"How busy is it tonight?" Maybe I can call in sick. I mean, I kind of need the tips from a Saturday night, but some things aren't worth the trouble.

"Don't even think about calling in." She snorts. "Harv would lose it."

"Fine. Thanks for the warning."

"Sunglasses and a scarf?" she says. Then she hangs up.

Like I have a scarf that would cover my whole face. I'm not a 1950s housewife, a bank robber, or a rancher in Montana. Besides, even if I do cover my face, how many other waiters are five foot tall with long black hair? He'd realize it was me and it would be even stranger because I'd tried to sneak past him.

I opt for walking really fast, but it's not a great plan. I've barely squeaked through the door when Harv stops me. "There's a VIP in there asking for you."

He's flipped my own people.

"He said you were the best waitress he's ever had," Harv says. "And he wants to set up his weekly board meetings here at our restaurant." He's beaming.

"Oh." So, wait. Am I a total narcissist? Maybe this isn't even about me. "Was he asking for me? Kiki said—"

"He wants you to wait on the board for their meetings, but they do them during the day and you usually take nights. You'd only have to switch to days on Tuesday, and you get Sunday and Monday off already, so I thought—"

"I'll do it," I say.

Making Harvey happy? That's a no-brainer. So what if I have to wait on a bunch of stuffy business people? It's not like he's asking me out. He was impressed with the *restaurant*, not me. I'm an idiot.

"Oh," Harv says. "And he was hoping you would wait on him tonight, too."

Well, crap.

"Chop chop," he says. "We have a VIP to impress."

Only, when I approach his table, Easton doesn't look like a VIP businessman. With the smile on his wickedly curved mouth, he looks a lot more like Dickie Greenleaf —Jude Law's most epic role.

"Bea," he says, smiling as he stands.

He's acting like he'd been waiting just for me, which has the other waiters looking and pointing.

"Easton," I hiss as I shake my head slightly.

He sits, thankfully.

I hand him a menu.

"I'm not sure I should really be waiting on you again today." I point at the empty chair across from him. "I ran off your last date, and even with your millions, they couldn't match you with a better one?"

"Your boss didn't tell you?" He lifts his eyebrows. "I told him I'd pay all the revenue you usually make for all the tables you usually wait on. Then you can eat with me." He jumps up and pulls out the seat across from him. "This one's yours."

5

EASTON

It's a grand gesture.

It's what Elizabeth told me to do when I told her I liked someone, but the girl wasn't interested.

Actually, first she laughed.

For a long time.

But once she finally stopped, she asked for details.

I made some up, because I wasn't about to tell her I was borderline stalking her husband's foster sister. I might sound like the villain in that scenario.

"You're hot," Elizabeth said. "I mean, I don't have junk genes, but you definitely got better physical appearance markers than I did."

I rolled my eyes.

"She probably thinks you're just interested in the chase." My sister shrugged. "Most rich guys are. Think about Bentley."

"Emerson's friend?"

"A family friend for all of them. He dated for a long time before he was ready to get married and settle down." Her air quotes for settling were funny. "And you're higher profile right now than he is, because your success is new, and frankly, because you're not quite thirty yet."

"There aren't many rich guys with a six pack."

Elizabeth glared. "You wish."

"Fine," I said. "A two to four pack. But if I cut two sodas a day, I could have a six pack."

"The point is, if she's Quality, and I'm guessing she is, then you want her to seriously consider you. To get her to do that, you'll have to convince her you really do like her. That you're not just another rich playboy who thinks he can have whatever he wants."

I thought about it all day long, and then I came up with a plan. I've never made a plan in my life that didn't have at least one contingency, and I'm not about to start. So my grand gesture was buying a date—which I understand could be perceived as a little creepy, but at least she gets a night off and some extra capital with her boss—and if that bombs, well, I'll have weeks and weeks of work lunches with the board to try and figure out how to smooth things over.

On the other hand, if tonight goes well, the board meetings will be bonus opportunities to see her.

Or maybe she'll come sit in on lunch with me. . . . Her boss did say she usually does the dinner shift. My hopes and dreams for my grand gesture all pause when Bea shows up.

Her shirt is crisp and bright white.

Her pants have a line down the front—freshly pressed.

In my entire life, I've never looked at any girl in a boring uniform and thought she looked amazing. Until now. But with her shining hair—albeit pulled back—and her petite figure?

Wowza.

And if I'd said that out loud, I'd sound like a seventy-year-old man. Someone who would wear suspenders unironically, for heaven's sake. I have *got* to remember not to use 'wowza.'

"Bea." I stand.

She's glaring. "Easton." Her head shake is slight, but clear.

I sit.

She hands me a menu.

"I'm not sure I should really be waiting on you again today." She eyes the empty chair. "I ran off your last date, and even with your millions, they couldn't match you with a better one?"

"Your boss didn't tell you?" I did tell him not to, but I've learned no one ever listens. "I told him I'd pay all the revenue you usually make for all the tables you usually wait on. Then you can eat with me." I hop up and pull out the other chair. "This one's yours."

All the blood drains from her face.

I'm so used to seeing her duck whenever she gets nervous that this is *not* what I expected, but I'm smart enough to know it's not good. When her eyes meet mine, she looks utterly horrified. "Please tell me you're kidding."

"You'll still—" I was going to say 'get paid,' but suddenly, that feels a little too *Pretty Woman* for comfort. I should have run my grand gesture idea past Elizabeth, obviously. "You'll still get to pick whatever you want to eat. And you don't have to choose my meals for me."

Oh my word. Next, I'll be telling her I can cut my own steak.

"Look." I step away from the chair and circle back around to my seat. "I really like you. I'm not sure whether you dislike me, or whether I've just startled you." I try to show her I'm sincere with my eyes, but I worry I just look constipated.

"Easton." She shakes her head, her enormous eyes welling with tears.

That's when I realize how badly I misjudged this.

Epic mistake level.

I need to backpedal fast, or I'll be dead in the water.

The line between grand gesture and stalker is razor thin, and apparently I'm on the wrong side of it.

"I'm kidding," I say. "I'll have the oysters and the scallops." I hand her my menu.

She stares at me for a second, and then she inhales sharply and nods. The second she walks off, I text her boss. THAT DID NOT GO WELL. I TOLD HER IT WAS A JOKE. IF YOU MAKE SURE NO ONE ELSE KNOWS ABOUT IT, I'LL STILL PAY THE SAME.

Two seconds later, I text my friend Matt. COME TO THE RED HORSE AT THE OPUS WESTCHESTER FOR DINNER. WE "HAD PLANS." 911.

He said he was golfing earlier, but I wouldn't care if he was skydiving. I'd barely care if he was going in for a job interview. . . I've saved him more times than I can count, so he can come eat a free dinner when I need him. He's eight years younger than I am—just out of school—so free food's usually enough of a draw on its own.

He gets here just as Bea's bringing my oysters, which is pretty impressive.

"Who's this?" Bea's eyeing him like he's a moth trying to eat her favorite sweater.

"I'm Matt." He holds out his hand, which is strange. No one shakes hands with their waitress.

I shake my head.

He drops his hand and sits. "Wow, this place is nice," he says.

"I fell in love with their food last night," I say. "I barely slept, thinking about their prosciutto and cheese."

He eyes my plate. "And then you got oysters?" Matt's going to get punched if he keeps making me look dumb. I've been doing plenty good at that myself. I definitely don't need help.

"I was waiting to order the burrata until you got here." I look up at Bea. "Maybe make it two orders. Matt eats more than most teenagers I know."

"How do you two know each other?" Bea asks.

"I signed up for a mentoring program as an alumnus. They assigned me this loser." I can't help my smile.

Bea quirks an eyebrow. "Let me guess. You both went to Harvard?"

"Hardly," Matt says. "This guy flunked out of Princeton. I met him at Rutgers."

Everyone thinks I flunked out, because to my parents that was less embarrassing than admitting we couldn't pay the tuition. They couldn't risk that anyone at the tuition office might recognize I was taking out loans, so Rutgers, which offered me a full scholarship as a transfer, is where I went.

"You're a Jersey boy?" Bea narrows her eyes. "Really?"

"I think I got an 'in state' scholarship," Matt says, "which is really just a discount. They waived the fact that I'm from New York to entice me to go." He shrugs.

"That's smart of them," she says. "Bring the good people, but don't make it entirely free."

"Good people?" I cringe. "Not sure Matt qualifies."

He throws his napkin at me.

My phone rings—there's some kind of problem with the supplier for one of our men's colognes. By the time I get off the call, Bea's back with the burratas. Matt wastes no time popping some in his mouth. "That's *amazing*," he says. "But it's small." He glances my way. "We're getting more food, right? With like, big portions?"

Bea laughs. "We're not exactly known for massive portions."

"Tell her whether you have allergies," I say, delighted that she seems entertained. "Then tell her your favorite meal of all time and where you ate it."

Matt frowns. "No allergies, not like my boy here."

I try to kick him and wind up slamming my toe into the central table support instead. It's hard not to wince, but I manage.

"Wait, you have allergies?" Bea asks. "You said last night—"

"No food allergies." I scowl.

"But he'll run like a scared little girl if he sees a bee." Matt slaps the table. "His little scream is hilarious."

I'm going to kill him.

"I'd mock him about it more often, but I swear, it was so scary that one time that if I were him, I'd screech too." He shakes his head. "Do you even remember anything from that?"

"Of course I remember it. My face swelled up," I say. "It didn't break my brain."

"You looked like Will Smith in *Hitch*," he says. "Actually, you looked worse." He's gesturing. "Your ears were like—"

This time, my foot connects with his shin hard.

"Like what?" Bea looks entertained at least.

"The swelling went down as soon as I got epinephrine on board," I say. "And I hardly think you're planning to sting me."

"You never know," Matt says. "She looks feisty."

Bea immediately ducks her head, and it's so stinking cute. She recovers quickly, at least. "You didn't tell me about your favorite meal yet," she says. "I'll need to know about that one and about your worst, too."

"Hmm." Matt frowns. "I guess I'm not that picky. I like pizza, and I like tacos, and I like hot dogs."

Bea chuckles. "You're really making me work for this."

Matt shrugs. "I'm not very fancy, I guess. You said you want my worst too?" He sighs. "This one time, my roommate dared me to eat some meat that had been sitting out—"

"Okay," I say. "I think we've heard enough."

Bea's shaking her head when she walks off.

"Dude, is *she* why you called me over here?" Matt's grinning like a loon. "Because if not, I call dibs. She's smokin'."

"Yes, I called you to help me." I scowl. "You could whisper, at least."

"Fine." Matt leans closer. "But dude, I'm not sure how well it's going. She seemed pretty annoyed."

"I had a plan." I fill him in on how my grand gesture backfired.

"Dude, that was a terrible idea."

"I figured that out right before she started bawling." I groan. "I'm hoping she believes that I was kidding," I say. "I did successfully set up weekly board meetings here every Tuesday, so I'll see her at least once a week."

"Wait, your plan is to force her to serve you for a work thing?" Matt's whole face scrunches up. "Yeesh."

"Is it really a bad idea?"

"You're tall, good looking, funny, and really smart.

Oh yeah, and you're freaking *loaded*. Why didn't you just ask her out?"

"I did," I say. "She said no."

Matt leans back, exhaling. "You really should have led with that, my man."

"Why? Does that give you a better idea?"

He shakes his head slowly. "If she knows all that and she still said no?" He shrugs. "Chick's probably gay."

"If she doesn't like me, she must like women?"

Matt looks pretty grim. "The other option is worse, honestly. Because the only other reason she'd turn you down is that she just straight up doesn't like you. You can fix a lot, but you can't fix someone being uninterested."

He's right.

It is worse.

Two seconds later, Bea waltzes over, setting a large round plate on the table. Up until now, they've all been square-edged, so this is new. It's loaded up with french fries, covered with bacon, peppers, and parmesan cheese, judging from the smell.

"Was this even on the menu?" I ask.

"It's a side, technically," Bea says. "Hipster fries."

"Hey." Matt frowns. "I'm not a hipster."

"I'm not usually someone who's angry," Bea says. "But our angry broccoli's still amazing."

"Just try the fries," I say. "You might have a new appreciation for hipsters."

Matt grabs an impressively large handful. I swear, it usually looks like the kid can unhinge his jaw. After he pops them in his mouth, his eyes light up. "Wow." He should not be talking with his mouth full, but he's barely more than twenty. "These are amazing." He's already reaching for more. "What's that little pepper?"

Bea's smiling. "It's a shishito pepper. They're really fun, I think."

"Is it citrusy?" Matt asks. "Or grassy?"

I reach for some to see what he's talking about, but he deflects my hand while simultaneously stuffing another pile in his mouth.

"I think we may need another plate," I say.

She's still smiling when she walks off.

A few minutes later, she returns, carrying three plates rather impressively. No tray. She sets the fries down first, shifting the now-empty plate she brought Matt, and then she sets the scallops down in front of me. I'd forgotten I even ordered them. I was kind of looking forward to her picking something for me again.

When she sets Matt's plate in front of him, his eyes widen. "What's that?"

"That is the forty-ounce tomahawk," she says, picking up the empty fry plate. "And it also happens to be the single largest and most expensive thing on the menu. Since your friend clearly called you over to cover for his earlier *faux pas*, I figured you'd enjoy sticking it to him on the price." She gives a little half bow and walks off.

Well played, Bea.

"She is feisty," Matt says. "The bad news is that she knows your grand gesture *was* a grand gesture."

She doesn't seem that angry, though. It makes me wonder whether it was the fact that I was pursuing her or my method that upset her. She seems a little shy. Maybe it was more that her coworkers knowing about something like that would be horrible for her.

Matt wastes no time slicing off a huge piece. Before he shoves it in his mouth, he asks, "After you strike out, mind if I take a swing?"

I throw a scallop at him.

I do regret throwing it after I take a bite. They're not quite as good as the burger Bea picked for me, but they're the best scallops I've ever had by a wide margin. I can't decide whether it's because I'm a burger guy, or whether I just liked that she picked it.

I'd probably eat Matt's weird old meat if she brought it.

Which is why I can't just give up, even if she really is gay. Or worse, if she's already decided she doesn't like me.

6

BEA

Jake's awake when I get home, reviewing his new script.

I ought to tell him that Easton showed up again. He'd be even more upset than I am, but for some reason, when I open my mouth to say the words, nothing comes out.

It's really more of an Emerson conversation, but I can't exactly call and badmouth Easton to his new brother-in-law.

"Tips good?" Jake asks when he looks up.

I shrug.

"My director wants to move filming up. I'd be starting two weeks earlier."

"You're leaving again?"

"I don't know. I've only been home for ten days. I told Dave I wanted a solid break this time. I could just tell him no."

"You could," I say.

"Why do you say it like that?" He drops the script on the coffee table and stands.

"Like what?"

"Like, if I tell them no, I'm Jennifer Lopez or something."

"I'm not saying you're anywhere near her level, but if you're making them delay their schedule because three weeks isn't a long enough vacation for you. . ." I can't help smiling. "I haven't ever had three weeks off."

"Filming's hard." He folds his arms.

"I know it is," I say. "Wanna come wait some tables for me?"

"It's not the same. It's draining for me the whole time I'm filming, on and off set. Plus, I have to live in a hotel. At least you get to sleep in your own bed."

"I have heard the Hyatt's a tiresome place to stay." I shake my head slowly.

"You're kidding," he says, "but—"

The computer dings.

"I've been checking," he says. "Nothing so far."

I don't get many emails, so I've been obsessively watching my email since I submitted my jingle.

Which is really stupid.

It's not like I really think they're going to reply twenty-four hours after I submitted my song, but they did say the applications were rolling and that they'd make their decision quickly after the deadline. I submitted mine right at the end, but surely not everyone procrastinates.

When I step close enough to see the computer screen, it's an email from someone about the upcoming local election. I groan.

"There's a special place reserved down below for spammers." He shakes his head. "They're like a plague."

"It's fine," I say.

Only, the finals is a few days away—they said they'll call back just a handful of composers and select from between us with the client's involvement. They can't take *too* long to notify us, right?

I shower, brush my teeth, and put on my favorite pajamas. I'm in bed, almost asleep when I hear it. Another ding. Checking now is dumb. I should go to sleep.

It's probably an email offering me twenty percent off Ann Taylor's summer line now that it's fall.

But then Jake starts shouting. "Bea! Get in here!"

My heart's hammering when I leap from bed and race into the family room.

"Dear Ms. Cipriani," Jake says. "We are pleased to inform you that your submission of 'Smooth like Jello' has been chosen to advance to the final round of the competition. Your presence is requested to present your jingle on Tuesday, September 7th, yada yada." Jake spins around slowly, a smile spreading across his face. "You did it!"

It takes me almost an hour to fall asleep after that. I'm too excited.

I dream of the final round, and when they pick my jingle, for some reason they hang a huge wreath of roses around my neck, like I'm a horse that just won the Grand Prix. The strangest part is that, for some reason, Easton Moorland's standing beside me when I win, beaming.

When I wake up, I check the time—late enough to call. I dial my boss immediately. "Hey, Harv," I say.

"It's pretty early," he says. "Aren't you usually still asleep at seven?"

"Did I wake you up?" I wince.

"No, but I was surprised. Today's your day off."

"I need to talk to you about Tuesday. I have a thing, and I just found out, and it's kind of late notice, but I was hoping I could—"

"No way," Harv says. "You have to come in at noon and serve Mr. Moorland's board. You agreed."

I forgot all about that. "My thing is at seven at night," I say. "So that's fine. I was wanting to trade my shift."

"Done," he says. "You're now working the lunch shift. It ends at 4." He hangs up.

All day, no matter what I do to keep busy, I keep seeing that ridiculous rose wreath and stupid Easton Moorland smiling at me. I'm not sure where Jake went, but I'm going crazy all alone in the apartment. I open my laptop, and before I have time to think about it, I find myself typing in the search box.

Easton Moorland.

I hate myself for looking him up.

It's not like it's going to change anything. He's too good looking. He's too famous. He might not be as recognizable as Jake, because who is? But any notoriety is too much for me. Plus, there's *no way* someone like him actually likes someone like me. I'm sure he only tried harder because I said no.

Guys like him probably *never* get told no.

I should have thought of that and found a way to just put him off. I could have said sure and then canceled. After a few scheduling issues, he'd have given up. He'd never have gone to the trouble of asking my boss for a Tuesday lunch meeting every week if I hadn't felt hard-to-get.

There are dozens and dozens of articles on Easton Moorland.

Most of them are pretty boring. I mean, I already know he's slaying in the business world. Reading about all the thoughts people have on why is. . .yawn. I know his parents and his sister's name. It's a little creepy they have them listed online, as well as the fact that his sister just married Emerson, heir to the famous Richmond fortune.

I do see the irony in the fact that I'm reading about him and yet that's why I don't want to date him. Because people like me read articles about him and I want no part of it.

I hate that this kind of information even exists.

And yet, I type in another search: Easton Moorland girlfriend.

I really hate myself for it, but I have to see what kind of girl he usually dates. Maybe he's left a string of broken-hearted waitresses in his wake. It might even be his usual MO. I bet there's, like, a warning posted online, telling all the support staff at the various places he frequents that he's a dirty perv.

Only, every single article says he's a self-proclaimed workaholic, and as far as they've been able to uncover, he's never dated *anyone*.

That can't be right.

I mean, I've never dated anyone more than a handful of times, but it's mostly because no one has ever been interested in me. When you're a mousy little nobody, people tend not to ask you out. Easton, however, is not mousy, and he's definitely not a nobody.

There's no mention of Miss Collagen USA, so clearly the tabloids miss some stuff. Maybe he's been paying someone to get all the torrid stories about him cleaned up. People do that in movies. Or maybe one of his old Rutgers cronies owns a search engine, and they suppress anything bad about him someone tries to print.

So far, the articles are setting off one red flag.

When I search for something on Amazon, and there aren't *any* bad reviews, I'm immediately suspicious. Did they pay for their reviews? How do they have so many good ones? Trolls are everywhere, and they like to complain. So if not a single person has left a negative review? It's fishy.

So it worries me that no one has anything bad to say about Easton Moorland. As a business mogul, I find it bizarre. Shouldn't he have lots of enemies? By lunchtime, it's still bugging me, and I realize that I have no choice.

I have to call Emerson.

He answers on the second ring. That must mean he wasn't doing anything too important. "Bea! I'm glad you called."

"Uh-oh," I say. "Do I owe you money I forgot about?"

"Funny," he says. "I was *just* talking about you."

"You were?" That can't be good. "Why?"

"Remember when we were kids how you were the only one who could fix that toilet that just kept running?"

Definitely not what I expected him to say.

"We called a plumber, but they can't come until tomorrow at four." Emerson sounds desperate, which is kind of funny.

"You know, if your toilet's running, you should really catch it."

"Wah wah," Emerson says. "Same lame jokes I remember."

"Did you want my help? Or was that a lame joke?"

"On second thought, that joke was clever. *So* clever. Ha, ha, ha."

It's annoying that the first time I call in at least a week, he wants me to come fix a toilet, but I do want to pry for information, so I'm not really any better. "I can't believe your grandmother doesn't have someone on speed dial to deal with any problem, including plumbing."

"Andre, her groundskeeper and handyman, is on a trip," Emerson says. "But even if he wasn't, this toilet is at the shelter."

Of course it is. Where else would they be on a Sunday afternoon? I swear, if Elizabeth wasn't such a kook about animals, I'd have thought she married Emerson for his money. The only thing that woman spends money on is horses and pathetic, unloved critters.

"If I come over, you have to *swear* you aren't going to try and fob one of those little fuzzies off on me."

"You know, the tiny Shih Tzu you liked is still here," he says. "He's actually kind of whimpering right now, and. . .what's that, Ivin? You miss Bea?"

I hang up.

On my way out the door, I glance down at my outfit. I'm still wearing the shabby plaid pajama pants and faded navy t-shirt that I slept in. Emerson got me the pajama pants a few years back for Christmas, and Jake gave me the shirt for my birthday when I was sixteen. It says, "Yeah, I'm short. God only lets things grow until they're perfect. Why are you so tall?" I would normally change before leaving the house, but I'm going to be working on a toilet, and when I'm done, they'll probably need help with the kennels.

The last time I went over, I ruined a brand new pair

of khaki capri pants Jake gave me for my birthday. They were designer, which he told me in a very high-pitched voice as I tossed the urine soaked and scratched pants in the wash. To be fair, I think his tone was less about my pants and their condition and more about the clothes he already had in the washer. Apparently he didn't want them marinated in my filth.

Anyway, I'm nearly to my ten-year-old Toyota Camry when Jake pulls into the spot next to me in his Nissan Z. He claims it's 'not flashy,' and that it lets him 'fly under the radar.' I might've believed him if it wasn't electric blue.

"Where you off to?" He scrunches up his nose. "Nowhere public, I hope."

Jake never leaves the house without looking like he's ready to walk onto the set of some commercial or other. Ironically, he often spends half of his movie scenes covered with fake blood or carefully designed grime, but in real life, he's pristine.

I heft my home repair tool bag across to the passenger seat. "I'm helping Emerson with a toilet."

"That's even worse than anything I imagined." He shakes his head as he walks past me. He throws a hand back in a half-hearted wave. "If you run into trouble. . ." He laughs. "Don't call me. I definitely won't answer."

"You're an amazing brother," I shout. "The best!"

He pivots from where he's standing on our threshold. "You know, that guy could hire a full-time plumber to just be on call, and no one would ever notice. Why on earth he needs to make his sister go over there to work on a toilet. . ." He's still grumbling as he walks through the door and disappears.

I think Jake's problem is that he spent so long taking advantage of people that he always thinks people are trying to bilk him. No one I know is more sensitive to someone else asking for a favor—he repays everything anyone ever does for him, and he expects everyone else to do the same. Not with me, but with literally every other person in his life.

On the drive to Emerson's, I intend to think about what kind of outfit I should wear to the finals on Tuesday. Instead, I keep thinking about Easton. What he does on Sundays. Does he work on weekends? What kind of pet he might have or want to have? Whether he likes helping at the shelter. Whether he's a good mentor to that kid.

It's the dumbest thing ever that after turning him down, twice really, I keep thinking about him. My one consolation is that no one else knows what I'm thinking. They can't see my pathetic dreams or my ridiculous thoughts. And if I'm planning to work in questions about Easton while I help my brother selflessly, well, there's no reason for me to feel bad about it.

Who would know what his love life is like better than Elizabeth?

That girl does not pull punches.

She does play dirty, though. When I walk through the door, there's a box of puppies in the entryway. "Seriously?" One of them has a bow around its neck like I've walked into some kind of Hallmark movie. "You guys are disgustingly obvious."

"You think we put cute puppies in a box there just so you'd see them and want one?" Emerson waves me through. "Please. Someone dumped those guys twenty minutes ago. People are the worst."

I crouch down. "They do look like little angels." The one closest to me clamps down on my index finger and I revise my assessment. "They're actually gremlins, aren't they?"

"We think they're some kind of German Shepherd cross." Emerson tugs on my shoulder. "But for real, thank you. This stupid facility has a septic, and it's one of the dumb newer ones with the water tanks that have to spray off. I was starting to worry we'd wind up with toilets backing up any time."

"I'm coming," I say. "Geez."

It takes me exactly two minutes to figure out that the handle on the toilet is jammed and won't unstick. "Bad news," I say. "This needs a new handle, and I brought an extra flapper, but I don't have that."

"How do you know so much about toilets?" Elizabeth asks.

"Well, my mom got high a lot," I say. "And when they thought someone was coming to catch them, they'd always flush their supply. Paranoid people do that a lot when they aren't even being chased." I sigh. "We didn't stay in nice places most of the time, so a lot of their toilets couldn't handle any extra stress. As a kid, I got pretty good at looking things up on YouTube so I could still go pee."

Elizabeth's face is incredulous. She can't decide whether I'm teasing.

This is just another reason Easton and I would be a total disaster. I wish I could ask about him without looking completely obvious, but I can't think of any way to do that, so I just say, "I'll head to the hardware store and be back in a bit."

"You do think you can fix it though?" Elizabeth asks as she follows me out of the bathroom.

"Pretty sure," I say.

"I can go with you." Emerson grabs his keys off the counter. "I can even drive."

Elizabeth narrows her eyes. "I'm onto you, mister. You just don't want to have to help me finish the kennels."

Emerson throws his hands up in the air. "I offered to come, remember? I could have stayed home."

"You can work on the kennels with me, and Easton can take her," Elizabeth says, pointing toward the front of the shelter. "I think he just got here, and he's useless with this kind of stuff, but he could at least drive her there for moral support."

My heart stops dead.

Easton's coming?

I want to cry—I'm wearing frayed plaid pajama pants and a ratty shirt. I mean, I don't want to date him, but so far he's seen me wearing my work uniform. . .and now this. If any part of him *did actually like me,* well, it was nice while it lasted, feeling desirable.

Not that I care.

Actually, this is probably better. I stick my chin up and square my shoulders. "Sure. Easton can take me. Why not?"

"Yes, why not?" Elizabeth asks. "You're doing us a huge favor, so you shouldn't have to pay for gas to and from the store." She raises her voice. "Easton! I heard bells jingling. That's you, right?"

"Yep." He pokes his head around the corner of the door, and his eyes widen. "Bea?"

I sigh. "Come on." I shove past him and toward the front door, the dogs in the front kennel yapping louder again now that we're walking past them. "You're driving me to the hardware store."

Easton's beaming. "Sure thing, boss."

When we reach the front door, I stop, turning slightly. I press my index finger toward his face, which is really high up. "You will not flirt. You will not ask me out. You will not even think about doing either of those things."

"Hmm." He cocks one eyebrow. "I can refrain from asking you out, but I'm not sure you can dictate my thoughts."

I ball my hands into fists. "I'm wearing pajama pants and an old shirt, because I'm here to fix a toilet."

"You're super cute when you're all growly."

"I'm not growly." I scowl. The gremlin puppies are crying and clawing, trying to get out of their sad little box, and I point at them. "They're growly. I'm firm."

He laughs. "I won't ask you out, I swear, but if you start flirting with me, I can't be held responsible for flirting back."

I roll my eyes and walk toward my car.

"I thought I was driving."

"Oh, right." I look around for his car.

He pulls out his key fob, and I'm shocked to see that he's driving the boring gunmetal Toyota 4Runner parked on the end.

"Really?"

He shrugs. "Elizabeth told me she needed help at the shelter. The last time I came over in something nice, let's just say I regretted it."

It's his equivalent of my pajama pants and t-shirt. Clearly he has more than one car, though, which I find somewhat entertaining.

"What?"

I shrug. "Nothing. It just wasn't the car I expected you to drive."

"What did you think I'd drive?" His eyebrows rise.

"Please don't say a Ferrari or something." He follows me over and yanks the door open.

"I can't say I'd thought about it much." I'd die before I let him know I was googling him. "I'm kind of surprised to hear you help at the shelter." I hop in the car.

He leans on the doorframe, his face only a foot away from mine. "I'll probably keep surprising you for a while yet, Beatrice Cipriani."

Before I can say anything, he closes the door and jogs around to his side. When he gets in, he acts like everything's totally normal. "Cornell's? Or Wallauer?"

"Cornell's," I say. "Wallauer's overpriced."

"Good to know." He's smiling for some reason. Maybe because the thought of economizing on a toilet handle is stupid to a man like him, and that kind of bugs me.

"You know, you'll do better in life by controlling your spending than just earning more."

"Really?" He lifts his eyebrows. "You think so?"

"Well, taxes just go up the more you make, for one. But also, no matter how much money you have, if you can't live within your means, you'll never be financially stable."

"I suppose that's true," he says. "And you're right about the government taking my money. Taxes are no joke."

"I guess," I say, staring down at my hands.

I expect him to ask me something, or to pry, or to talk about the upcoming board meeting. He surprises me again by simply driving. He's just. . .quiet.

Neither Emerson nor Jake is even capable of that. When they're with me, someone has to be talking. The silence is kind of nice. I didn't expect to be almost *comfortable* in his presence. Or at least, I'm not climbing out of my skin like I usually am when he's at work, watching me.

When we reach the hardware store, he follows me inside, observing without interfering. I've just picked the handle that I think is the right color and size when I hear someone giggling.

It's two women. One of them is older, and one is close to my age. "—understand how people can go out in pajamas. Seriously."

"You know, Bea, I've never understood how people could express their opinions about others in public without being embarrassed about how rude they are." Easton glares. "Especially when they're clearly jealous of the person they're talking about."

The women look horrified, but they walk the other direction.

"You shouldn't have done that." I walk straight toward the checkout.

"Why not?" He's jogging to catch up. "They were being really rude."

"I *am* wearing pajamas. I didn't think I'd be coming shopping—I was fixing a toilet. But it wasn't the flapper; it was the handle. It's my fault. I shouldn't be dressed like this in public."

"It's your fault that, what? That you're wearing perfectly acceptable clothing that covers your body entirely?" He snorts. "Do you know what kind of trash some people wear? Sometimes they leave their booties or who knows what else just hanging out."

That makes me laugh. "I suppose some people do wear questionable things."

"I've never commented on their decisions, and those people can butt out about what you're wearing. I'm the person who's out and about with you, and I think you look cute. Their opinion isn't wanted." Before I can pay, he swipes his card and drops the handle into a bag.

"Are you saying *your* opinion on what I'm wearing does matter?" I arch an eyebrow.

"I mean, clearly it doesn't to you, but if the person you're here with isn't embarrassed, and you're covering the relevant parts of your body to be decent in public, then you shouldn't let them drag you."

"I'm not their mother." I snatch the bag and walk toward his 4Runner. "It's not my job to teach them anything. I take the path of least resistance when I'm in situations like that."

"Noted."

"Wait." I stop at the car door, my hand already on the handle. "What's noted?"

"That you prefer to ignore rude people, rather than confront them."

"It's not like we'll be going to Cornell's often."

"Well, I'm not sure about that," Easton says. "My sister's shelter is a bit of a mess, even after the remodel. We may bump into each other a lot in the next decade."

I can't help laughing about that, because it's true. Things there break a lot, which is the nature of a place that has people flowing through it constantly. It's probably even more true of places that take in animals.

"It looks like they're just as shameless about using you as they are with me."

"Only when they can't get a plumber on the line," I say.

"Actually, they've never called me to help before," Easton says. "I was telling Elizabeth this morning that I had a crush on you, and she said that the next time she saw you, she'd text and tell me to rush over."

I freeze.

Easton's eyes are steady on mine.

I blink. "You—you're kidding."

He smiles. "Of course I am." He unlocks the car, and this time, he lets me open my own, but he doesn't walk around to his side until I've closed my door.

On the way back to the shelter, he's totally normal—no jokes.

Part of me wonders whether I imagined the flirting, but it's happened too many times now. So when he pulls into a parking spot and cuts the engine, I break the silence. "Easton."

He turns toward me, a half-smile tugging on the edges of his mouth. "Beatrice."

"No one calls me that," I snap.

"Why not? It's pretty."

"Let me rephrase. Only my mother and my grandfather call me that, and I hate it."

"Bea it is," he says. "Sorry to have stepped on that landmine."

"It's fine." It's really weird I even told him that. Usually I just cringe and ignore it. Always, actually. I *always* cringe and let it go.

"My parents call me Eastie whenever they want something. It may not be the same, but I hate that, too. I'm not three years old."

"Do your parents ask you for stuff a lot?"

"Like fixing toilets, you mean?" he asks.

I shrug. "Sure."

"Not really. They do ask me for money pretty often. Always have."

"Usually I think it goes the other way, but mine was always asking me, too." My mom took any two dimes I managed to rub together as a kid, so I guess I get it. But once I got older and had a job, she was downright hostile and persistent. "You should shut that down fast."

"What?" Easton frowns. "Shut what down?"

"Do you know what enabling is?"

His frown deepens.

"It took me a lot of therapy to learn that when I give my mother money, I'm enabling the behaviors that led to her asking me for money. I thought I was helping, but it does at least as much harm as it does good. It only took a half dozen times of me refusing point blank and telling her I'd only give her food before she quit asking me."

"My parents aren't junkies." He hops out of the car.

He's out talking to Emerson when I finish fixing the toilet handle. I wash my hands—their soap is mostly donated I know, but the bubble gum smell is annoying—and head back to the front. "I survived the gauntlet," I say. "Your ploys didn't work."

"What?" Elizabeth doesn't quite get my humor yet.

"I passed through the portal of puppies, and I'm leaving without one."

"You're leaving?" Easton asks.

I nod.

"Oh. Well."

"Hey, what happened with that jingle contest?" Emerson asks.

I want to kick him.

"What jingle contest?" Easton asks.

"Bea plays piano like. . .well, like the Piano Guys or something. She's amazing, and she's always making up songs, too. She entered this jingle contest, or at least, she was going to."

"I did," I say.

"And?" Emerson asks. "When do you hear back?"

"I made it to the finals," I say softly. "It's on Tuesday."

"Yes!" Emerson wraps me in a bear hug. "That's amazing, B."

"I mean, there are five of us, and we have to perform the jingle ourselves for a live audience so they can choose the winner." I tilt my head and widen my eyes. He knows why that's not great for me.

"Oh, shoot." Emerson grimaces. "I'm sorry."

"Why?" Easton asks.

"I can't sing well, for one," I say. "But also, I hate performing. I'm good at writing music, not at putting on a show."

"Can you have someone else do it for you?" Easton asks.

"Are you offering?" I ask.

"Oh, heavens no," he says. "I sound like the seagull in *The Little Mermaid*."

"He actually does," Elizabeth says. "His voice is an assault."

"Bea's not bad," Emerson says. "It's just that since she was a music major, she always compares herself to these opera quality singers."

"I'd love to come watch and support you," Easton says.

"Me too," Emerson says. "What time is it?"

"It's at seven at night," I say. "But I don't think we can take an audience."

Emerson frowns. "But surely—"

I shake my head. "I'll email and ask, alright?"

"Swear?" My brother does not let things go. It's one of his most annoying traits. He holds out his pinkie.

I slap his hand. "I swear, idiot." Even if we pinky

promised last week, he should know better than to do it in front of anyone else.

"I'm really proud of you. I mean it."

"And I'm impressed," Easton says. "I really want to come see you too. I'm a great clapper."

"A great *clapper*?" Elizabeth frowns. "Why are you being so idiotic?" She turns to me. "He's not usually this corny, I swear. Actually, the only time I've ever seen him act this dumb was when I brought my friend Andie over and. . ." She freezes, and then she turns very slowly. "No freaking way. Do you *like* my adorable sister-in-law?"

7

EASTON

"*ike* her?" I force a laugh.

I'm going to kill Elizabeth.

I don't think they can take my business away for murdering someone. I can hire someone to run it while I'm in prison, surely. Right? I can't believe she's bringing up her stupid friend Andie from high school.

"I mean, it doesn't matter whether I do or not," I say. "Because when I asked her out, she turned me down."

Elizabeth's laugh is a little unhinged. "Holy Kibbles and Bits."

I don't know another adult in the world who uses mock swears that revolve around dog food and cat treats, but that's Elizabeth. "If you don't shut up, I'll shove kibble into your big mouth."

"I better get going," Bea says. "I should practice for Tuesday." She ducks out of the door so fast that I'm worried she might get whiplash.

"I think my sister might like you too," Emerson says. "I've never seen her act quite so startled."

"You must be kidding. She turned me down."

He shrugs. "That's just Bea. She turns down everyone. That's why she never goes out on any dates."

"Wait, you need to explain," Elizabeth says.

"When we were like seventeen, my friend Holden asked her out," Emerson says. "She said no, and he was pretty upset. When I asked her about it, she said he was clearly kidding."

Elizabeth frowns. "But he wasn't?"

Emerson shakes his head. "I told her he was serious, and she said she could tell he wasn't really serious. Not really."

My sister frowns. "Does she have low self-esteem?"

"What do you think?" Emerson asks. "Her mom ignored her half her life, and then her grandfather criticized everything she did, including being quiet."

"So she never dates?" I hate myself for asking, but I can't help it. "And she's not dating anyone right now?" It did occur to me that she might have turned me down because she's already got a boyfriend. The idea makes me feel vaguely ill, but I'd rather know.

It's always better to know, right?

"No way." Emerson shakes his head. "She's a really great person, but I don't think she's ever really dated anyone. I mean, she's had a few dates here and there, but no guy ever took her out more than a handful of times, and almost all of those were setups."

"How is that possible?" I can't believe that's really true. She looks like a goddess.

"Honestly, I blame Jake. He's not big on sharing, and he's a little off-putting. Add that to her propensity to think no one *really* likes her, and you have someone who's impossible to take out."

"Is he in love with her?" Elizabeth asks. "Because he's really weird around her."

"Jake hasn't had much in his life, and he thinks Bea is his." Emerson shrugs. "She's the only person he even listens to, and I think it's more like a dog protecting his only beloved toy."

"That's not a no," Elizabeth says.

"I've wondered myself whether he might love her," Emerson says. "But if Jake Priest wants something, he takes it." He sighs. "I think if Jake *is* in love with Bea, he doesn't know it himself."

"Wait, do you really like her, Easton?" Elizabeth says. "Because part of me was wondering if maybe you were gay."

I roll my eyes. "It's so dumb that if a guy doesn't have time to date or an active interest in someone in particular, every straight person they know assumes they're secretly gay."

"I mean, it's not a big deal now," Emerson says. "Most people who are out, they're just out. Right?"

"I have no idea," I say. "But that's not why I haven't dated much. I'm definitely not interested in guys, unless Bea's secretly a guy."

"This is so weird," Elizabeth says. "Nine million girls out there and the only one you've ever liked is my sister-in-law? Is this a prank? Because if so, it's a good one."

I grab the door handle. "Thanks for the support," I grumble. "I thought you'd be happy for me, but whatever."

Elizabeth runs up and throws her arms around me. "I'm sorry." She presses her head against my chest. "I am happy for you, E, I swear."

I sigh slowly.

"Bea really is stunning, so I can see why you'd like her. I was just surprised."

"And if it goes badly. . ."

"It would be a little weird for me, sure," she says. "But it's not like you two will fight at our baby shower, for instance. Right?"

I look down at her. "What are you saying?"

"I thought we weren't telling people," Emerson says. "I didn't say a word to Bea, even though I was dying to when she started talking about those puppies."

Elizabeth spins around and immediately starts wheedling. She's got this down to an art. "I'm so sorry. It's just, I was kind of moody with him just now, and I didn't want him to leave mad."

"You're already using the baby to get out of sticky situations? Really?" Emerson asks.

"Do we know if it's a boy or a girl yet?" I ask.

"Girl," Elizabeth says.

"Boy," Emerson says.

I frown. "Are you having twins?"

"We don't know whether it's a boy or a girl yet," Elizabeth says. "We decided to wait and be surprised, so we just have hunches."

"That's dumb," I say. "It's a surprise no matter when you find out."

"You're dumb," Elizabeth says. "It's disrespectful to say whatever you think."

She's so snarky, always. I imagine it'll only get worse once she has a baby to protect. "Just for that," I say. "I hope it's a boy."

"Rude," she hisses. "You know how much I love watching babies trying to crawl in floofy little dresses."

"It's going to be a *boy*," I shout as I head out the front door.

Mom's going to crap a brick.

The Richmond heir, being birthed by one of her children. I swear, I need to stay away for at least two weeks after they tell her. Mom's annoying enough without hounding me about having a child. When I'm not stuck working over the next day and a half, I'm looking for funny parenting reels and memes and sending them to Elizabeth.

What on earth is Instagram for if not this?

But really, I'm trying not to think too much about Tuesday—the lunch I'm dragging the board to so that I can see her again—and the fact that I have heard exactly nothing about attending her competition finals. I really can't think of many things I'd rather do than go and see Bea perform a song she wrote.

Finally, on Tuesday morning, the idea hits me. I shouldn't just sit around and hope she invites me. I should be proactive. I didn't build my business into what it is by hoping people would call and offer me opportunities. I created the opportunities by badgering, cajoling, tricking, and forcing people into giving me a chance.

About twenty minutes of searching yields the information that there *is* a final performance for the Jello Jingle Competition, and the finals are open to the public. I text a screenshot to Emerson, and he responds with, IT'S A DATE. He's a pretty decent brother-in-law. I mean, that's funny. He knows I want to date his sister, and he's making a date with me to go cheer for her. Irony and a pun.

I do wonder, briefly, whether it might be a mistake to go without an invite, and I decide to feel her out at the lunch.

Which, thanks to the distraction of my research, it's time for.

When I walk in, the host walks me, along with the three board members who arrived at nearly the same time, into a side room. "We're excited to welcome you to our facility," the thin man says. "Right this way."

Several other board members are already there. "This menu's great," Mr. Dressel says, already poring over the items listed. "I'm thinking we should order a handful of appetizers, and then by the time everyone's here—"

"Actually," I say, "our waitress today has an amazing gift. If you answer a few questions, she can pick the very thing from the menu that you'll like the most."

Mr. Dressel arches one eyebrow. "That sounds. . .unlikely. How could anyone else know what I want better than I do?"

"For one, she might know the menu better than you." Mrs. Yaltzinger sits. "I think it sounds interesting."

"Me too," Mr. Jimenez says. "I'm not sure about you, Frank, but I always seem to pick the wrong thing. The person next to me usually has something better than what I chose."

"That's because I make better decisions than you," Mr. Dressel says. "It's nice that you're finally admitting it."

"You certainly don't have to let me choose for you." Bea's standing in the doorway. "But if you're not sure what to order, I'm happy to help." Her half smile is perfect. As the last few board members wander in, she explains to them that if they'll answer a few basic questions, she can select their meal. Or they're welcome to order for themselves.

Fifteen minutes later, everyone's orders have either been placed or prepared, and a brawny guy in all black is helping her unload appetizers from large trays.

"For you." She's smiling when she sets scallops down in front of me. They look different than the ones I ordered for dinner over the weekend.

"I didn't see those on the menu," Mr. Dressel says.

Bea shrugs. "Sometimes the item someone would like most isn't on the menu. I'm close enough to the chef that he'll often make things that have been specials in the past for me." She shrugs. "But the menu items are also all wonderful." She sets his Wagyu beef tartare in front of him. "You chose one that I never pick for anyone, since it's not one of my personal favorites."

"See?" Mr. Dressel shakes his head. "That's a flaw. What if the only thing I'd like would be the beef tartare?"

"In my experience," Bea says, "that type of person never asks me to choose for them, so they always get just what they want anyway."

Mrs. Yaltzinger laughs. "She's got you there, Frank."

"Well, now that we all have our food," Mr. Dressel says, frowning, "we should get started."

"But we need to see whether she was right," Mr. Jimenez says. "This dangling bacon tower is weird. I'm surprised she chose it for me."

"Yes, I was definitely not expecting oysters," Mrs. Yaltzinger says. "I've never been brave enough to try them."

"It's the apple cucumber mignonette that makes these special," Beatrice says. "Well, that and the fact that you're going to try three east coast oysters, and three west coast oysters. I think you'll quickly discover which you prefer."

I go ahead and slice a scallop in half and pop it in my mouth. Unlike the buttery, seared scallops from the menu, these are light, almost sweet. I'm quite sure I can taste citrus, as well. While I'm chewing, I watch as everyone else tries their appetizers. I'm not the only one sighing with delight.

"Fine," Mr. Dressel surprises us all by saying. "Scratch my order for the entree. Surprise me with something you'd choose."

Bea nods slowly. "Alright." When she starts to back out, Mr. Dressel objects.

"Don't you need me to answer your questions?"

"You said you had no allergies," she says.

"But what about the others? My favorite and worst meal?"

Bea's smile is smug. "I've been able to observe you long enough that I think I can do without the answers."

A moment later, she slips out, but that doesn't keep us from talking about her.

"Not gonna lie," Mr. Jimenez says. "When you said we were doing our board meeting over lunch, and then you named the place we'd sent you for that failed setup, I thought maybe you had lost your mind. But this food." He shakes his head. "And having someone choose for you. . .it's brilliant."

"I'll withhold judgment until I see whether she brings me that ghastly burger," Mr. Dressel says.

"That's what she brought me," I say, "and it was amazing."

But the next twenty minutes are quickly consumed with their ideas for launching a women's line. By the time I shoot down the third one, I can tell they're annoyed.

"Who has heard of the brand Express?" I ask.

Most of the board members scrunch their noses. At least they know what I'm talking about.

"That's not a high fashion company," Mrs. Yaltzinger says. "They're nothing like us."

I shake my head. "They were a designer label at one point," I say. "Perhaps not couture, but designer at least.

Back in 2001, they took the first misstep on their journey toward being delisted from the stock market because their stock price fell below a dollar."

It's a horror story in fashion.

"Do you know what that step was?" I glance around the room.

They shrug. They share meaningful glances with each other. They look down at their empty plates. A few drain their glasses. None of them look my way.

But finally, Mr. Jimenez says, "Just tell us."

"They had two arms at first. Express was for women. They poured millions upon millions into creating that brand. It sold extremely well. However, their men's line, Structure, always lagged. Some said it was a misallocation of advertising dollars. Some said the designers they used weren't as in touch as those who did the women's side." I did a whole project in school on the rise and fall of Structure and Express. "The CEO in 2000 was tasked to bring the men's line up to par with the women's. Instead of redesigning or refreshing, he decided to take what worked—the Express name—and transition the entire men's line to become 'Express for Men.'" I can't help my cringe. "It was an unmitigated disaster. All the dollars they'd poured into making Express a recognizable name for women made it anathema for men. That, coupled with a few years of safe but disastrously boring clothing, built out the coffin. A lot of people blame the leadership in the past five years, but it was already in a steep nosedive that very few could have pulled out of."

"What's the point?" Mr. Dressel's never patient. Not ever.

"I understand your insistence that we launch a women's brand, but doing it the wrong way would be far worse than having no women's products at all." I look around, meeting each person's eye.

As if on cue, the doors open behind me, the various aromas of our food slamming me in the face. Beatrice has excellent timing, unsurprisingly. I told her I wanted longer than usual in between each visit so we could conduct our meeting, and she nailed it. It makes me wonder whether she was waiting outside the door listening in.

"As the best latency spotter in the market right now, we really need your insight into women's couture so we can figure out what to target," Mrs. Yaltzinger says. "But you went on one date and have refused any more."

"That's because," I say, "I've already identified a girl I'd like to date. I need a little time to win her over." I glance behind me.

Bea freezes for a beat, and then she sets a plate in front of me. "Lobster risotto," she whispers. "I had chef swap out the snow peas for asparagus."

"Your chef—David Burke, right?—is brilliant," Mrs. Yaltzinger says. "That looks amazing."

"David designed this menu," Bea says, "but one of his up-and-coming sous chefs has been handling lunch. Her name is Julietta, and she's like a savant with vegetables. She smells them for twenty minutes each morning, tossing the ones that don't pass muster into a big bin."

Mr. Dressel frowns.

"But for you, sir." She walks toward Mr. Dressel, taking him his food right after mine. She's already figured out the pecking order. She places his plate in front of him and steps back. "Native lobster and Crab Imperial." She tilts her head. "Hasn't been on the menu since last fall, but a fresh catch of beautiful lobsters came in this morning, and I thought you'd appreciate them."

She doesn't wait for Mr. Dressel to take a bite. She's already off, serving Mrs. Yaltzinger her seared ginger salmon, and then Mr. Jimenez his bison short ribs.

A few moments later, and no one's grilling me about the women's line. They're all oohing and aahing about the food—and Bea's taste. "How do you do it?" Mr. Dressel finally asks, and then he *licks* his finger off. Clearly she really bowled him over with the lobster and crab thing.

"You want my secret?" She arches one eyebrow. "This is my job, sir, and you want me to give away my secrets?"

He sighs. "I suppose not."

We haven't made much progress—maybe about as much as I've made with Bea—by the time she returns for the final time. "I know that none of you asked for dessert, and most people don't want it after lunch. But I could tell that three of you really needed just a *bit* more." She sets a wooden board with skewers on it in front of Mrs. Yaltzinger, Mr. Jimenez, and Miss Lundgren. "These are called dessert pops. There's a champagne-infused berry, a macaron, and the best truffle cake ball you've ever had. The dips on there are to die for."

"What about me?" I ask.

"You're already too sweet." She flounces out.

When I go to grab the check, she's talking to some-one. I'm pretty sure she's not actually waiting for me, but it almost feels like it. "Hey, you did a great job today," I say. "There's a reason I asked for you. I knew they'd love the select-their-food-for-them trick."

"None of our other waiters do that," the host says. "A few of them have tried, but it went. . .not as well."

"I asked for her secret," I say. "But she wouldn't share it."

"Sometimes she refuses to do it," the host says. "But when she's *on*? It's pretty amazing."

Now I really want to know how she does it. I pay with the company card—board meeting—and then pull her aside. "Come on," I say. "Now that no one else is around, surely you'll share how you do it."

She rolls her eyes.

"Easton," Mrs. Yaltzinger catches up to me. "I just talked to Ursula. I know the last date was not a love connection, but she has some ideas, and I think if you give her a chance, you'll see that she's great at her job. She learned a lot from your feedback last time, and she has a few strong candidates. You can even take a look." She holds up her phone. "I really like this lady, who runs a salon on the West side."

"He really did meet someone, you know," Bea says.

My heart stutters.

"She's pretty shy, but he met her on his last date."

"Did he?" Mrs. Yaltzinger's eyes light up. "Tell me more. Is she pretty? Did she look fashionable?"

Bea shrugs. "She actually looked pretty plain to me. Definitely not a stylista."

I snort. "She's breathtaking." I can't help staring. Even in her work uniform, her flawless skin, her waterfall of hair falling from her high ponytail down her back, and her full, pursed lips are just. . .stunning. There's no other word that fits.

"She's small and mousy," Bea says. "But Easton seemed to really like her."

Mrs. Yaltzinger sighs, staring at me without the slightest idea that Bea is talking about herself. "I'll give you a week. If you're not dating someone officially by then." She points. "You'll let us try again."

I nod slowly.

But when Mrs. Yaltzinger wanders off, I pounce. "How about you open the door a little. I only have a week."

"Huh?" The little wrinkle between her eyebrows is adorable.

"Just let me in a little—you can see what you think."

"It's not that I—"

"I know your jingle finals are tonight, and I want to go with you."

"The thing is, Jake's already coming to help me," she says. "He's—he gets—I don't think it's a good idea if—"

"I'm not scared of your brother," I say.

She bites her lip.

It's so cute. "Just give me a shot. If I make things hard for you on your big night, you can refuse to talk to me again."

"I wouldn't normally take him with me," she says. "Jake makes most things harder. I know he hasn't been that nice to you, either, but he's really connected, and he's also painfully talented with music, entertainment, all of it."

I'm sure he is. I actually hate that she's right. "It'll be fine," I say. "Tell me I can come."

"Fine," she says.

"I should also confess that I might have mentioned the details to Emerson."

She rolls her eyes. "That's fine. He probably would have pried them out of Jake anyway."

I'm on my way out the door when something hits me. I have no idea what to wear. "Hey, so what are you planning to—"

But when I turn around, she's already gone.

8

BEA

I always panic when any kind of performance looms.

What was I thinking, telling Easton he could come? It was *almost* as bad as when I told that woman he works with that he did have a girl he liked. I must have lost my mind.

She's breathtaking.

Is there a chance that he really thinks that? Or is he a lot smoother than Emerson and Elizabeth seem to think he is? Emerson says he's not a player—quite the opposite. He says Easton has never played at all.

He says he's a bench-sitter.

Just like me.

Sometimes I believe it. Others, like when he's commanding the attention and respect of an entire room full of savvy business people, I have no idea how that could possibly be true. He reminds me of Uncle Bentley, but even more focused. Before he realized how he felt about Aunt Barbara, Uncle Bentley was a dating disaster, so it feels like it's much more likely Easton just doesn't show his family that side of who he is.

But to tell him that it was fine if he came tonight?

Complete idiocy on my part.

I'm already so nervous that I can barely breathe. The thought of Easton watching me completely embarrass myself is horrifying.

"I can't go," I whisper.

Jake wraps an arm around me and steers me back into my bedroom. "Not in that, you can't."

"I like these pajamas," I protest.

"The little pink cats wearing tiaras are very cute." Jake shoves me toward my bed and starts rummaging around in my closet. "This selection is appalling, you know. One of these days, you really need to take me up on my offer to buy you some clothes that aren't outdated and frumpy."

"In order to do that, I'd have to go somewhere in public. I avoid—"

"Don't I know it." Jake's shaking his head. "But sadly, your best option is this." He chucks a cream and white striped sheath dress at my head. "Put it on." He walks out the door without even looking at me to see whether I agree.

That's how he's always been. "What about the blue dress with the—"

"No." Jake doesn't even bother raising his voice. "Just put that one on. We're already cutting it close."

With the way he drives, we won't be close—we'll be early. I grumble as I drag my pajamas off and pull my dress over my head. When I come out, the dress a little tighter than I like, Jake's still shaking his head.

"What now?"

"You are not wearing those." He points at my wedges.

"They're comfortable," I say. "And I won't fall on my face in them, which is an undervalued attribute."

"If you aren't wearing something that's miserably uncomfortable, you aren't ready yet." He sighs as he brushes past me and starts chucking things out of my closet. "This is really, really shameful." He spins around, thrusting a pair of boring camel heels at me. "Really? *Steve Madden*? How old are you?"

"Old enough to remember when you wore Steve Maddens," I mutter.

"I *never* wore Steve Maddens."

"You wore Birkenstocks, and that's worse."

Jake laughs. "Put these on, and when you win in spite of your horrible wardrobe, you're going to let me take you shopping, finally."

"I won't win," I mutter. "And now I'm going to have blisters on top of it."

"A lot of whether you win with something like this comes down to your attitude." Jake grabs my shoulders and lifts me up an inch and a half. He stares me right in the eyes. "You will look right at those judges, and you will keep your chin up. Like this." He keeps staring.

"That's creepy," I say.

He laughs. "Be creepy, then, and smile." He releases me and lifts his hands past his face, his smile lifting at the same time.

"That's even scarier."

"This is a million-dollar smile," he says. "And yours has got to be worth—"

"At least half that?"

He snorts. "I was gonna say twenty bucks, but yeah. Let's go with a half-mil."

I punch his shoulder. "You said you'd sing while I play."

"I said *if* you choke up, and *if* they allow it, I'd sing it for you."

"The rules don't say you can't have someone else sing it," I say. "It just says it has to be performed on stage."

"But if I go up there, we'd have to share the credit," Jake says. "It did say that, and do you really think they want a movie star to win their prize?"

"Your agent would lose his mind."

"I'll do it," Jake says, "if that's what you need." He drops his voice. "But this is supposed to be *your* time to shine, not mine."

"I hate spotlights," I say.

"Oh, I remember." But he stops grumbling and ordering and he walks quietly alongside me to his ridiculous car. At least his car gets me there early, and if I'm queasy from the speed, well, we aren't late.

As we're walking in, I notice Emerson and Easton, standing shoulder to shoulder just inside the double doors of the auditorium. "Bea," Emerson says. "You look great!"

"Don't say that." Jake groans. "She'll insist she doesn't need any new clothes if you compliment her."

Emerson smiles. "Plebians like Bea and I don't need new outfits every time we leave the house."

"Exactly," I say.

"New clothes aren't always a bad idea," Easton says. "Sometimes they help you feel ready for whatever you're facing."

"I don't want to agree with you," Jake says. "If you could do me a favor and not say anything smart like that, it would be great."

"Not all of us can be uniformly stupid," Emerson says. He turns toward Easton. "Jake's never been accused of saying smart things."

"Not without a team of writers to script his lines, at least," I say.

Jake rolls his eyes, but when we walk into the main auditorium, I'm surrounded by three handsome men who all want to see me succeed. It's more than a lot of people can claim, I'm sure. "Thanks for coming," I say.

A moment later, I have to leave the audience area and take my place on the stage. Jake jogs along with me until I reach the stairs. "What'll it be, Hornet?"

"You're right," I whisper. "If you come, I'll never know whether I won, or if Jake Priest did."

He beams. "Go sting 'em, Bea. You got this."

Only, when I reach the stage, I realize I totally do *not* have this. No one else looks even half as nervous as me. Actually, they all look like pros.

There's a very good looking, probably very gay man next to me. His eyebrows are perfectly shaped, his nails are buffed and polished a dark, navy blue, and there's a thin, tasteful kohl line above and beneath each of his large eyes.

Makeup.

The man next to me has better makeup game than I do.

I can't believe I did nothing to touch up my makeup after work. I probably look like a preteen girl.

But then the lights click on, and it's go time. The woman who stands up and approaches the podium has a large cascade of absolutely gorgeous, rich mahogany curls that are pinned up on one side and flow freely on the other. That's the reason I don't notice her face until she turns outward and starts talking.

She's been badly burned on her left side, from her forehead all the way down to below her nose. Her hair covers some of it, but there's plenty that's still visible. It looks like ripples of wax are running down her face and then it swoops out and down her neck, disappearing into the top of her asymmetrical gown.

Perhaps the most distracting part of her burns is the stunning beauty of her face on the non-burned side. It's like an artist painted a masterpiece of epic proportions, then upended a bottle of turpentine over one corner. It actually makes me sad, looking at the perfection of her features on the right side, compared to the left. I can't help thinking that, although on the outside my life looked just fine, I might understand her better than most.

My damage just isn't as obvious to everyone who sees me.

When she opens her mouth, I almost forget about the disfigurement. She has the smoothest, lightest, loveliest speaking voice I've ever heard. "Welcome to the finals of the Jello Jingle," she begins. She explains how stiff the competition was, and that tonight's prize includes a job—the Jello Jingle—as well as a cash prize, a small scholarship for some training, and the mentorship from a partner at one of the nation's leading jingle firms.

I can see why they chose her as tonight's emcee. She's poised, well-spoken, and she has a beautiful speaking voice. "I'm delighted to announce that we have talented artists here with us tonight from across the globe. Our first finalist tonight, Dmita Frost, hails from Liverpool, England. She's here in New York while completing a study abroad program for another four months, and this is her first time entering any musical contests. Please join me in warmly welcoming our contestant from across the Pond."

Everyone claps as the petite black woman stands up and approaches the spot our emcee just vacated. She's not playing the piano—but her recording playing from the speakers sounds just fine. Her jingle's short and sweet, but her lungs are powerful. The melodic line is weak, and the words are a little frivolous, but her performance is clearly an A plus.

Next up is another shorty—do all short people go into music these days? His hair's long and shaggy and almost covers his eyes. But when he starts his song—also using the option of a recorded accompaniment instead of the piano behind us—I can see how he made it into the finals. His words are punchy and memorable. If his tune is a little forgettable, well, we all have our strengths. His voice isn't compelling, but it's pleasant enough.

Next up is a very tall, very strong woman with arms that look at least as big as Emerson's, if not quite as large as Jake's. "My jingle came to me at my niece's birthday party." Unlike the others, she's seated at the piano, and when she starts to play, I have to work not to cringe. Her dynamics are all over the place. Choppy. Loud and then soft.

But the melody is killer.

It's the only one so far that I might find myself humming next week. And that's bad, because that's my biggest strength. I was hoping no one else's would be catchy.

I'm hoping they call the very pretty gay man next, because I like going last. But when they call my name, I stand up, my legs working exactly as they should, blessedly. I walk toward the piano as calmly as possible, and then I sit, staring at the familiar keys.

It's a Steinway S, a pretty common baby grand, and it usually has a rich, full sound, even in a large room like this. I adjust the microphone a bit—it was far too high, thanks to that tall woman—and then I close my eyes for a beat, counting off and then starting, specifically not looking out at the audience at all.

So much for Jake's admonition to catch the judge's eye.

There are many things, including most social situations, where I choke. There are times when I'm downright paralyzed. But with a piano in front of me, I never panic. Touching these keys has always been the place where I feel the most at home. For someone who didn't have a home at all for a long time, that's not nothing.

After I play the opening stanzas, I open my mouth and sing the simple, clear words. My voice has never floated. It has never soared. But it's serviceable, and I don't embarrass myself, at least. When I stand up, the audience claps pretty vigorously, which is always nice.

The last performance is probably technically the best. The guy sits at the piano too, and his navy-painted fingers move deftly across the keys. He flubs a spot and then another, but all-in-all, if I were a judge, I might pick his. It's catchy without being annoying, and he has a nice, clear voice that doesn't distract from his message, which is that Jello creates happy memories.

I'm bracing myself for bad news when the brunette with the burned face stands up. "Now, we didn't tell you that audience votes actually compose ten percent of the scores for each jingle, and I'll be the one performing the winning jingle on Jello's behalf. So now that we've heard each song from the creator, I'm going to perform them myself. At the end, we'd love it if you could go to the website listed on the screen behind me and vote for the jingle you think is the best."

It was interesting to hear the jingle from each creator, but it's a real *experience* to hear it sung by this woman. Her face may have been damaged, but her voice.

. . It's like listening to Michelangelo work on the Sistine Chapel.

I'm convinced that each new jingle's perfect, just because of how she sings it. I'm surprised they chose someone with such indescribable beauty to sing something designed to be catchy, but it somehow makes something corny sound classy.

Then she sings mine.

When I was comparing it to the others, it was hard. I mean, I was doing the playing and singing, so I couldn't really listen. But as a less biased onlooker, I realize that mine is good.

Technically, the balance is perfect.

The words are catchy—Jake really helped there. They're corny, but not painful. The melody is perfectly strung. For the first time, I wonder whether I might win. Once she sings the last one and asks everyone to vote, my hope is floating dangerously high.

It's not about the money.

I mean, money's nice, but it's more about the chance to work with an agency. It's about adding this to my resume and possibly springboarding from this into a real job. I've been out of school for almost three years now, and I've made no real inroads toward getting the kind of work that I want. I help my teacher with her small, side-gig jobs.

But I'm not paid, and my name's never on anything.

This could be it.

When the woman approaches the podium again, an envelope in her hand, she's smiling. "As many of you know, we have three industry judges, and their scores are worth fifty percent of the rating. The audience votes are worth ten percent, and Jello allocated the other forty percent to me, as the voice of their brand."

That actually surprises me. I should have read more closely.

She pulls the paper out of the envelope. "Today's first runner-up will receive a cash prize of five hundred dollars and a recommendation from our organization. Her melody was my very favorite, and her skill is undeniable. I was very impressed by Beatrice Cipriani."

It takes me a second to realize. . .that means I lost.

In fact, I'm so busy processing my disappointment that I don't even hear who won. Everyone else is clapping, and I'm just sitting in my seat, staring straight ahead like a zombie.

"Beatrice?" Someone's poking me.

It's the gay guy next to me. "You're supposed to come up with me."

He stops poking and just grabs my wrist, dragging me across the stage alongside him. "You got second place."

I force a smile. "Congratulations. Your jingle was amazing."

He shrugs. "Yours was better. I'm not sure how I won."

But then we're both bowing, and people are clapping, and someone is handing me a manila folder. The next few minutes pass in a blur of papers and smiles and murmured questions. I try to answer them all properly, but I'm not sure I've ever felt quite this numb.

Until I'm on my way toward the edge of the stage, finally. I'm sure Jake will be there, and Emerson. . .and Easton. I can feel my cheeks flush.

Because I lost.

They all came to cheer for me, and I lost.

"Beatrice," a voice calls. A lilting, mellifluous voice.

I turn slowly, and the melted-face woman's smiling at

me. "Beatrice, I hope you'll allow me just a moment." She gestures, and I follow her toward the side curtain.

"Yes?" I blink. "Did I miss something? A signature?"

She shakes her head. "No, but I wanted to explain."

"Explain?" I'm still feeling numb, and I'm clearly missing something.

"Your jingle was the best," she whispers. "I knew it. The audience knew it. You should've won."

For a brief moment in time, the sounds around me are all amplified, like the world that has been on pause comes screaming back to life. "What?" I must have misheard her, or worse, hallucinated.

"Your song was the best," the woman says. "But you'll get the scoresheet later, and you'll be able to see that I scored yours much lower than the others. Without that, you'd have won." She sighs. "I wanted to tell you why."

My heart hasn't been this crushed by anything since. . .well, maybe since the night I met Emerson and Seren and Dave for the first time. "You—why?"

"Your jingle was good. You have real talent." She leans closer. "I'm stuck doing jingles—things where I can't show my face. But you." She sighs. "The sky's the limit for you. I torpedoed you in this because this kind of thing clearly isn't where you should be. It's not even where you want to be—I saw that in your face when you were up there. You need to give up on jingles and write *real* music. Release all that sound that's banging around in your head. The world needs quality music from real, pure musicians like you."

After gutting me like a wriggling carp, she smiles and waltzes off.

9

EASTON

I liked Bea before.

I really did.

She was classy, poised, funny, smart, and of course, absolutely beautiful. But now, after watching her up there, it's like I'd never really seen her, not really. Not who she was inside. When she sat in front of that piano, she came *alive*.

I'd been looking at a Picasso hanging in a smoky old hotel.

I just saw the masterpiece on display in an exhibit at the Louvre.

What baffles me is, when her song was clearly the best, why didn't she win? "She was robbed," I say.

"I agree," Emerson says. "Do you know what happened?" He turns toward Jake, who's sitting on his other side. "I'm not a musician, but wasn't hers the best?"

Jake's frowning.

"I won't say anything when she comes down here," Emerson says. "But I think they picked that other kid just because—"

"Jingles are strange," Jake says, "but I watched the people in front of me, and the people over there." He tosses his head to his left. "They were all voting for her."

"See?" Emerson shakes his head. "Something weird's going on."

"Winning runner-up is still pretty amazing," I say. "They said there were over two hundred and fifty applicants."

"And all the finalists were good," Emerson says. "But still."

But then Bea's climbing down the steps near the stage, and she's walking toward us. We scramble to leave the seats and greet her, but as she gets closer, it's clear that she's trying really hard to act like she's fine when she's not. I may not know her very well yet, but even I can see that.

"You were robbed," Emerson says.

She shakes her head. "It's fine. The competitors' songs all sounded amazing."

"Still." Jake wraps an arm around her shoulders. "Yours was the best. Everyone around us agreed. Maybe next time you'll actually let me take you shopping before so you look the part."

Bea frowns. "If they can't recognize my music because my dress cost thirty bucks at Ross Dress for Less, then they should—"

"Whoa," Emerson says. "Your super rich brother offered to get you something nicer and you turned him down?" He shakes his head. "That guy who won was wearing some kind of designer, I'm sure."

"Versace," I say.

"Right." Emerson smacks his forehead. "I forgot we have the king of couture right here with us."

"Hardly," I say. "I run the business side."

"But you're wearing a Givenchy suit," Jake says.

"That's because I never know when I might be photographed," I say. "There's an actual designer responsible for curating my wardrobe, and most of it comes from our lines." I lift my arm. "Like these cuff links." I can't help chuckling. "I'm a walking billboard."

Bea looks pained. I can't believe I'm standing here talking about our cuff links when she's been cheated.

"Sorry," I say. "The point is that all three of us agreed. Your song was amazing, and the real loser today is Jello."

"That's true." Emerson drops to a hissed whisper so loud he may as well have just kept talking. "Doesn't it violate their duty to Jello? I mean, if this song is worse, won't their sales be worse too?"

Bea's smile this time looks real. "Actually, we all had to sign something saying that whoever submits gives them permission to use their song, so they could still use mine."

"That's crap," I say. "If they use yours, you should sue them."

Jake arches one eyebrow. "I bet they do use yours, though. It was catchier, and I'm not just saying that because I stayed up half the night working on it with you."

I really hate that guy. It's like he takes every opportunity to. . .wait. "You were up half the night with her?"

"I mean, that's normal, though." Jake's smile is smug. "We live together. You did know that, right?" He drags Bea just a little closer. "Hornet's a pretty decent cook, so when Emerson got married, I told her if she kept cooking, I'd pay Emerson's share of the rent and mine."

"You also kind of made his room your second closet."

Bea shoves his arm off. "So, you know. I don't feel guilty about it."

"I do help her with her stuff when she needs it," Jake says. "And this jingle was really good." He shrugs. "Maybe you should have had me sing it."

"Speaking of singing, you said you don't sing well," I say. "But you sounded great."

"I tell her that all the time," Emerson says. "She's not an opera singer like that other lady, but she has a great voice."

"I'm really fine," Bea says. "I got five hundred bucks, which is the most money my songs have ever made."

"How much of that do I get?" Jake asks. "Like, a third?" He bites his lip, his expression boyishly impudent. I can see why all the girls gush about him, but I don't have to like it.

"Stop badgering her," Emerson says. "As if you'd take any of her money."

"Beatrice, right?" The guy who won swaggers by. "There's a big party in the room next door. You should stay and celebrate, too. Your song was really great."

"Better than yours," Jake says. "Must be nice to have people on the inside."

"Wait," the guy says, his jaw dangling for a moment. "Are you—Jake *Priest*?"

Jake frowns.

"What're you doing here?" The guy beams. "You should *definitely* come to the party."

Jake rolls his eyes. "My girl, Bea wouldn't—"

Bea jabs him with her elbow. "Thanks for letting us know. We'll definitely head over. And huge congratulations to you."

"Wait, is Jake Priest your boyfriend?" the guy asks. "That's *insane*."

"He's my brother," Bea says.

"*Foster* brother," Jake says, slinging his arm around her shoulders again. "And roommate."

Bea rolls her eyes, but doesn't shove him away again. "We'll be there in just a minute. Congrats again."

The guy's still staring at Jake, but he does finally walk away.

"That must get annoying," I say. "Having people recognize you everywhere."

"It's even worse when it's a gaggle of girls," Bea says. "They cling."

"Can you believe her? We even *live* together, and she could just tell people she's my girlfriend so they'd leave me alone, but she refuses to help me out."

"One day you'll have a real girlfriend," Bea says. "And she wouldn't appreciate me pretending that you have one now."

"Doubtful," Jake says.

She ducks under his arm and heads for the side door the guy just disappeared through. I take my chance to circle around Emerson and Jake and take a spot at her side. "You seem to handle disappointment pretty well."

She looks at me sideways, her lips twisted. "I've had a lot of experience, and I've had plenty of examples of how unattractive it is when someone doesn't take things well."

"Jake?" I can't help imagining what Jake throwing a tantrum looks like.

"She's talking about her mom," Emerson says. "Her birth mother."

She shrugs. "Not a surprise that I have a birth mom who's a mess, probably, since you know they're my foster brothers."

"Well, I thought it was impressive. A lot of people would be too bummed out to go to a party."

She frowns then. "I didn't say I'm not bummed, but I'm too angry to get depressed."

"Angry?" I wouldn't have thought she was mad. She looks fine. "Why?" I lean closer. "Do you think something weird happened?"

Jake grabs two drinks off a tray and offers her one.

Bea, who's quite small and has always seemed quite reserved, knocks the martini back in one smooth motion. "Thanks."

Jake looks floored, like he didn't expect she'd take it.

She hands it back to him and grabs the second drink too. "I needed that." She looks right at him. "That woman who was the emcee?"

"She sang like. . ." Jake whistles. "I've never heard a voice like that."

"Well." Bea swears under her breath. "She told me that my song was the best, and that I would have won, but she intentionally voted me last."

Jake's entire face falls. "She—what?" His voice is way, way too loud. Plenty of people are looking our way now.

"Unless you'd like to broadcast this," Emerson says, "we should take this down quite a lot."

"Right." Bea takes a small sip from her second martini. "Anyway, she told me that I'm *too good* for jingles." She swears again. "Can you believe that?"

"I knew something was weird," Jake says. "I do think you ought to sue them, especially if they use your song for their ad campaign. That's not her decision to make."

"I mean, technically, it's exactly her decision to make," Bea says.

"But if you want to do jingles, you should be able to

do them. That's so unfair." Emerson grabs a bright pink drink off a tray.

I grab one, too.

"Those are mocktails." Emerson points at a sign. "I don't drink, but you might want something else."

"I'm fine with a mocktail," I say. "But why did that woman say Bea's too good? Don't they want people who are good? I don't understand."

"Jingles are. . ." Jake sighs. "In the musical world, jingles are usually written by people who lack talent, or at least, that's the reputation they have."

"They're for people who have given up on making it writing real music," Emerson says. "Which is stupid. Plenty of people like jingles, and sometimes they're better known than most any other song on the radio."

"Right?" Jake asks. "Where does she get off saying you should be doing something else? You entered the contest, and it's a free country."

"But," I say. "If that's true—do you really *want* to do jingles?"

Bea lifts her head slowly. "What do you mean?"

"Why are you doing them instead of writing regular songs? Yours was the best—so could she be right? You're young. You're certainly not out of time. And you have a job."

"You have some nerve," Jake says. "You barely know her."

"I've wanted to do jingles for a while," Bea says.

"If you knew her at all, you'd already know that," Jake says.

"But Emerson just said they're usually for people who have given up on their dreams." I'm not looking at the guys. I'm looking at Bea, and she's staring down at her feet, the hand holding the martini a little loose. In fact, the edge of the glass is a little slanted, with the liquid approaching the edge. "That's not you, right? You haven't given up?"

"Hey." Jake steps closer, his chest puffed out. "You need to watch your mouth."

"Why?" I'm still watching Bea. "Am I right? It seems to me that the woman up there might know more than I do about music, and maybe she saw something in Bea or her song that made her feel like she needed a push."

"Giving the win to someone who doesn't deserve it isn't a magnanimous act," Emerson says. "It's an assault, and Bea doesn't like singing in front of people, unless she's in a group. She would never want to perform her own music, and that's how the industry works."

"I'm just saying that sometimes the people who know us the best don't realize what we really need." Bea's still looking at the ground, but I think I might be right. Maybe the reason she's so upset is the woman was right. "Is there another contest you could enter?" I ask. "Or maybe—" I spin around to face Jake, who looks ready to clock me on the jaw. "You must have contacts. You could help her find someone—"

"You think I haven't offered?" Jake shakes his head. "Hornet doesn't want any of that. It's not who she is, so back off before I *back you* off."

I throw my hands up in the air. "I'm not trying to pick a fight here, but. . .it looks like all of you have already decided what she needs. Sometimes we don't know what we can do until we try."

"Thanks so much for the pep talk," Jake says. "As foster kids, we really needed your silver-spoon brand of cheerleading so we could aim high and really fulfill our potential."

"Alright," Emerson says. "That's enough insults. Easton just met Bea—and me too, for that matter—and he means well."

"I do," I say. "And I think that lady did, too. Just something to think about."

"I've thought about it," Bea says softly, finally lifting her face. "But Jake's right." She grimaces a little. "I'm— my voice—I'm good at jingles, and it's a good fit for me. I'm happy writing them, and I'd love to have a job doing it." She shrugs. "She was wrong." She downs the second martini.

And then two more.

Given that she weighs a hundred pounds soaking wet, I'm guessing she shouldn't have had four. When she reaches for a fifth, I intervene. "Whoa there, thirsty. Let's see how those hit you before downing another, huh?"

Jake had one drink and hasn't had another sip. "I've got this, Richie Rich. You can go."

"Is this a habit for her?" I can't help wondering.

"I've never seen her drink before," Jake says. "Which is why *I've got this*."

"Wait, she never drinks?" So that woman really did upset her.

"Her mom—" Jake shakes his head. "Actually." He snorts. "It's not really any of your business."

"I don't mind taking her home," I say. "I have a great hangover—"

Bea bends in half and throws up, right next to my shoes.

Jake laughs. "Go on. Tell us about how good your egg and molasses milkshake is, Richie."

I roll my eyes.

"Okay, Hornet. Time to go." Jake reaches for her, but she shoves him away.

I want to ask why he calls her hornet, but I feel like it's one of those things I'll eventually figure out. That's when it hits me—Bea. Bee. Not very creative, but it has the feel of something that probably started back when they were kids.

She shocks all of us when she reaches for me. "Easton."

I straighten and let her grab my arm, being sure to flex my forearm just a bit. You know, it can't hurt to put my best arm forward. "Yes?"

"I need to talk to you."

"You do?" She nods, and then she straightens, sort of, her head canted to the side. "Over there." She points at the corner, and then swivels around. "And then you'll take me home, right Jakey?"

Jake snorts. "Of course."

Bea starts walking, but she looks a little less than steady, so I take her arm and steer her toward the corner she pointed out. "Alright," I say. "We're here. What did you need to tell me?" I stupidly hope it's something. . .well. Something good.

"You asked before." She looks up at me. "How I do it."

Huh?

"At work." She nods slowly. "I told you it's a secret, but it's not. Not really."

Does she mean how she chooses what food for which person?

"I work at a place where pretty much everything is good. When I have one of the not-good chefs, I refuse to do it."

I suppress my laugh. "Okay."

"People just want to be special."

She's right about that.

She presses her hand against my chest, looking up at my face. "I wanted to be *special*."

I want to tell her that she is. I want to tell her just how special I think she is, but I doubt she'll remember a word of it.

"But for the people." She frowns. "After I rule out everything they're allergic to, I usually give them something they never had the guts to try—as long as it's good, because they'll love it." She shrugs. "Easy peasy."

"But if they never had the guts to try it, they could hate it."

She shrugs. "Sometimes they do." She presses her finger against her mouth. "Shhhh."

I chuckle this time.

"But usually people eat that weird thing they haven't had because it's *good*." She leans against me again, her hand surprisingly soft. "You have a really nice stomach."

Two pack for the win.

I can't help it. I laugh out loud. "Do I?"

"It's pretty special." She's frowning. "I can't go out with you, though, because you *are* special." She leans even closer. "It's the same reason I don't write music."

"Why?" I had no idea she'd hand me the keys to Bea Cipriani while drunk, or I'd have tried to booze her up sooner.

"Everyone wants to be special, but the only special thing about me is that I can disappear."

"Disappear?"

"I'm so *not-special* that I just. . ." She snaps. "I'm invisible. People don't even notice me. I'm really good at that. It's why I'm a good waitress."

She can't really think that. "None of the other waitresses could do what you do—and you had the best jingle. You're not invisible. You're spectacular."

"The other waitresses that tried to copy me were really stupid." She's beaming now. "I mean, a little bit, you have to be able to read the room. But mostly it's just that my gimmick makes them feel special." She hiccups. "And the food has to be good. Did I say that?" She shrugs. "That's it." Then she sighs, leans against me, and closes her eyes. "You really do have a special chest." Her hands flatten against me. "And your stomach is nice."

"I think it's time for Sleeping Beauty to head home." Jake grabs her arms, and she swivels.

"Jakey." She smiles. "Yes, let's go home to sleep."

He pats her back. "I think it's a good thing you never drink, Hornet." Before I can say a word, he slings her up over his shoulder and carries her out, her shoes dangling from her toes, but miraculously not falling.

It's not how I thought the night would go, but at least I have a goal, now. The next day at the office, I call an emergency meeting of the board.

"I've had an idea for branching out," I say. "And I think you're going to love it."

"I don't love being summoned here like I'm your secretary," Mr. Dressel says.

"What couldn't wait for next week?" Mrs. Yaltzinger asks.

"What's the number one rule for couture?" I ask. "More than anything else, you find success if you have this one thing."

"Exclusivity?" Mr. Dressel asks.

"Endorsements," Mr. Jimenez says. "Celebrity endorsements."

"None of those things hurt," I say. "But the reason exclusivity matters, is that people want to feel *special*.

The reason celebrity endorsements work is that people think celebrities are special, so they want to be like them too. . .so they can also feel special."

The entire board stares.

"Think about it." I stand up and start to pace. "When we limit releases, it's not because we only *want* to sell a hundred of something, or a thousand. We'd always like to sell a million of everything. But for most of our products, there aren't a million people who could afford them. To sell that many, we'd have to lower the price so everyone could afford them. And if it's a watch or a men's dress shoe that everyone can afford?"

"No one wants it," Mr. Dressel says. "That's the problem with any kind of discount brand. The lower you make the price, the more you sell. The more you sell, the less exclusive it becomes, and the less people will pay, cannibalizing your profit."

I nod. "You've all heard of personal shoppers. It was a huge fad for a while, and in fact, there were lots of online companies capitalizing on it. They offered 'online shoppers' for any budget. They're trying to turn a profit from people who have less money to spend, but they want them to spend it on the products those shoppers choose."

"Sure," Mrs. Yaltzinger says. "High-end stores like Nordstrom and Saks have always had personal shoppers."

I nod slowly. "So we're going to offer to partner, on an invite only basis, with several of the best women's lines, and we're going to tell them we want thirty percent of their gross revenue. . ."

"Why would they partner with us?" Mr. Jimenez asks. "We're their competition."

"Not for women's goods, we're not. Instead of having

our own line, we're going to offer a very exclusive service to women that's only available to those who are sponsored by a man in their life who's an existing client of ours." I smile.

"How will we do that?" Mrs. Yaltzinger frowns.

"We'll send emails *only* to people who have placed an order with us, and if someone's wife *wants* this service, she'll encourage her husband—"

"To buy from our men's line," Mrs. Yaltzinger is smiling now. "So it will increase existing sales and create a new revenue stream."

"Exactly," I say.

"And it's exclusive," Mr. Dressel says.

"They have to be 'special' to even be eligible for this service," I say. "And once the women have been matched, they'll meet with one of our elite team of magic makers."

"Magic makers?" Mrs. Yaltzinger frowns. "That sounds like a Disney thing."

"Fine. Pick another name." I wave my hand through the air. "It doesn't matter. Each one of them, and there won't be many, will be stylish, well-versed on every single item we're able to sell, and will be trained to find things that will be flattering for every body shape."

"How will that differ from any other service that Nordstrom or Saks offers, other than being more limited in their selection?" Mr. Jimenez looks skeptical.

"Those people are peddling outfits. We're going to promise people that we'll create a new look for them. If we select them as a client, they *will* stand out at whatever event they choose to attend. We could even call it Rough Diamonds." I beam. "I love that, actually."

"How can you be sure it'll work?" Mr. Dressel asks. "What if people hate it?"

"We'll have a full refund guarantee," I say, "because we'll demand that from our suppliers."

"Who would agree to that?" Mr. Jimenez frowns.

"Who wouldn't, if their products are really as amazing as they say?"

"I don't know," Mrs. Yaltzinger says. "I doubt they'll be keen to accept returns on things people have already worn."

"They already do," I say. "Nordstrom has one of the most generous return policies in the world, which is how used designer heels wind up at Nordstrom Rack."

"But—"

I shake my head. "We have zero responsibility for coming up with our own lines, our own production, or our own products. We get to skim the profits off of others, and in the future, we can certainly roll out our products, one line at a time should we choose to incorporate them."

"The upside seems good," Mr. Jimenez says. "If you think you can convince the other designers to partner with us."

"I know people who run almost every team, and one thing they've all been saying is that competition has been fierce lately. I think they'll fall all over themselves to be chosen." I lift my eyebrows. "Why?"

"It's also external validation that they're special," Mr. Dressel says.

I nod slowly. "Now you're getting it."

It's interesting that Bea gave me the idea for our new women's fashion revenue stream, which will hopefully allow us to leverage our good name for men's clothing, jewelry, and accessories, to make a profit from women as well. She may think she's invisible, but she's the opposite.

She shines.

I intend to show her just how stunning she really is.

Sometimes the only thing standing between invisible and show-stopping is the spotlight.

10

BEA

I'm closer to thirty than I am to twenty, and I've never been drunk. . .until last night. I've really only ever had a sip of alcohol here or there by accident before now. After my own experience with inebriation, I find that I have *no* idea why my mom drank so much. I don't even remember feeling good, and the day after is just *horrible*.

My head's pounding when I wake up and shower, and it doesn't improve, even when I drink what feels like a gallon of water. The Tylenol and Ibuprofen are just barely starting to kick in when I drag myself into my room to get ready for work. Maybe because my head hurts, or maybe because I'm tired, or maybe because I'm depressed about last night's epic failure, but I finish getting dressed faster than ever before. I could leave. . .but I'd be almost half an hour early.

I decide to check my email on my laptop before I go. If I make the font larger, that might help my head. Only, when I get my email up on the screen and sort through all the spam, there's one bolded subject line that mocks me.

Here's a good one

It's not really a great subject line, not compared to the million marketing emails that are always clamoring for my attention. They're usually offering me free things, discounts that will save me oodles of money, or something that's very *limited time*! *Act now*!

But this one is from a name I now know.

Octavia Rothschild—the woman who crushed my hopes and dreams last night. Now she's dropping into my email like we're old friends? A good one of what? What on earth would she have sent me?

My little cursor arrow hovers over the subject line for a second, then one more. But finally, I click. Because unlike all the free deals and limited time sales I casually delete, I care what this woman thinks.

⊱❦⊰

Dear Beatrice,
     You might still be angry with me, and that's okay. The things we most need to hear usually make us the most mad. But I wanted to at least reach out and offer my aid. You may not want anything to do with me, but I'm actually pretty good at figuring out which lyrics work, and I'm good at tightening sloppy lines. I'd be happy to grab lunch—I'll pay—and go over any song ideas you may have.

     Even if you don't want my help on any of that, which I would understand, I think you should consider entering a contest like this one (link below). Best of luck releasing what I know is already waiting inside of you.

     Best,

Octavia

B *est?* Is she kidding? She tells me I should have won, tells me she intentionally caused me to lose, and then she tells me she'd be happy to *help*? If I could hate someone who sings like she does, I'd hate her twice.

Since I can't quite bring myself to hate anyone with that kind of unparalleled musical talent, I sit, fuming, until I realize that I'll be late for work. Now I have a real reason to curse her out as I head in for work. I'm on my way out when Jake's door swings open. "You're leaving?"

"I do that every day," I say, "almost. More's the pity."

"Well." He looks me over head to toe. "You look alright." He nods. "No worse for wear, at least."

"I suppose one night of drinking won't wither me entirely."

He smiles. "Not entirely."

By the time I reach work, it's raining. Of course it is. Maybe I can blame the rain for being late. I throw the strap for my bag over my shoulder and prepare to sprint from my car to the back door. My phone dings, and I almost ignore it, but it could be Harv. If he's already mad I'm late, I should know before I rush headlong into a lecture.

I whip it out and tap the message app.

It's not Harv. It's not anyone from work. It's a number I don't know, but I'm guessing it's someone who got my number from Emerson.

SAW THIS AND THOUGHT OF YOU. YOU'RE TOO SPARKLY TO BE INVISIBLE FOR LONG. There's a link.

It must be from Easton. No one else knows what happened.

The link is for the same stupid song-writing contest Octavia sent me.

I consider texting back the word STOP, because my phone blocks any number that I text that to. . .but I feel like Easton would just find a workaround. He's probably friends with Verizon's owner or something.

Or, if I'm being really honest, I'd admit that I don't actually want him to stop texting me. I was kind of excited when I realized it was from him.

I'm not nearly as excited that his text was encouraging me to write non-jingle songs. It feels like there's some kind of conspiracy of people who don't even know me but know what's best for me. They seem to feel like they can simply encourage me a little, and suddenly I'll burst out of my little shell to belt out bestsellers.

I blame the stupid inspirational movies like *Coyote Ugly* where stupid junk like that is always happening. It's always the introvert who hides in their room and works remotely until they overcome their *weakness* and suddenly can be more. Better.

Where's the story for the introvert who *likes* the idea of working in her room? Why can't I be perfectly satisfied with it? Extroverts who want to be in the spotlight must secretly rule the world, and that's why they're shoving their values off on other people. By the time I calm down enough to make the mad dash into the restaurant, I'm already braced for Harv to yell. Instead he waves me over with a smile on his face. "I didn't think it would be you," he says.

"I'm sorry?"

"Theo overstaffed this shift on accident, but we didn't notice until it was about to start. So we figured whoever got in first would work, and whoever showed up later would get to take the night off."

That is *not* what I expected to hear. "Uh. Okay."

"You're usually early, so I figured you'd be working. Will it leave you in a bind if you take the day off?" Harv asks. "Do you need the money? We could just do smaller sections, but—"

"It's fine." I did just win five hundred bucks. But on the way back out to my car, I don't even bother jogging. I walk, slowly, as the rain pelts my face and hair, drenching my entire body. By the time I get to my car, I realize that I'm crying.

It's been a while since I've done this—rain-cried.

Rain used to be my favorite. I could cry as much as I wanted, and no one would even notice. It was the best cover story for having too many feelings—feelings that don't always fit in my body like normal people's. That's my real trial. I feel too much. Always have.

Thanks to my mom, I learned early how to choke them down.

But sometimes, they overflow, and when they do, I'm always grateful for a nice rain storm. I stand beside my car for a few moments before I feel ready to get in and drive home. I'm parking when my phone bings. I kill the engine and check to see who's messaging me now. Will it be Jake or Emerson telling me to cheer up, or Easton again with another stupid pep talk?

Toss up.

But it's not any of them.

It's Seren. I CAN'T EVER KEEP UP WITH YOUR WORK SCHEDULE, BUT I MISS YOU. LUNCH? DINNER? TELL ME WHEN AND WHERE.

That makes me smile.

Seren always makes me smile. She makes everyone smile. She may have the saddest story I've ever heard, but she spreads joy like she's a hose and joy is water. Everyone in her life is better for knowing her. I wish I was like Seren.

I'm more like a hose that sprays Eeyore-vibes.

That thought makes me laugh for some reason. And the laughter turns into crying again. If I go inside, Jake will bug me until I want to strangle him, trying to cheer me up. The problem with trying to cheer someone up is that it's so forced, so in your face. Seren's not like that. She just quietly exudes calm and happy energy. I could really use some of that emanating happiness right now. I JUST FOUND OUT THEY DON'T NEED ME TODAY, I text back. HAVE TIME NOW?

OF COURSE! I JUST MADE A BIG PAN OF LASAGNA, BUT DAVE IS WITH KILLIAN AT A MEET.

I'LL BE OVER IN FIFTEEN.

It's more like twenty, but when I pull down the drive, like always, I wonder why it's been so long since I drove home. I spent most of my life thinking I didn't have a home. I didn't find this one until I was almost a teenager. I thought I was so broken I could never be of use to anyone.

Dave and Seren, and Emerson too, honestly, glued me all back together. I'll never be like someone who wasn't shattered, but I can usually function well enough that people can't tell how broken I am. And it's all because of this place—these people.

Even stepping out of my car helps me breathe easier.

Seren understands what I need. She never ever pushes me to do things I don't want to do. In fact, when we were younger, I'd come home crying sometimes about some project I couldn't fathom doing. Before I came to live with them, I was never at any one school long enough to worry about grades. But once I moved here, I realized I was pretty behind.

Group projects and class presentations practically left me covered in hives.

Seren went to bat for me and had the school provide something called 'accommodations.' It meant they had to find me an alternative assignment that I could do without wanting to crawl in a hole and never come out.

When I walk through the door, looking like a drowned cat, she holds out her arms. "Oh, Beebee."

I rush into her arms.

She hugs me tightly, never asking any questions. Then she releases me. "Need a change of clothes? Or are we marinating for some reason?"

Most of my analogies are music ones, but all of hers are something to do with food and cooking. In spite of that, she herself is very thin. In fact, she looks like a movie star. Always has. It's in her blood. My mom probably passed me a genetic disposition to be an alcoholic, whereas Seren got movie-star genes. Her grandmother was one of the most famous movie stars of her era, and the mansion Seren and Dave run as an inn used to be her family home, staffed while she was growing up with five full-time employees.

She had a very different childhood than I did.

And yet she gets me. When I finally emerge, wearing her slightly-too-big clothes, I feel like a totally different person. She always smells like lilacs, for one. I used to think it came from spending time in her garden, which she's always working in when she's not baking, but I think it must be a perfume. She smells this way year round.

But I smell like her right now, and I love it.

"Ready to eat?"

She didn't mention rolls, but of course she made those, too. I swear, it's a miracle everyone in this family isn't a thousand pounds. "Thanks."

"We should set up some kind of weekly dinners. I wonder if we could find a day everyone could come."

"I'd love that," I say. And I mean it. I think we all would. "What about Sundays? I get Sunday and Monday off every week."

"I'll text Ardath, Emerson, and Jake right now." She beams. "What about Bentley and Barbara? Should I invite them? Or no?"

"Of course," I say.

"It'll be more chaotic, but their twins are so stinking cute."

She's not wrong about that, but family chaos is the good kind. After eating two plates of lasagna, even though it's the vegetarian kind, and three rolls, I lean back and cry Uncle. "I'm so full you could stuff me for Thanksgiving."

Seren smiles. "Good."

"You didn't go to Killian's meet?"

"It's in Philly, and I had to be here to meet the contractor."

"What contractor?"

She sighs. "We're remodeling the *Oceans Beneath Us* room—there was a busted pipe, so it moved to the top of the list. We've been waiting on this tile—it's period, and it's perfect—for three weeks."

"A lot of people ask for that room, too."

Seren nods. "Less than used to, but yeah. People still like that movie." She looks almost sad. I suppose it's inevitable that the pool of people who loved her grandmother will shrink with time, but I can see why it would bum her out. It's not about the money for Seren—it never has been. I've rarely met someone who cares about money less than she does.

"Thanks for texting me." I look at my hands. "I had a rough night last night."

Seren drops a hand on mine. "I'm sorry."

She never pries. It's just not her way. "I was a finalist for a jingle contest, but I lost."

"Oh, Beebee. I wish you'd told me—I'd have come and cheered."

"Emerson and Jake went," I say. "But having them there when I didn't win made it harder." It feels nice to say that. I'm not sure if she'll understand, but it's true.

"I would have been proud if you'd gotten dead last." She really would have been, I'm sure.

"I got first runner up," I say. "I did win a five hundred dollar prize."

Her eyes widen. "Bea! That's wonderful. How many contestants were there?"

"A lot," I say. "I should be happy, I know. But the woman who gave me the news told me that I should have won." I grit my teeth.

Seren blinks. "I don't understand. Was it political?"

I shrug. "Nah, I don't think so." I want to tell her— and I don't. Talking about it hurts, but I think she'll get it. So I explain what she said, and then I tell her how Easton was there, and what he said.

"Wait, Easton—Elizabeth's brother?" Seren frowns. "Why would he go? Did he know another contestant?"

I sigh. "No, he came to support me. I ran into him at the Red Horse."

Seren nods slowly. "Okay."

"He asked me out, and I said no."

Her eyes widen, but she doesn't say anything.

"I—he was there on a date with some supermodel with these huge, fishy lips." I pucker.

"That's definitely not you."

"Thanks," I mutter.

Seren leans back, laughing as she drops her hands flat on the table. "I meant the fish lips." She lifts both eyebrows. "You're definitely lovely enough to be a super-model, but you might need really, really tall shoes."

That makes me laugh, too.

"But Bea, why was he there if you turned him down? And why would he tell you that the woman might be right? It feels. . .bizarrely overreaching."

"We did get along pretty well when I took care of him on his failed date," I say. "Miss Collagen USA left in the middle of the meal, and then he flirted reasonably well. And then. . .he set up a weekly board meeting at our restaurant, so I talked to him some then."

"Oh?"

"And I might have led him to believe I might have *some* small interest."

"Okay."

"But he's wrong about the song things, and so was that Octavia woman." I whip out my phone. "Look— one of them emailed me about this song-writing contest, and the other one texted me. Why do people think I don't know what's best for me?"

Seren drops her hand over mine again. "They care about you, and most people can't see past their own damage to navigate someone else's."

It's stuff like this—these profound things—Seren just drops them around like stray musical notes kind of pouring all over from a bucket full of sound. "I think they probably do care, but they want me to be successful in the way they measure it. They don't accept that what *I* want is also fine."

"Are you sure that writing non-jingle songs isn't what you want?"

That surprises me. Of all the people in the world, the last one I thought might side with them was Seren. "Wait, do you think they're right?"

Seren tilts her head. "It almost feels like *you* do."

"What have I said that might possibly be taken that way?"

"You're awfully upset," she says, "for something you don't care about."

I sit back and think about it for a moment. Could she be right? Am I incensed because I'm *scared?*

"You know what masking emotions are." Seren shrugs. "And maybe that's not what's going on, but anger's a pretty strong mask."

Sometimes I hate all the stupid cognitive behavior training Seren's had. Alright, maybe that's not true, but I do hate when it feels like someone is analyzing me, even when I asked for it. "You think I'm angry because. . .I'm afraid of writing anything but jingles?"

"You wrote a song first, you know," she says. "Not a jingle, but a song."

"For you," I say. "For your birthday."

"And then Jake used it for that contest and won."

"That song may have been what broke him out, but it was the least played song on his first album."

"Still." Seren nods. "It could have broken *you* out."

"I didn't want that then, and I don't want it now."

"Alright," Seren says. "And that's fine."

"I know you think working at the restaurant is a waste of my talent."

"Have I said that?" Seren stands and picks up our

plates, but she pauses with her face just a few inches from mine. "I've always thought that anything you do, as long as it makes you happy, is exactly what you should do, even if it's collecting trash."

I should get up and help her, but I don't. I sit like a scarecrow, not moving, not shifting even a stray piece of straw while she moves around me. Clearing the table. Putting leftovers in the fridge.

"But let's say that's right." I stand up. "Let's say I should write songs."

"Okay, let's say that." Seren wipes her hands on a towel. "Then what?"

"Why would people I've barely met be the ones to point that out?"

"Sometimes it's the people who don't know you as well who can see what you need most. They're impartial and unbiased."

"Is that what you think?"

"Does it matter what I think?"

"It does to me," I say. "A great deal."

Seren sets the towel down and crosses the room. She brushes a hand against my cheek. "I think you're exceptionally talented, but I've never been sure whether you'd be happier writing songs and living a flashier life—whether you should push through that childhood trauma and move past it—or whether you're someone who has always and would always have wanted a quiet life at home." She gestures around her. "I love my life. I make lasagna. I care for the inn and my children, and it's everything I ever wanted. I didn't have trauma as a child, but back then, I never wanted people staring at me and complimenting my face." Her voice drops to a whisper. "But I don't want to project my desires on you. You might not want what I want."

There's no one I'd rather be like. "What if I do?"

"There's no shame in that," Seren says with a soft smile. "But you're every bit as amazing and just as much my daughter if you *do* want something different." A tear rolls down her cheek. "That's what true love is, I think. Wanting your child to succeed in whatever way *they* want to succeed, and helping them do it in any way you can."

"Mrs. Stevens seems really happy, writing jingles," I say. "And she never has to leave her family room to do it. She teaches there, too."

"Mrs. Stevens is a gifted teacher, and I think she really likes you," Seren says. "But she's also using you—has been for years."

"What?" Today's apparently the day for Seren to say a million things I never expected. "How so?"

"She told me about two years into teaching you that you were the most talented songwriter she'd ever met." Seren sighs. "Then she proceeded to have you help her sell dozens and dozens of jingles." She shrugs. "You were happy with it, so I never intervened, but I've thought she was taking advantage of your talent for a very long time. She should have found you work years ago, but she's selfishly told you she couldn't help."

"But—"

"You're her competition," Seren says, "and she's not nearly as good as you, so she has kept you under a proverbial rock."

"But she said if she ever heard about—"

"About a job?" Seren arches a brow. "And in *years*, she's never once heard about a single job you'd be a good fit for? She's never once recommended you?"

I feel like an idiot. My own mother thinks I'm a dupe.

"You've always been afraid to try things," Seren says.

"I probably should have pushed you more—then you'd know that failure isn't the worst thing in the world."

"What's worse?" I ask.

"Never trying." Seren walks past me into the family room and sits down. "You know I lost my husband many years ago in an accident."

I follow her over. She never talks about this.

"One thing I almost never tell anyone is that I was pregnant when the bus crashed." She meets my eye, and I can see the wreckage. "I lost that child, and I lost my uterus, which ruptured in the accident."

"I'm sorry."

Another tear rolls down her cheek and she swipes it away. "For a long time, I thought I'd never be a mother. Even after I'd managed to resurface from the grief of losing my parents, my husband, my grandmother, and my siblings, that thought would throw me back under. I didn't know how to breathe after that. I'd lost my little girl, and I'd never have another. Not ever. I couldn't."

Now I'm crying too. Again. And there's no rain to blame it on.

"But Beebee." She's smiling through her tears. "I didn't know yet." She's shaking her head. But when she opens her arms, I fall into them. Against my hair, she says, "I didn't know that I didn't need that uterus. My children were already out there, waiting for me to find them."

She holds me for a moment.

And then she says, "But first, I had to take a really big risk."

I sit back, watching her.

"I had to love again—and it felt absolutely terrifying. Dave's such an easy person to love, but it felt. . .it felt impossible. Until it wasn't." She shrugs. "Loving him opened the doors for me to meet and love Emerson, you, Jake." She smiles. "All of you came into my life because I took a risk. A really big risk. A scary risk, each time."

After Seren dries her tears, she turns on one of our favorite movies. *Sabrina*—where a girl is hung up on the younger playboy brother, but she eventually falls for the crusty old businessman. By the time it ends, I feel glued back together reasonably well.

On the way home, I keep flipping radio stations. None of the songs sound quite right, so I finally shut the radio off. Driving home in silence might sound depressing, but it's not. It's just what I need. And when I get home, I breathe a sigh of relief that Jake's not home.

Because there's a song that's trying to claw its way out of my head, so I sit down in front of the piano and start banging it out.

11

BEA

Songs have always taken shape in my head.

I used to sit, huddled, while my mom and Joe did whatever noisy and disturbing things they did. She dated a lot of guys, and I couldn't ever keep up with their names, so they all became Joe. It bugged Mom at first, but eventually she stopped caring about that, too. Whenever Joe and Mom did things that made me feel sad, I would plug my ears and hum.

At first, my sounds were messy and unformed, like when a little kid sits at a piano and insists they're making music.

But eventually, the songs improved. When I moved in with Seren and Dave, I would sing them sometimes, when I thought no one was looking. Seren caught me once, and they put me in piano lessons straightaway. That's when the songs in my head really started to take shape. With inspiration from the greats, I started understanding pitch, key signatures, octave runs, and so much more.

A new world opened to me, a world I'd always longed to navigate.

But my music rarely came with words.

Words were tricky. Emotional. Dangerous.

That made jingles perfect—no serious themes meant no danger. I kept things simple. So when I sit down to form the music crowding out the rest of the thoughts in my head, I can't help shaping it around the rubric I usually create. I bang the notes into quick stanzas, with a repeating line that should be easy to remember.

Only, the song doesn't want to do that. Not this time.

I wrestle and wrestle with it, but it keeps wriggling free. It gets longer. It gets more complicated, and then a harmony starts to form above it. Finally, I decide that if I write it down, it'll listen better to what I want. But after jotting down page after page of notes, I realize it's still growing. I crumple them up and throw them in the trash and collapse into bed.

When I wake up in the morning, it's to a very strange sound.

Jake took a year of haphazard lessons before the piano teacher fired him. He absolutely *cannot* play piano.

He's *horrible*.

And yet, he's playing the song I wrote, or at least, he's trying to. I bolt upright and run out of my room. "What are you doing?"

"This song is great," he says, not turning away from the piano. He's taped the pages together, and he's squinting at them as he painfully tries to press the right keys.

"Stop," I say. "That's an assault." I rub my eyes. "What time is it?"

Jake does stop, thankfully, but when he turns, he's smiling. "I'll stop. . .if you play it for me."

"No way." I back toward my room.

"Alright. Have it your way." He starts plonking down on the keys, missing a flat.

I cringe. "Stop. Please, stop."

"Play it for me, Hornet. Please."

I groan, but I decide anything's better than being tortured.

He shoves over as soon as I get close, and he's beaming. "Yay."

I roll my eyes, but I start to play, not even bothering with the sheet music he never should have pulled out of the trash. I change a few things that I realized were wrong last night before drifting off.

"Ooh, I like that." Jake's bobbing his head. "And right here, what if you did this?" He hums a harmony, and it's a little better than my first idea, but it's clunky, so I clean up the bridge note.

"Or." I play the new version.

"You're a freaking genius."

It's a good thing I don't need to see the keys, or I'd be in trouble every time he makes me roll my eyes. But it's actually kind of fun, writing the song with him.

"What's this for?" Jake asks. "It's too long for a jingle —and don't take this the wrong way, but it's too good."

I sigh, my fingers freezing. "I don't know."

There's a knock at the door, which surprises us both. Other than our family, no one really even knows where our apartment is. We keep it that way on purpose —it's why we have it all in my name. Gas. Power. Internet. Water. The lease. The media's relentless with him. We even have two covered spaces for his flashy cars. He's not here that often with all his filming, but when he is, we're used to keeping to ourselves as much as possible.

"Are you expecting someone?" I ask.

He shakes his head, but he does eventually hop up and jog to the door.

I squeak. "I'm in pajamas. Hang on." I barely duck behind my door before he swings the front door open, and I hear it.

A voice that I am *not* expecting.

"Elizabeth said you guys lived here," Easton says.

My hands tremble. What's he doing here? I press my ear to the door.

"Bea's not home," Jake says. "Sorry, dude."

"Oh." Easton sighs loudly enough that I can hear it. "Well."

"Yep. Sorry." Jake'll probably close the door in his face.

"Am I wasting my time?"

Okay, that I did *not* expect.

"I came to apologize, because I went overboard, clearly. I know I don't know her very well yet, and I know you guys know her way better, but even I can tell she's enormously talented. You have to give her that much."

"She's the most talented musician I've ever met," Jake says.

Could he really mean that?

"But until she believes it, she won't ever want to write songs," Jake says. "The one song she ever wrote won a contest and broke me out." He snorts. "It's the whole reason people know the name Jake Priest."

"Are you serious?" Easton asks. "Then why aren't you pressing her—"

"I'm a complete jerk," Jake says. "I always have been, you know. I don't even remember a time when I didn't piss off everyone I met."

"Why does she put up with you?"

"I have no earthly idea," Jake says. "I really don't."

"But if you told her to try writing real songs," Easton says, "she might listen."

"I'll never pressure Bea to do anything. Not ever," Jake says. "If you'd ever met her biological grandfather, you'd know why."

Jake closes the door then, and I slump to the floor, dropping my face on my knees. My grandfather. He never asked me to do anything.

He ordered.

It's his job, to be fair. He orders everyone. He's not mayor of New York anymore—now he's the governor. He only got worse with the promotion, if you can call it that. He hated my mom worse after he changed jobs, anyway. She kind of fell off a cliff after that campaign, but she's always been his biggest liability.

And they're the reason Seren and Dave could never adopt me.

He's the reason I can't call them Mom or Dad. If I ever slipped and said something on record, on a video, anywhere. . .Grandfather would lose it. I shudder. He's made it very clear what he would do to me if I do anything to harm his career.

Is that what's been holding me back?

More than being afraid I'd fail, have I worried that Grandfather wouldn't accept it if I started singing? I have no doubt he'd find it an unfitting career for a young lady, but would he really get angry? What would he do?

What *can* he do?

He's threatened to shut down Seren and Dave's inn before. If I ever let on that I lived with them, that the mayor's granddaughter was in a foster home, he said they'd pay for it. But would he really make good on that old threat? It's always been easier to be quiet and keep my head down. It's always been easier not to make him angry.

But thinking about that kind of makes me furious.

And that helps me finish the song.

When I walk out, Jake's there, watching me like he'd watch someone who just lost their job or got dumped. "You alright?"

"Fine." I sit at the piano and start to play.

It's right.

I can feel it.

It takes me a few hours, but I compress it all into an AABA format, and I add a coda at the end, complete with a lift for the last few lines. Now the scary part—I have to add words.

"What just happened?" Jake asks.

I startle.

He's been here this whole time?

"Did you just write a whole song—start to finish—in two and a half hours?"

"Of course not," I say. "It has no words, and I started it last night."

Jake's shaking his head. "That was amazing."

I roll my eyes. "Stop."

"I failed you." Jake's always kidding around, but he doesn't look like he is right now.

"Stop," I say. "You're being weird."

"You looked—" He sighs. "You looked *possessed*."

"I'm sure I always look like that when I'm composing."

"I know you probably need to go to work soon, but. . ." He whistles. "That was something to watch."

"Work!" I swear under my breath and scramble to get ready, nixing the shower. After dropping yesterday's shift, I cannot be late. But even as I pull on pants and button down my shirt, the song's still rolling around in my head, like it's seeking for lyrics.

Something scary is happening.

Words are forming.

Words that fit the melody *and* the harmony. Words that mean something. Words people could dissect to try and figure out what I'm feeling. Words that will betray who I am to people I don't even know.

Words that could come back to bite me.

I'm too afraid to write any down, and I don't have time in any case. But as I screech into my parking spot, there are a few words I can't seem to help typing out. They aren't lyrics, but they're just as scary.

After completely ignoring him for a long time, I finally text Easton back. IF YOU STILL WANT TO. . .I COULD MAYBE GO ON A DATE.

My finger trembles as I hit send, and then I stuff my phone in my pocket and jog into work. There aren't any extra workers today, praise be, and my shift is pretty uncomplicated. At least, until my very last table.

When I reach it, Easton's sitting there.

There's a huge bouquet of pale pink roses wrapped in bright mauve paper on the table in front of him. "Why, hello," he says. "You know they tried to give me another waitress?" He shakes his head. "I set them straight." He's smiling.

To my great dismay, so am I.

"I told them I'm unable to select my own food, and I only trust one person to feed me."

I offer him a menu.

He laughs. "No thanks."

"You are ridiculous."

"You're not the first person to tell me that," he says. "But you are the cutest."

My face heats immediately. "I have three questions you need to answer."

"You can't remember my allergies?" He quirks one eyebrow. "Really?"

"No." I shake my head. "I remember your answers to my other questions, but these are new."

"They are?" He nods. "Alright, go ahead." He folds his arms. "I'm ready."

"Why are you here today?"

"To eat." He grins. "Next question."

"Is that the only reason?"

"I heard the florist had too many flowers." He tosses his head. "I thought I'd help them out."

I open my mouth, but he cuts me off.

"Ah, ah, this is your last question. Think carefully."

"What?" I snort. "You said you were here *to eat*. I hardly think that counts as a real answer."

"Isn't that why most people come to restaurants?" He leans closer, and I can't help noticing how sharp his jaw is. How bright his eyes. "I mean, it was a lie, but you should probably believe your guests as a general rule."

"I can't order you the perfect food if you lie to me." But my heart's definitely racing, and I want to hear why he really came.

"I don't care about the food. I didn't come for it at all. I came to see someone. That's my honest answer."

"You should always answer me honestly."

"The thing is, I want to." He sighs, bracing his hands on the white linen tablecloth. "But I'm worried that if I do, this girl I'm crazy about will spook." He leans closer. "She spooks easy."

I'm *for sure* blushing now. "What if she told you she wouldn't spook?"

"Is that your last question?" He's smirking.

"I guess it is."

"Here's the thing." He nods. "I'm not someone people tell 'no' very often. I mean, I used to be. When I was growing up, my family was kind of a joke. My dad's not the best in business, and most people had figured that out. But now? My business does well, and I'm, well, I'm reasonably successful." He smiles. "But I really, really like this girl. She works here. You might know her. I think people call her Hornet."

"Not people," I say. "Only one idiot."

"Well, she told me she'd let me take her out." He's beaming. "When I saw that, I got so excited that I just *had* to see her. Only, she didn't send me the selfie I asked for."

I whip my phone out, and sure enough, he texted me back. Eleven times. I close my eyes and shake my head. "I was working."

"I knew that," he says. "So I thought, why not show up here and see that gorgeous face in person."

"Has anyone ever told you that you're ridiculous?" I drop my voice to a hiss. "Most people can't afford to come here once a month. You should not be coming this often."

"You're lucky. Your new admirer could come here every day and it wouldn't make a difference to him."

"You'd probably get fat though," I say. "And then you'd have no chance. I'm shamelessly interested in your six pack."

"You are?" The corner of his mouth turns up. "I might need to get a video of you saying that. You know, for my sister. She insists my stomach is not very impressive, but if you like it. . ."

Oh, no. I can't believe I said that once. There's no way I'd repeat it. And if Emerson saw it, I would die.

"No, I mean, if you—if I thought." I inhale and shake my head. "Never mind."

"I'm not sure I can let that one slide," he says. "Maybe I should take you to the beach on our date. Put this stomach on display and see what you think."

"Stop," I say.

"Look, when you're fighting an uphill battle, you need every advantage you can get."

"A battle?"

"Love's a battlefield, baby—surely you've heard that."

"Baby?"

"I heard it." He cringes. "Look, not every swing is a hit."

"But three strikes and you're out," I say. "And that was—"

"Don't say it was three. One, maybe." He zips his mouth closed.

I laugh. "I'll be back in a moment with your appetizer, sir. I've got other tables to check on."

"I'll be here, making sure your flowers don't get stolen."

He's utterly absurd, but he's growing on me. Which he shouldn't be. We're a terrible match, but apparently this day is about me doing all the things that usually scare me.

A few moments later, when I circle back around and drop off his appetizer, Easton frowns mightily. "Really?"

"What?" I tilt my head.

"Did I make you mad?" He looks at his plate forlornly. "*Broccoli?*"

"It's called angry broccoli," I say. "And it has a bit of a kick. Brace yourself."

"Unless it has a bit of a completely-different-food underneath it, color me disappointed."

"You did show up unannounced," I say. "And you're being a bit of a pain."

"Ah, so this is a punishment appetizer."

"It's not even an appetizer," I whisper. "It's a *side*."

"But last time, at least I got the hipster fries."

"Last time, you were being less annoying." I shrug. "Eat it or you risk offending your waitress."

He pokes it. "How bad is that, really? Just offending her? Or, like, would not eating it downright tick her off?"

"Just try a bite, little boy, or I'll send you to bed with no dinner."

He sighs, but he saws off a smallish chunk and pops it in his mouth. He chews, chews, and swallows. "It's not a homerun," he says, "but it's not a total disaster."

"Since you seem very very opposed to broccoli, I guess I'll take it."

"You know, if my mom saw me here, she'd say I must really like you. When I was a kid, she couldn't get me to eat a single bite of the stupid little trees. That's what I called them."

But when I circle back around with his meal, the entire plate's clean. "Did you throw it in a plant or something?" I ask. "Or flush it? I'm pretty sure our toilets can't handle that. I'd like a little warning if it's going to back up. I can tell Harv who to bill."

"Oh, I don't know," he says. "I imagine your toilets here are pretty powerful."

"You didn't really flush it, did—"

"Relax," he says. "I ate all of it so that when you meet my parents, you can tell them about what I did to impress you."

"You're kidding."

"Not even a little bit," he says. "Trust me. Nothing

would tell them how much I like you more than my will-ingness to choke down broccoli."

I'm laughing as I start to walk off.

"Wait. You didn't tell me what this is."

"It's the burger from the first night," I say. "You've been a pretty good sport about everything. I figured after getting stuck with broccoli, you should get some-thing you really like."

"But it's the same thing I already had."

"You're a problem child." I shake my head.

"How about this?" He points at the empty seat. "You eat this with me, and then you can bring me something else."

"But you'll have to wait even longer, and I can't afford to sit down and share a meal."

He hands me the burger. "Just take a bite every time you come by."

Our fingers brush when I take it—can't leave him hanging, plus I'm starving—and my heart lurches. "Fine. Just one." But it's a big bite, and the burger's even better than I remembered. I close my eyes. "Man, that's good," I finally say.

I grab my second bite a few minutes later after I drop off another round of drinks for the table next to him. And when his pork chop with Portuguese clams is ready, I get a third. "This is kind of fun," I admit.

"Really?" he asks. "Because this girl I like works nights, so I'm kind of always free. I could do this every night."

I press a finger to his mouth. "Don't even think about it."

His eyes light up and he looks at my finger as his mouth curves into a half-grin.

I yank my hand away and wipe it on my apron.

"You sure about that?" He hands me the burger again.

By the time he's finally done eating, it's time for my shift to end.

"How about it?" he asks. "Stick around and eat dessert with me?"

I already told him I'd go on a date. How much worse is eating a dessert with him? Still, I feel like I have to ask for permission. "Lemme make sure it's okay."

It takes me a minute to track down the manager.

"Your boyfriend—who keeps coming and buying all kinds of things—wants you to finish your shift by eating with him? Food he'll be paying for?" My manager Phil rolls his eyes. "Go ahead. Do it every night if he wants." As I walk off, I hear him swear under his breath and mutter, "I miss the honeymoon stage of dating."

A moment later, I carry out two strawberry arnaud lookalikes.

"What's this?" Easton asks.

"Have you ever heard of the Strawberry Arnaud?" I ask.

"Should I have heard of it?"

I set his down in front of him, and then I walk around and sit across from him. It's strange. . .and kind of amazing. "This famous restaurant in New Orleans offered it for a while. It was a million dollar—or three million, I suppose—dollar dessert."

"It was—what?" His eyes bulge. "Did we really need two?"

"Relax," I say. "The guy I'm dating says we can eat here every night." I can't help my grin.

"I mean, how many million is it?" He looks a little sick. I can't tell whether he's playing along, or whether he's nervous.

"This one's twenty dollars," I say. "But it doesn't come with any hidden extras."

He exhales dramatically.

"When you read on the restaurant's menu about the dessert, it goes on and on about the fine Louisiana strawberries, the port wine reduction sauce, and the creamiest ice cream." I point at the desserts I brought. "This one has all of that. Ice cream, strawberries, and a port wine reduction infused with citrus."

His brow furrows.

"But the famous one came with a massive diamond engagement ring, and for a while it was a pretty famous way to propose if you were, you know, uber rich."

"Are you trying to send me a message?" He arches one brow.

"No way," I rush to say. "I just love strawberries, and I've always wanted to try this."

He laughs. "I'm kidding, Bea. Calm down."

But actually, as I sit there eating ice cream and strawberries, I'm the opposite of calm. For the first time in a very, very long time. . .I'm hopeful. Things in my life are scary, but they're also exciting.

A Sunday night isn't the ideal time for a date, but I didn't want to wait until Monday, and I'm not sure that would really be any better anyway. When the girl you like works nights, you take what you can get.

It took me a while to figure out what to do on our date.

First dates are a lot of pressure when you like the girl —it's a little like picking appetizers and entrees for someone that you want them to like. But I'm virtually certain I'll win her over with my plan. I have very little to work with that's in any way adjacent to the musical realm. I wasn't kidding when I said I sound like the seagull from *The Little Mermaid*. Honestly, that might be a little generous. He, at least, had moxie.

I do have one single card to play.

I'm thinking the element of surprise will help me, so my text is a little vague. I'LL PICK YOU UP AT 6. WEAR COWBOY BOOTS IF YOU HAVE ANY.

That precipitates a volley of clarification texts from her, all of which I ignore. Where's the mystery if I tell her via text what we're doing and why I chose it? No, it's better if she stews a little. I've given her the relevant information. It'll either go over really well, or it'll be like the time I tried to rent out her entire area at work.

I'm really hoping for the 'well' option. I must be due, right?

I check my clothing at least six times in the mirror before I decide I should text someone. I have no idea what my stylist would say, so I don't ask her. I text Ace a photo.

OH MY—WHAT ARE YOU WEARING, TEX?

REMEMBER THAT CLASS I TOOK IN UNDER-GRAD? I'm hanging all my hopes on the fact that my professor gave me an A, and now that I'm almost out of time to even change clothes, I'm starting to panic.

Ace calls me. "What are you doing right now?"

"She agreed to let me take her out," I say.

As my best friend, Ace was the first person I told when I met Bea. "Took her long enough."

"Things that are worth it take effort."

"So you keep telling me," Ace says. "But I prefer easy conquests." Some girl's laughing next to him.

"You don't say." I snort. "But listen, do I look okay? Ask your date."

"She wants to know how rich you are," Ace says.

I hang up. Clearly any advice he gives me won't be any good. "Okay," I say to myself in the mirror. "It's going to be fine. She agreed to go out with you, and if nothing else, she'll see that you put effort into this."

Right? Probably.

I give a lot of thought to which car to pick her up in. I could use the 4Runner again. She seemed surprised, but she knows about it. She probably drives something a waitress can afford, but I'm absolutely positive her brother Jake drives something expensive. I know Emerson doesn't care much about cars, so I'm wondering whether she'll like a more expensive car or be repulsed by it.

At the end of the day, what woman hates money?

I almost take the 911, but in the end, I pick the XC90. It's not flashy, but it's roomy and nondescript. It's the safe call, and I feel like I should play some part of tonight safe. When I pull into a spot in her apartment complex beside a truck, I'm glad I picked the car I did. Jake's outside with Bea, and he's kicking her tire. Neither of them sees me, which allows me a moment to spy on them.

"This thing's a hunk of junk, Bea. I swear, why won't you just let me buy you something that runs?"

"Because you'd get me something horrible."

"You could just take one of my two cars," he says. "I don't need both."

"Like I said. Horrible." But she's smiling.

"Pick what you want, then," he says.

She sighs. "I can afford the car I have, as you well know."

"I have more money than I need, as *you* well know, so —" He cuts off when he sees me.

Bea follows his face to mine. "Oh." She glances at her watch. "Shoot."

She's wearing a very cute sundress, but she's definitely not wearing boots. At least she's wearing cute flats that are close-toed.

"I don't have cowboy boots," she says, "and I was going to try and find a pair at Goodwill, but then my car wouldn't start and—"

"Who gives a girl shoe requirements for a date?" Jake scowls. "Starting off on the wrong foot, man."

Bea kicks him. "Stop being rude."

"Ow." He's limping as he hobbles toward the apartment. Maybe that's why he keeps glaring at me, but I doubt it. I have a growing suspicion that Jake's feelings for Bea aren't entirely brotherly.

"Are these shoes alright?" Bea looks nervous.

"They'll be fine," I say. "I'm sorry I stressed you out."

She shakes her head. "No, you didn't. But then you didn't respond about *why* I needed them, and I was worried." She takes in my outfit—Lucchese boots, dark jeans, a belt, and a grey western shirt with snaps in place of buttons. "Are we going to some kind of costume party?"

I can't help laughing. "Something like that."

"Huh?"

"Are you ready to go, or do you need to go back inside?"

Bea snatches her purse off the top of her car and walks toward me. "No, let's steer clear of Jake. He's always in a bad mood when I ask for a ride."

"Seems like he'd be happy to fix your transportation problems."

Bea sighs, following me to my Volvo. "Jake's always extra. You just have to learn to say no around him a lot."

"At least he means well."

"He still thinks his whole career took off because of one stupid song I wrote." She snorts. "It was his face, his talent, all of what makes *Jake Priest* that won. It had very little to do with my song."

I remember that single, I think. "Was it the one about lemons?"

She pauses. "You remember it?"

"They played it like twenty times a day for a while," I say. "Everyone remembers it."

"Well, anyway, movies are a way better fit for him, I think."

"Because he didn't really write the song?"

"He's just a better actor than a pop star." She shrugs. "He really likes acting, and he's great at it. I suppose you could say his life prepared him to be good at it."

I'll have to ask more about that one later. What kind of life prepares someone to be an actor? Was he a circus performer or something? "Are you curious where we're going?"

"I assume that was your goal." She hops in the car before I can decide whether to be cheesy and open her door.

I rush around and climb in my side to start the car. "It was, I guess, but only because I wanted you to spend today looking forward to our date."

She's staring out the window, so I have no idea what she's thinking or whether she's annoyed.

"Maybe that was the wrong plan. I could have simply started early and tried to monopolize your time all day."

Her head whips toward me. "Oh, no, that would've been bad. I had to do all my laundry this morning."

"Oh, darn. That was a missed chance," I say. "I wonder what you look like when all your good clothes are dirty." I eye her outfit. "You could have been wearing American flag pants and a kitten shirt."

"Or an old Pink Floyd shirt and Sponge Bob boxers. You never know."

At least we're chatting just fine. In fact, the thirty-minute drive to City Slickers flies by, and as we pull up, Bea peers at the street signs. "Where are we?"

"I haven't been here for a while," I say. "I'm a little worried I'll make a fool of myself. But. . ." I cut the engine and climb out.

She looks at me over the hood of the car. "City Slickers?"

I point to the line below it. "Dance hall."

"Dance?" Her eyebrows rise and her lip twists. "As in. . .we're dancing?"

"Not a fan?"

She shrugs. "I mean, I'm not *not* a fan, but I've never been before."

"Don't worry," I say. "Most of the heavy lifting falls on me, I swear."

"And you know how to dance?" She lifts both eyebrows. "Because that surprises me, to be honest."

I laugh. "It was my favorite class one semester."

She stares.

"Okay, fine. Two." I start for the door, and she catches up. I think about going for her hand, but it's too early. She's too skittish.

And I'll be holding it a *lot* in a few minutes if things go as planned.

"They also have amazing tacos," I say. "The proprietor started this as a Tex Mex place, but they decided to add some things to bring more people in, and. . ." I gesture for her to go ahead of me.

It's usually hard to get a table, especially on Sunday nights. They don't do country dancing every night, but they do Friday, Saturday, and Sunday. I called ahead, however, and with a little *persuasion*, they agreed to hold us a spot.

"Mr. Moorland," the host says, waving us through.

As we eat our tacos, Bea watches the dancers. Her tapping foot is a dead giveaway that she's musical. She may not know how to dance, but she knows rhythm. Unfortunately, she also appears to be getting more and more nervous about the dancing part.

"I've already had a lot of fun," she says when I finish my second taco. "I'm not sure—"

I stand up and hold out my hand.

"But my purse."

"It'll be fine, I promise."

She frowns, but she does stand, and then she places her tiny hand in mine. That same zing I felt before runs from the place where her hand touches mine, all the way through my entire body.

Until this moment, I wasn't sure it was real.

I've seen enough movies where you feel that little zap, but in thirty years, I've never once felt it myself. I thought maybe that's what happened before, but it was so quick that I didn't trust it.

But tonight?

Touching her makes me want to dance, so we're in the right place. And just then, a song ends. I have to drag her, practically, but we slide out onto the dance floor. When the next song starts, it's *This Kiss* by Faith Hill, and it's a good one to start with.

Watching her face as my hand slides around her waist and my other hand wraps tightly around her hand, moving her around the dance floor in time with the music. . .it's everything I hoped it would be. She's easy to move—not fumbly or resistant—and once we start moving, it's like she and I are the only ones out here.

That's always been my favorite part. The world disappears.

Her cheeks are rosy, and by the end of the song, she's smiling.

"Not too bad?"

"You're a wonderful dancer," she says. "I'm very impressed."

But the next song's starting. "Shall we keep going?"

She doesn't pause. She just nods.

I whirl her away. The faster songs, the slower ones, she never asks to sit down. Hours pass, and my feet start to complain, and still, we keep dancing. Finally, I get a small stitch in my side, and I drag her back to our table.

"Were you really not tired?" I ask as we're both chugging our waters.

She shrugs. "I'm on my feet for more than eight hours a day for work."

I smack my forehead. "Duh. I should've known."

"What?" she asks. "Sitting at a desk and ordering people around all day didn't prepare you for this?"

I laugh. "I may not be able to walk tomorrow."

"Why didn't you stop sooner?" She looks genuinely worried.

"It felt like I'd drifted into Faerie," I say. "I would have danced all night."

"I'm sorry you felt chained to it."

"Nothing like that," I say. "I just didn't want to let you go." I can still feel her in my arms—the most perfect thing I've ever felt.

Our eyes lock, and for a moment, it feels like she thinks the same thing. All around us music blares, people bustle, and glasses clink. But here, at our table, it's like the tiny sphere of isolation that exists on that dance floor has extended to wrap us up again. It's just Beatrice Cipriani and me, our perfect moment. Her eyes are wide, her lips just slightly parted, and the only way this could be better is if there wasn't a table in between us and I could kiss her.

I'm trying to figure out how I can make that happen when my phone rings, the stupidly loud jangle breaking through our bubble like a hammer to glass. I ball up my hand, my jaw tightening. Why didn't I turn the ringer off?

"Do you need to answer that?" Bea glances down at it.

I hit the volume down button to silence it, but it starts ringing again almost immediately. It's Ace. He's going to keep calling until I pick up. I groan and swipe to answer the call. "What?"

"Where are you?"

"I told you," I hiss. "I'm out."

"Oh, right. With Cinderella."

Sometimes he's really obnoxious.

"Look, I just found out that Waterman's having a party, and the rumor is, he has some cash to invest. I really want to convince him to invest with me."

"Why do you need money?"

"I want to hire some new developers," he says. "Only—"

"I don't care," I say. "Good luck."

"Wait," Ace cries. "Don't hang up. I heard you got invited to the party."

"So?"

"You're not going?"

I snort.

"Okay, but you *could* go, and you could take me with you."

"This is a you problem," I say. Only Ace would be so self-centered that he'd call me on the first real date I've had in a decade to ask for a favor.

"Easton, I wouldn't ask if it wasn't serious."

Sounds like Ace needs more than just a few developers. I exhale. The night's been great, so maybe I should end on a high note. Leave her wanting more. "Fine."

"Thank you. Should I come get you?"

"No." I can drop Bea off and swing around the loop faster than heading home. "I'll go straight there myself. Give me a little bit."

"Need to go?" Bea doesn't look upset, but she does look curious.

"A large part of my job, unfortunately, is knowing the right people, and it's taken me years to meet some of these people, and even more to convince them to take me seriously." My parents didn't do me any favors, there. "My buddy Ace—"

"I heard," she says. "He wants you to introduce him to some people at a party?"

"A party he can't get into without me," I say. "So if you don't mind if I—"

"It's fine," she says. "I'll go with you. Unless you think I'm underdressed?"

I blink. She'll go with me? I thought she hated stuff like that—I was sure this would be the end of tonight. But if we keep hanging out after the party. . .I could take her to get dessert or something. And if I'm not in a big rush, I might be able to kiss her.

No.

I *will* kiss her. Screw Ace and his demands. I'll get him into the party, and then I'm bailing. This is still my night. I smile. "Sure. Great. We don't need to be there more than a few minutes."

"Okay." Her smile's shy, and I love it. More than I should, probably.

It feels like she's smiling just for me. I think that's the thing that I like the most about her. I've never in my life felt as special as I do when I'm with her. When she smiles, when she glances my way, when she turns and her eyes meet mine. . .it feels like the world is ours.

BEA

I don't date much. It's not that I don't want to, but mousy girls aren't asked out very often. When we are, it's usually by guys we don't want anything to do with.

The last time I had a date, a little more than six months ago, it was with a guy who came into the restaurant. He was with his parents, celebrating a new job, and at the end of the meal, he asked for my number. He was reasonably cute, so I figured, why not?

That date became my *why not* going forward.

He was pushy. He was grabby. The whole thing ended with a slap and an uber.

But this date? I wish he *would* hold my hand. I mean, he did, while we were dancing, but not after. Even so, it's going so well, it's almost made me regret not dating more. I thought real life never mirrored the movies, but this is coming pretty close. Even the dancing, which I thought would be just awful, was really fun.

I'm not going to lie—it's pretty hot that he can dance so well, and thanks to my sense of timing, it was easy to follow his very clear lead. I'm not a huge country music fan, and it was still a really fun night. So when he says his buddy Ace needs help getting into a party. . .I realize he means to take me home.

But I don't want to go home yet.

This is why they tell kids to stay away from addictive substances. Once you get a little, you just want more, but here we are. I'm already jonesing for more time with Easton.

"It's fine," I say. "I'll go with you. Unless you think I'm underdressed?"

At first he looks a little surprised, probably because I told him I don't like big social events. After taking a moment to catch up, he rallies. "Sure. Great. We don't need to be there more than a few minutes."

"Okay." I'm not sure what else to say. I don't want to sound pathetic. "Are we going, then?" I stand.

"Right. Yes." He stands up, too, and then he leads me out, one arm hovering behind me to make sure no one bumps into me. It's pretty cute—and it feels like he's claiming me.

I don't hate it.

I'm honestly a little surprised by his cars. He's not much older than Jake and me, and Jake bought a sports car with his first paycheck. I suppose it makes sense that a savvy businessman would want a less flashy car than a movie star, but still. A 4Runner and a Volvo? At least the Volvo's comfortable, and of course, it runs well. That's the primary concern for me, honestly. Mine is temperamental.

I just figured if a guy had more than one car, at least one would be flashy.

"Why don't you let Jake buy you a car, really?" Easton asks, clearly also thinking about cars.

"It's a slippery slope with him," I say.

"Meaning?"

"Have you ever been around little kids?"

"That feels non-sequitur," Easton says.

"For the non-Ivy League person in the car. . ."

He laughs. "I'm not an Ivy League graduate either, but non-sequitur means something's kind of a disconnect. In other words, I asked you about Jake and then you asked me about little kids." His eyes cut sideways briefly before returning to the road. "What do they have to do with each other?"

"I've done a few rounds of being a 'big sister,' and I also have a much younger foster brother. In my experience, the key to forming successful relationships with kids is establishing boundaries and then holding them."

"Okay." His brow's furrowed.

"Jake's like a little kid. . .on crack."

"He does drugs?" Easton's smiling, so I'm assuming he knows that's not what I'm saying.

"Jake had an interesting childhood," I say. "If absolutely terrible childhoods interest you." I chuckle. "He doesn't really like anyone."

"Except you."

"I mean, he tolerates Emerson, and he loves Dave and Seren same as we all do, but yeah. I may be the only person he truly likes, even in the family."

"And?"

"His whole life he's had very little, so now that he does have stuff, he wants to hoard it." I look at Easton's profile. "Or give it to me."

"It sounds nice. I mean, your car doesn't run, right?"

I sigh. "My car's old, and I thought it just needed a new battery, but it's still having problems with a new one, so I think the starter may be bad. The thing is, I can always take the bus if I have to, and repairing an old car is way, *way* cheaper than buying a new one. Right?"

"But if he wants to buy you one, it would be free, so why say no?"

"First, it's not free to me either. I'd have to pay much higher insurance on a new car. But beyond that, money always comes with strings."

Easton nods slowly. "And if you let him buy you a car?"

"He'll want to keep going," I say. "You heard him talking about buying me clothes. He wants to get me a new phone. He's always complaining about mine because the photos aren't great." I shrug. "It's fine if my photos aren't the best quality. The world's not suffering from a shortage of high-res photos of Jake Priest."

"I guess not," Easton says.

"If I really, really needed something, I know he would get it for me, and that's nice to know."

"Or Emerson."

"Or Dave and Seren," I say. "I have no shortage of people willing to help me, and that's one of the reasons I want to do things on my own."

"Must be nice."

"Don't tell me you don't have people who will help you," I say. "Your family is money money money."

"Not exactly." Easton sighs, and his hands tighten on the wheel. "It was mostly smoke and mirrors growing up." He shakes his head. "Mom and Dad never let us tell anyone, but our family was usually one step away from bankruptcy. Dad's not very good at business, and it wrecked everything, over and over. As a teenager, I decided I'd figure out how to do the opposite of what he did."

"Oh?"

He nods slowly. "Even though it was against school rules, I sold candy to kids at school. So much candy."

"Candy?" I can't help chuckling again. "Sounds. . .lucrative."

"I know it sounds stupid," he says. "That's actually why it worked. No one suspected me of really doing it to make money. I turned it into a joke. 'How bad do you really want my Snickers?' or 'Are you hungry enough to pay twenty bucks for this Butterfinger?'"

"Wait, you're serious?"

"I paid for my own college by selling candy for way more than it was worth to a bunch of spoiled kids in high school and sticking every last dime in a savings account my parents didn't know about. Only, my second year of school, Dad found it."

I'm completely shocked. Emerson mentioned that Elizabeth's family had struggled, but I didn't think it was with money.

"Anyway, it was less embarrassing to tell people I'd partied too hard than it was to say my parents found my college fund and used it to keep from filing for bankruptcy, so everyone thinks I failed out of school."

Maybe no one's life is really as easy as it looks.

"I do have some great friends, like Ace, who will do whatever they can to help me." He's staring straight ahead like he's a little embarrassed. "That's why I'm driving over to help him. He'd do it for me."

"But your parents aren't the rock they should be for you."

"Not exactly, no."

"Do they still raid your savings when they run into trouble?" I shouldn't be asking. It's none of my business.

"It's not exactly the same anymore," he says. "But the

whole reason I started my own company is that I wanted to make so much they could never spend through it all."

"But their spending is the problem," I say. "If you can't get that under control—"

"Trust me," he says. "Unless they start ordering the New Orleans strawberry thing every night, they can't outspend me. Not anymore."

"I guess, but they probably still feel like an anvil around your neck, dragging you down."

"We live in the land of opportunity. I just got pretty good at swimming." He shrugs. "Honestly though, it's fine."

I kind of hate his parents, but I don't mention that. Before I can think of anything else to say, he turns into a neighborhood—the houses are gargantuan. They're as big as Seren and Dave's inn.

"Whoa."

"Yeah, there's a reason Ace wants to meet this guy."

"How do you know him?"

"He taught me tax law basics at Princeton before I left."

"Are you the kind of nerd who still talks to teachers?"

Easton laughs. "I guess so."

"So am I," I admit. "But only three of them. The ones who really taught me the most."

"Really?" He turns to face me. "Interesting."

"Well, not lately, I guess. I haven't had much to tell them about."

"You could tell them about winning runner-up in the jingle contest."

I shrug.

"But you won't, because you didn't win."

"Sometimes it's hard when people really think you're

talented," I say. "Harder than if they just thought you were nice."

"I get that," he says. "Expectations can be the worst."

"Exactly."

When I hop out of the car, I notice that Easton's jogging around to my side. His smile's a little sheepish. "I wasn't sure whether opening your door would be corny."

"My dad—Dave does it all the time."

"Why don't you call them Mom and Dad?" Easton asks. "Unless that's a rude thing to ask. Emerson does."

I sigh. "It's not much of a first date topic, but for now I'll just say that my family's very complicated, and I have to be careful what I say and to whom."

His brow furrows, but he doesn't press further. He does, however, offer me his arm, like we're characters in a period piece.

"Do people walk arm-in-arm these days?"

His shoulders droop a bit. "Maybe not."

"Who cares?" I slide mine through the crook in his elbow. "Maybe we'll start a new trend."

"If we're starting new trends, my stylist will want you to wear very specific things." He's smirking, so I know he's teasing. Probably.

It's a good reminder that as much as my grandfather can be overbearing, people do watch Easton. I'll have to see how bad it really is. Because right now, his visibility feels like his only flaw, and that scares me. There must be other substantial problems with this guy that I haven't found yet.

A perfect guy is great in theory, but I don't believe he exists, and if he did, there's no way he'd like me. I'm as flawed as they come.

"Oh good." As we approach the house, Easton waves

at someone. It's a guy I've seen before, and it finally hits me where. He's Elizabeth's employer. She did mention the event was for a friend of her brother, and the first time I met Easton was at this guy's video game party. "Ace." Easton tosses his head at him.

Ace smiles at me. "And you must be Beatrice, Emerson's sister. Right?"

I nod. "That's me."

"You two do not look even a little bit alike," he says.

"They're not blood related, idiot," Easton says. "Foster siblings."

"Ah, right. Sorry." Ace winces a little. "I'm Ace. Sticking my foot in my mouth a lot is kind of my thing."

Easton nods. "That tracks."

"This guy has been bailing me out for a long time now, so he knows better than most."

"But Ace would give up his left arm for me if I needed something," Easton says.

"Hey now," Ace says. "Let's not get hasty. I'm left-handed. Maybe my right, but never my left."

"You're left-handed?" Easton asks. "How did I not know that?"

"He's a lousy friend," Ace says. "I doubt he'd even sacrifice his pinky toe for me if it came down to it."

But now we're at the front door.

"Ready?" Easton whispers. "I swear, we won't stay long."

But from the second we walk through the door, people are waving at him. "Easton, my man," a man in his forties says almost right after we walk inside.

I release him, partially because it makes him look a little crazy to be standing with my arm hooked through his, but also because the lions are all coming for him, and I run from lions as a general rule.

"I'm going to get a drink," I say.

Easton freezes. "Jake said you don't usually—"

I wave him off, smiling so he knows not to worry. "Not a *drink* drink. Just something to hold in my hand. Go ahead. You can find me over there when you're done." I gesture.

Only, he grossly underestimated how in-demand he'd be. It's been at least thirty minutes, and every time he tries to break away from a group of people, someone else snags him. I actually almost feel sorry for him. He's definitely trying to leave, but he's popular.

Meanwhile, I'm making sure this end of the punch table does *not* blow away. It would make a huge mess inside this massive house if it did. With such powerful air vents, you never know what could happen. Sometimes I set my drink down, with a napkin under it so no one inadvertently grabs it. Sometimes I hold it.

I'm flexible.

"You look as bored as I feel," a man in dark slacks and a sky blue button-down says. He's handsome in an Italian-model kind of way, with longish hair falling across his face.

"Not bored, no," I say. "In fact, it's been pretty entertaining just watching the people in this party. I think the clothes they're wearing probably cost more than my parents' home."

The man's lips are twitching.

"And I mean that on a person-by-person basis."

"You might not be wrong." The man holds out his hand. "Tyler Osborne, Piper Communications."

"Oh, Tyler, I hate to disappoint you, but you're currently talking to the most boring person in here." I lean closer. "My shoes came from DSW, my dress is from

Nordstrom Rack, and my watch?" I lift my wrist. "It's a hand-me-down from my sister."

He smiles. "You're actually more interesting than I expected."

"Oh?"

"Didn't you come in with Easton Moorland?"

Ugh. "Yes, but we're just friends. His sister's married to my brother."

"You're family, then," Tyler says.

"I guess," I say, "but not really." I shrug. "I won't be here long, so you'd be better off getting to know someone more connected, I assure you."

"What do you think about Easton's company?"

"What?"

"Sacrifice Nothing," the man says. "That's the name."

"It's kind of a stupid name," I say. "I mean, everything in the entire world that matters requires some kind of sacrifice, right?"

He tilts his head. "How so?"

"I get that it appeals to people who have never had to give anything up, and I suppose that's the whole idea. Their overpriced stuff is for people who want to have it all, but really, they're fooling themselves."

"Are they?" Tyler smiles.

"Let's assume the money they have to spend to buy something from that label isn't already the trade-off because they just have so much. They're also clearly valuing things that won't really bring them joy. The overpriced clothes and shoes and watches are just another empty patch for the holes in their soul."

Tyler nods slowly. "Wow, you really don't think you're his girlfriend."

I chuckle. "Nope."

"You're not like all the people who buy Easton's brand, then?"

"Vapid, you mean?" I ask. "Spoiled?" I shake my head. "I certainly hope not."

The man spins around then, hissing. "Did you get all that?"

When I follow the direction he's looking, I see a woman holding a camera. She throws him a thumbs up.

"What on earth. . ." But Tyler's shaking his head. "The weird thing is, when we asked Easton who you were earlier, he had a slightly different answer."

"Who are you?" I ask.

"I told you," Tyler says. "A reporter with Piper Communications."

I thought he was just another wannabe businessman trying to network, but he did tell me he was with a communications company. I just didn't think—reporter. "Look, I was spouting inane party nonsense."

"I thought you sounded eloquent," Tyler says. "You certainly look poised. And I think the bit about how you're wearing DSW shoes was especially cute. Relatable."

"I don't give you permission to post a video with me in it."

"Sadly for you, New York is a one-person consent state, which means the only person who has to give consent is me, since I was also on video."

I want to strangle him. "Alright, what do you want?"

"You know," he says. "I actually feel a little bad. You two are kind of cute."

"If you feel bad, just delete the video."

"Can't do." Tyler frowns, and a moment later he disappears entirely.

"Hey you," Easton says. "Ready to go?" He glances

behind me and to the left. "We should go fast, because I think that's Patrizio Bertelli, and if he realizes I saw him, I'll be stuck. I've been waiting to hear back from him for two days."

"You can talk to him," I say. "It's fine."

"I'd rather talk to you." He's smiling as he leads me out the front door.

"Easton," someone says.

He starts jogging. "Quick. It's like a pack of wolves in there."

But once we reach the car and shut the door, it's quiet. Too quiet.

"Hey, so. . ."

"Yeah?" He turns, leaning across my body to click my seatbelt into place. "What?" His face is inches from mine. "Everything okay?"

I swallow. "The thing is—"

He's staring at my mouth. His eyes are fixated on it. Is he going to kiss me? Do I want him to?

I need to tell him about the whole Tyler thing, but in this moment, I can't find a single word. His mouth lowers toward mine, and a tiny sigh escapes.

The corner of his mouth turns upward, and he bites his lip. "Bea."

"Yeah?" I look up at his eyes, but he's still looking at my mouth.

"You have the most beautiful mouth I've ever seen." And then he kisses me, pressing his lips against mine.

My hands shoot up to grab his face, and he shifts a little, his mouth slanting across my lips. Our bodies are pressed tightly together, probably because of the enclosed space, but I like it. I *like* it, like it.

He doesn't try to plunge his tongue into my mouth. He doesn't try to suck my face off. He just kisses me gently, persistently—his lips moving softly against mine —and my heart soars inside my body.

"Easton," I whisper.

He releases me and drops back into his seat. "I did it." He's smiling.

"Did what?" I raise one eyebrow. "Did you have a bet?"

"Yes." He's beaming now. He shifts so he's looking at me again. "A bet with myself."

"With yourself?" That's too cute. "What were the terms?"

"I promised myself I wouldn't chicken out."

"Do you chicken out a lot?"

He shakes his head. "Not really, but I've never been this excited or this nervous about kissing someone in my entire life."

"Me either," I admit.

And now he's *really* beaming.

"The thing is," I say. "Something happened at the party I should tell you about."

"Oh yeah?" He's leaning toward me again. "Was it something like this?" When he kisses me again, I forget all about stupid Tyler.

But maybe I shouldn't have.

My stupid board has called an emergency board meeting. I'd like to complain, but I can't, seeing as I did the same thing.

"What was so urgent?" After my date last night, I couldn't sleep, I was so excited. Six a.m. came especially early this work week. My eyes are still burning, even after my commute to the office. "You all look exceptionally crabby."

"You should have been the one calling *us* in here," Mrs. Yaltzinger says. "To explain this." She points at the television on the wall.

It's black.

"You need me to explain how a television works?" I frown. "I can just call tech support to—"

Her phone must have been buffering or something, because a video blares to life just then. It's Bea's gorgeous face, standing by the punch table last night. At first I'm confused, but then I hear what she's saying.

"My shoes came from DSW, my dress is from Nordstrom Rack, and my watch?" She waves it at the guy she's talking to. "It's a hand-me-down from my sister."

The guy, who's smiling at her rather creepily, bugs me. I didn't even notice him hovering around her last night, but now I want to know who he is.

"What do you think about Easton's company?" he asks her. "Sacrifice Nothing—that's the name."

"It's kind of a stupid name," Bea says. "I mean, everything in the entire world that matters requires some kind of sacrifice, right?"

It *is* kind of a stupid name, but I would never say that publicly, and it's awkward that she did. Awkward, but ultimately, not really that big of a deal.

I turn toward Mrs. Yaltzinger, but she points. "Keep watching."

The man I now kind of hate tilts his head. "How so?"

"I get that it appeals to people who have never had to give anything up, and I suppose that's the whole idea. Their overpriced stuff is for people who want to have it all, but really, they're fooling themselves."

"Are they?" The jerk's smile is so smug I want to smack it off his face.

"Let's assume the money they have to spend to buy something from that label isn't already the trade-off," Bea says, "because they just have so much. They're also clearly valuing things that won't really bring them joy. The overpriced clothes and shoes and watches are just another empty patch for the holes in their soul."

Shoot. That's pretty damaging. The *holes in their souls?* Come on, Bea. A little less pretentious coffeeshop critique and a little more thought about what kind of people you're talking to would be nice.

She was, after all, at a party full of my friends.

The man knows he's got her, I can tell. "You're not like all the people who buy Easton's brand, then?"

"Vapid, you mean?" she asks. "Spoiled?" I shake my head. "I certainly hope not."

Alright, that's pretty bad, but when Mrs. Yaltzinger shuts it off, I breathe a tiny sigh of relief. It's not the first bad press we've dealt with, and this sort of thing always blows over.

"This is who you're dating?" Mr. Dressel stands up. "This woman who goes on television and criticizes the people who buy your brand?"

"A woman who wears DSW and Nordstrom *Rack*?" Mr. Jimenez says. "Really?"

I shrug. "So she's frugal. People should appreciate that she's relatable."

"Oh, plenty of people do," Mr. Jimenez says. "In fact, they're touting her as the Evita of the fashion industry."

I snort. "Does that make me an authoritarian dictator?"

"You think this is funny?" Mr. Dressel asks. "We told you to find a girlfriend so you could grow the brand. Instead your girlfriend, so-called, is desecrating it."

"Be careful what you wish for, er, demand?" I sigh. "You're all overreacting."

"You have to break up with her immediately," Mrs. Yaltzinger says, "which should be immediately obvious. Most of the rabble who are jeering and commenting on her video aren't the type of people who would buy Sacrifice Nothing, but who knows what else she'll say?"

"Look." I don't get angry often, but when I do. . . "You barged in here and started ordering me to date to inspire a launch I had no desire to make. Then you set me up on a date with an awful woman who I couldn't bear for even a full meal, much less more. And now that I have met someone, someone I really, really like, you're telling me I have to dump her, because what? Because she's not a socialite who has thousands to blow on over-priced luxury goods?"

"Like it or not, you're the purveyor of those over-priced luxury goods." The vein in Mr. Dressel's forehead is throbbing. "So, yes. We're telling you to dump her."

"Or else?" I ask. "Or else. . .what?"

"You retained control of your company since the IPO," Mr. Dressel says. "Mostly. And I hoped it wouldn't come to this, but I'd just like to point out that you your-self retained only forty-five percent of the stock."

"My parents own another ten percent," I say. "And there's no way—"

"Hello, Mrs. Moorland?" Mrs. Yaltzinger says. "And Mr. Moorland. Are you there?"

"Hey, Eastie," Dad says. "I'm sorry to hear that this weekend's party was a bit of a mess."

"But you know, when we make messes, we have to clean them up." Mom has never once said anything like that to me before. In fact, I've spent the better part of my life cleaning up *her* messes.

"If we have to force you to dump her, we will," Mr. Jimenez says. "But we'd rather this not get nasty." He's smiling, but I've never hated him more.

"I think this meeting's over." I walk out, heading for my office. The second I close the door, I call my parents. Dad ducks my call, but Mom picks up.

"Hey, sweetheart," Mom says. "I'm sorry that got ugly in there. It was really unnecessary."

"You can't be serious about telling me to dump her, right?"

"Of course not," Mom says. "But you have to admit that it's complicated."

"I gave you those shares so you could use them as collateral on the home loan you needed. How is any of this complicated? They're *my* shares." My hands are balled into fists at my side, the phone pressed against my ear by the force of my shoulder.

"The thing is, we needed that loan because your dad had an unparalleled opportunity to go in on an investment, and well."

The investment failed.

It's literally the only constant in my life. If there's a bad idea, Dad's the first to sign up. Mom persistently refuses to stop him. She's usually standing beside him waving pom poms.

"What are you planning to do if he lost the loan money?"

"The only way we can pay off the house note is to sell the shares," Mom says. "It's really our only remaining asset. Unless you happen to have some money you could lend us."

I grit my teeth.

Those shares are worth millions and millions of dollars. I don't have that much money just lying around, not without selling shares myself. I do have a few investments I could possibly sell off, but even that takes time. "You told them you'd vote with them, though, when I *gave* you those shares for a company *I made.* . .why?"

"They told us that this girl—she could devalue the entire company. If that's true, we can't *afford* to support you in dating someone like that. We need those shares to hold their value now more than ever, and so do you. You just can't see it, but we're trying to help you make smart decisions."

I'm not even disappointed. I should've expected something like this, honestly. "Thanks a lot, Mom."

"But darling, surely you understand that the kind of

woman you date reflects on all of us, and your sister married a Richmond, so now more than ever—"

I hang up.

And then I call Bea.

She doesn't answer, so I call again. And again. And again. Finally I stop being a stalker and send her a text. HAVE YOU SEEN THE VIDEO?

I'M SO SORRY.

I close my eyes. She has seen it, and clearly she feels bad. There's no way that she would have said anything like that to anyone she thought might—it hits me then that the video was likely doctored to make it look even worse than it was.

This is my fault, of course, for having such a stupid business model that someone speaking the truth could devalue my entire brand. Sacrifice Nothing *is* a pretty vapid brand name. Anyone who has lived for more than a dozen years knows that important things—most things worth having, in fact—require some kind of sacrifice.

But rich people are my target demographic, and the idea of never compromising and never giving up anything appeals to them. Never mind that most of them have sacrificed time with their families, their ethics, and likely also their souls for the money they spend on my products. That's the reason this whole thing is such a big deal. Rich people are the only ones who can afford my products, so we can't afford to have them feel criticized by the face of the brand.

I NEED TO SEE YOU.

THAT'S A BAD IDEA, she texts back. LESS BEAT-RICE IS YOUR ONLY PLAY RIGHT NOW.

I'M NOT SUGGESTING WE POSE FOR A BILLBOARD AD, THOUGH IT WOULD BE A BEAUTIFUL SPREAD WITH BOTH OUR FACES

ON IT, AND I'VE GOT JUST THE SLOGAN. "HOLE IN YOUR SOUL? TRY *SACRIFICE NOTHING*. IT'LL PATCH IT FOR A HOT MINUTE."

She doesn't reply.

COME ON, BEA. AT LEAST LET ME COME BY.

Why am I asking? I know where she lives. She doesn't respond, but I don't need her approval to bang on her door. I take the Volvo again—the XC90 is my least attention-grabbing car, since I left my 4Runner at Mom and Dad's. It's not like I'm Jake Priest or anything, but given the current status with the trending video, it would be nice if I wasn't seen running right over to her house.

When I knock, I expect Jake to answer and yell at me, so it takes me by surprise when Bea yanks the door open. "What?"

"Hey! You answered."

"I'm not some hotshot with a butler," she says. "I always answer my own door. You're mistaking me for Emerson."

She's making jokes, so it can't be that bad. "Look, I'm sure that guy baited you, and I know—"

"I'm an idiot," she says. "Given half a chance, I'll always say the wrong thing."

"But in this case, everything you said was true."

"Thank you for not being angry," she says, "but I know that must have been embarrassing for you, and I'm really sorry."

"No, what's embarrassing is that my board is so angry that they want me to dump you." I run my hand through my hair. "They're being so stupid and unreasonable about it."

"We weren't together in the first place," she says,

"which is what I said to the half a dozen reporters who have tracked down my number."

"Bea."

She shrugs. "Your board's right. You can't be tied to me, not with this mess I made. It's only because of a connection between us that it's even newsworthy."

"That was the best date I've had. . .ever. You had fun, too, I know it."

"I did," she says, "but not enough fun to destroy a multimillion dollar company."

I roll my eyes. "Destroy? It's not made of paper mâché."

"I'm not trying to sound arrogant," she says. "I'm just trying to take responsibility. What I said—it was unguarded, and Easton, I say stuff like that too often. I'm not good at things like this. There's a reason your board doesn't want you dating a waitress."

"Beatrice?" A man behind me is peering around my shoulder.

Bea closes her eyes and mutters, "I should've just stayed in bed today." Then her nostrils flare, and she squares her shoulders. "Easton, it's time for you to go."

"You must be Easton Moorland," the man says. He's tall, he's broad-shouldered, and he has a winning smile, for an older man. It's a smile that has been used a *lot*, a smile that most everyone in New York knows. "How unfortunate to find you here."

"Why are you here, Grandfather?"

Bea's grandfather is the governor of New York? Seriously?

"You may not be tapped into social media, but I am, and let me tell you, darling, you are *trending*."

"Easton." Somehow, she turned my name into a plea. "Later. Okay?"

"Swear you'll answer when I call, or I'm not leaving," I say.

She nods. It's small, but it's there.

"Good. He's leaving." The old man beams. "And as long as you stay away from him, you just took the first step in your life toward making your old man proud." He's beaming. "You're a woman of the people. If we play this right, you could probably even run for office yourself."

"There's nothing on earth I want less than that," Bea says.

I'm chuckling as I walk to my car. For a waitress the board doesn't want me to date, she sure seems to have some interesting secrets, and I intend to discover every last one of them. If anything, I'm more intrigued than ever.

＊ 15 ＊

BEA

When I was young, I adored my grandfather. He always had a scratchy face, and he smiled a lot. I remember people taking photos of us, and I don't remember him yelling. I've never been sure whether he just didn't yell as much back then, or whether I blocked it out.

Either way, as I got older, he definitely yelled.

A lot.

And whenever he showed up, my mom got angry. She also always got stuck in rehab, which meant that I went home with Grandpa. No one could see me while I was staying with him unless I was dressed and pressed like a doll, and I could never do anything but smile and nod. He was very clear on that. I've since wondered whether the people we met thought I was a halfwit.

I'll never know what Dave and Seren said to convince him that they could be adequate foster parents, but he kept them on a very short leash. The promise he extracted from me as my part of that deal was that under no circumstance would I ever call Dave and Seren Mom or Dad—no one could know that I was their foster child. The world could know that I was staying with them for a short time, and that was all.

Anything else would result in my removal from their care.

I could probably call them whatever I want now, but some habits die hard. I'm afraid of the dark. I'm still irrationally worried that there might be monsters under my bed, and I'm still afraid of my grandfather. I know too much about what he's capable of, and I'm under no delusions that he'll go easy on me because we're related.

Grandfather will always do whatever is best for him. Period.

"I will never run for office." I block him from coming inside. "I don't think we have anything else to discuss."

He frowns. "I'm coming inside."

I shake my head. "My roommate's sleeping."

"You mean the Fansee's troubled foster kid?" He scowls. "That Jake boy should not be your roommate."

This isn't a new argument. He's always hated Jake. It's not personal. He hates anyone being near me who might attract attention that could possibly circle back to him. He dislikes anything he can't control.

"I'll provide you with an apartment—a nice one, in The City."

I hate when New Yorkers call New York City *The City*. It's *so* arrogant, like comparatively, no other cities matter. "I'll pass, but thanks."

His lip curls. "You know what your problem is?"

"Wait, I only have one?"

Now he's really annoyed. "Right now, your smart mouth is not appreciated, miss."

"I'll make note of it."

"You were taught better than this."

"Was I?" I cross my arms. "You taught me never to let anyone push me around."

"That doesn't apply to me." He narrows his eyes.

I shrug. "That part of the lesson didn't take. What else did you want to say?"

"You will not see that boy again." His eyes harden, which is impressive since they were already downright flinty. "Am I clear?"

"See him, as in clap my eyes on him? Or see him as in go on a date and kiss?"

The wrinkles around his lips deepen. "What did I say about the smart mouth?"

Egging my grandfather on is always a bad idea, but if I don't push back at all, he gets even worse. It's a delicate balance, pushing back just hard enough to get him to leave me alone. "I apologize," I whisper. "I just didn't get much sleep with all the drama over the video, and I don't want to wake up Jake. He has a shoot later."

He sighs. "Well, if you're going to bed, I'll assume you heard what I said, and you plan to listen." He waits for me to disagree. After a moment, when I don't argue, he nods and huffs before leaving.

I never promised him a thing, but in his mind, I sure did.

Not that it matters. Whether I do what he insists or not, all Grandfather cares about are the results. People liked me in that video—only rich people got annoyed. And they're mostly annoyed at themselves for being soulless, not at me for pointing it out. Which means it's good for his image to be connected to me. It could have just as easily gone the other way.

That's what makes me a wild card.

Nothing I do is premeditated, and I certainly never know how people will take it. My safest play is the same as it's always been. Stay home, keep my mouth shut, and stay away from any kind of attention. Emerson—the Richmond heir—and Jake do *not* make it easier. The last thing I need to do is start dating the latest fashion wonderboy, but he's just *so* cute.

Waking up to a dozen messages from friends and coworkers about my internet fame wasn't wonderful. But Easton rushing over here to make sure I'm okay? Reassuring me that he's still interested, even though I was a complete mess? Telling me that he doesn't care what his board thinks?

It's pretty cute.

Even so, it's *early*, and it has not been a great day.

Thankfully, Jake's not actually home. That means I can go for a run alone, which I do. I feel a lot better once I've worked up a sweat, and while I'm in the shower, I have an idea for a song. When Jake finally does walk through the front door, looking like maybe he had an early morning shoot, I've got almost the entire chorus worked out.

"Hey, listen to this."

I start banging away without thinking or even really more than glancing his way. "And then I was thinking I'd transition like this." I play my coda, and then the first two lines of the verse. "It's blocky, but maybe if I. . ." I trail off, erasing a line and cleaning it up.

"You are—"

I snap my head back, surprised Jake's standing just behind me. He crossed the room without me even noticing.

"What?"

His hand brushes the hair hanging down my back. "Your hair's sopping wet. The entire back of your shirt is soaked."

I shrug. "I had this idea while I was in the shower, and I just wanted to get it down."

"It's even better than the one you wrote the other day," he says softly. "I'm impressed."

"Do you really think so?" Then it hits me, how to finish out the opening lines. "Oh! What about this." I play them all together, and then I plunge into the chorus. "I even had an idea for words. What do you think about these?" I clear my throat. "Don't judge my voice, because I just had a yogurt."

"Bea, stop with the self-deprecating crap about your voice. You sound amazing. Just sing."

That surprises me, but I shake it off. "Okay. Here goes." I swallow, and then I launch into it. "Walking that fine line, but it's never enough; When the one who makes you small is so rough; Nothing you do will ever earn a smile; You should really quit caring, at least for a while."

I hunch my shoulders then, hearing just how corny it sounds.

"You know what? Never mind. The lyrics need work."

Jake drops a hand on my shoulder. "That was—it was *really* good, Hornet. I mean it."

I turn around slowly. "Are you just being nice?"

He shakes his head. "Not even a little. I know your grandfather came today. Is that what inspired this?"

"How do you know—" It doesn't matter. "It was and it wasn't, actually. I am talking about him, kind of, but I think the song's because of Easton. You know, that video's a mess, but he wasn't even mad. I embarrassed him, and I criticized his company, mocking everyone who buys his brand, really, and instead of getting upset with me, he came over to make sure I'm alright."

Jake frowns.

"I guess it made me realize what people *should* do. It's what I've never had."

"I don't criticize you," Jake says.

I sigh. "True, but you don't push me, either. I'm writing songs, plural. Not a song. I'm halfway through my second in a week. Maybe I'll enter that contest after all."

"You were mad about it," he says. "You said that woman was a jerk."

I shrug. "Maybe I needed someone to believe in me, even when I don't believe in myself."

"I do," Jake says.

I roll my eyes. "Oh my gosh, Jakey, stop. Not everything is about you."

"This isn't about Easton, either, though." He shoves his hands in his pockets. "If you're writing songs, then *you're* writing them. Not that guy."

"Fine," I say. "I'm writing them."

Jake finally smiles. "Well, good for you. I could put in some calls to see who's running the contest, and then—"

I shake my head. "No thank you."

"Some things haven't changed, I see."

"I guess not." But I'm smiling back at him. No matter how much he annoys me, I can't stay mad long. Jake's just like that. Not with everyone, but with me. Although, I do think it's the same boyish charm that women all over the country fall in love with on the screen. It's just even stronger in person.

I go back to the piano, tightening a few things, working on a transition and then playing the whole thing again, start to finish. It takes me a minute, but I get it all down on paper, too. When I finally finish, I lean back and sigh.

"That was really amazing to watch."

I nearly jump out of my skin. Jake's sitting on the sofa, doing *nothing*.

"Were you watching me that whole time?"

"More listening than watching, but yes. Why?"

"It's. . .weird."

"It was kind of amazing. Once you're big, and I have no doubt you soon will be, I'm going to tell people at parties how I was sitting in the room next to you while you wrote this one."

"Jake." I roll my eyes. "You're ridiculous."

"And like all my other outrageous stories, this one's true."

"There is *no way* you were dropped off by helicopter and then skied your way down the Sierra Nevadas with Ashton Kutcher."

"Don't forget the wounded dog we found and carried to safety."

I'm laughing now. "The fact that anyone believes that story makes me doubt the future of humanity more than anything else I've heard. *Jellyfish* have more brain cells than someone who believes that."

"Fine, Ashton and I didn't exactly find the dog that way, but *this* one really will be *true*." He stands and crosses to sit next to me on the piano bench. "And Ashton tells the same story, by the way. His agent made it up. I'm just following orders."

"What actually happened?" I ask. "Twisted ankle?"

Jake sighs. "More embarrassing."

"Oh, now I really need to know."

"I can't tell you. I signed a form saying we'd stick to the same story—the one you've heard."

I slug him on the shoulder. "You're an idiot."

"But look—the one thing about my life that's not

made up." He points at the paper where I've jotted the song down. "That's the real deal, Bea."

I'm not good at taking praise. I have no idea what to do with it. Luckily, it doesn't happen often, so I can usually just shrug it off. It leaves me poorly prepared for moments like this—raw, real. Thankfully, my phone buzzes. I can't help hoping it's Easton. Which is stupid.

When I realize Jake's phone also buzzed, I'm a little disappointed.

ANNOUNCEMENT: WE WILL NOW HAVE A WEEKLY FAMILY DINNER ON SUNDAY. I'LL HOST EACH WEEK UNLESS SOMEONE ELSE CALLS IT. I'LL TAKE REQUESTS FOR DINNER. FIRST COME, FIRST SELECTED.

Seren's as cute as ever.

"What is this?" Jake says. "Like anyone wants to go back every Sunday."

Only, I can tell by his half-smile that he's as happy about it as I am. I start texting right away. SPAGHETTI AND MEATBALLS.

Jake's head whips sideways. "Hey, now. You're not fighting fair."

"She said first request gets picked first." I shrug. "Snooze and lose."

For someone who said he doesn't want to go back, his fingers sure fly over the front of his phone. THAT PASTA IN A GLASS DISH WITH THE SUNDRIED TOMATOES.

Now I'm laughing. "For the love, Jake."

"What?" he asks. "No one else makes it like that."

"It's because Seren made that up with whatever ingredients she had in the fridge."

"She made it every week after that for two years," Jake says. "I know she can make it again."

"She calls it Jake's Pasta Casserole, you know," I say. But that reminds me to ask. . . CAN WE BRING PEOPLE?

IF WE CAN'T, Emerson texts, I'M NOT COMING. :P

"They are joined at the hip now," Jake says. "Pathetic."

"That's kind of what marriage is, dummy."

"Who did you want to take?" Jake frowns. "That annoying Easter guy?"

"You know it's East*on*."

"I thought after that video, you two would be done." He plonks at the keys on the piano, making a terrible noise.

"Stop." I drop a hand on his. "My ears."

He turns, his eyes intent. "I'm serious, Hornet. Are you still going to date him?"

The question surprises me. "I mean, I don't love that he's in the public eye, and my grandfather says I *have* to stop seeing him right away." I roll my eyes.

"You won't date anyone who's a public figure, right?" He's staring at me in a weird way. "You always said that. Always."

"That was always Grandfather's thing, but I'm beginning to wonder why I have to listen to him. I'm an adult, and I'm old enough to make my own decisions. It's not like he can take me away from Dave and Seren anymore." My laugh's bitter. "Even now, I can't quite bring myself to call them Mom and Dad without correcting myself, at least, not unless I'm talking to Emerson."

"He always called them that so easily." Jake sighs. "But I think your grandpa might have been right about Easton."

"Why don't you like him?" My brow furrows. "I thought you were kidding at first, but you really do seem to hate him."

"It's not that I hate him." Jake looks back down at the piano keys. "It's just that. . ." He drops his voice until I can barely hear it. "I hate that *you* like him."

"Why?"

He turns slowly, his eyes blazing. "Because I'm in love with you, you idiot."

I laugh. I can't help it. It's ridiculous. "Jake." I swat at his shoulder.

But he catches my hand. "And that, that reaction's why I've never told you."

I yank my hand away and slide to the edge of the bench. "Stop it."

He shakes his head. "I've always loved you, Hornet. You'd know it, if you just—"

I stand up. "Jacob Kingsley."

His frown is intense. "No one has called me that in more than ten years."

It's his real name. Not many people even know it anymore. "I know you, and I've known you so long that I know the you most people have never even met." I put my hands on my hips. "I know you better than you know yourself." I really do think that's true. Insightful isn't a label many people would slap on Jake Priest.

"And that's why I love—"

I shove my finger against his mouth and he freezes, his eyes focusing on my finger until I yank it away. "Stop. I mean it."

"Beatrice." He won't stop looking at me like that. It's unnerving.

"I'm toxic," I finally say. "My family. My baggage." I

shake my head. "You and I were never a good idea. Not for even one minute. Not then, and not now."

"Even when we met, you knew what I was," he says. "You always knew."

"And that's why we're a bad fit. It's why you've never asked me out before now, not even once. Not in all the years you've been a part of my life."

"I was scared about losing you," he says. "But I would do anything, fix anything, change anything to be with you."

I sigh slowly. "Ah, Jake." I wave him over and sit back on the piano bench. Then I drop my head against his shoulder. "You're scared. That's the first true thing you've said."

"What?"

"Now that I like someone, and I mean, *really* like someone, you're scared. Just like the little boy I met so many years ago."

"What are you even saying?"

I'm staring at the music I wrote today, the music I've been too afraid to write for, well, for my whole life. "Jake, you have exactly one person you really trust."

"You." He nods. "You get it."

"I do, and in all that time, if you really were in love with me, brash, brave, over-confident Jake, do you really think you'd never have asked me out? Kissed me?" I turn to face him.

He looks confused.

"Jake Priest doesn't dither. He's not crippled by indecision." I press my index finger against his nose. "But now you're worried that you're about to lose me."

His voice is broken when he whispers, "I can't lose you, Bea." It cracks when he says, "I can't."

"I know." I wrap one arm as far around his shoulders

as it will go. "And you never will. Not ever. Do you hear me?"

"But we're not really family."

I hate how small his voice is, and I hate that he doesn't already know this in his bones. "No one on earth could be more my brother than you are." Tears pool in my eyes. "Not even if I found out I had a secret twin whom Mom sold to the circus. You'd still be more my brother than he was. Nothing will ever change that. No matter what you do, no matter what you say, no matter who I date or kiss or marry, you will always be my brother."

"But Emerson left." Now he's crying. Jake Priest, whom I have never once seen cry when a camera wasn't rolling, is sobbing next to me. "He just left, and now we never see him anymore."

"Oh, Jake." I wrap both arms around him, and he cries against my shoulder. "He's not gone. You just haven't gone to see him, and you haven't invited him here."

"He's a Richmond now."

"He is, *and* he's still a Fansee, just like you and me, in our hearts. In our souls."

We stay like that for an awkwardly long time, but eventually Jake gets it together, and he straightens. "It would be great if—"

"I don't need to tell anyone," I say. "The fact that you bawled on my shoulder will go with me to my grave."

"The Ashton Kutcher thing is more likely," he says.

Now I'm really laughing. "You're such an idiot."

"And you must really like that Easter guy."

"I hate when you do that."

"What?"

"Using a name you know is wrong."

"You love it, Hornet. You can admit it."

He is *so* annoying. "I feel really sorry for whatever girl you really do fall in love with. She is in for a truck-load of misery."

"You know it," he says, smiling. "I'm not sure if she's really out there."

"I think she must be," I say. "I mean, God made you, so he'd have to make a woman who's such a doozy that she can handle you, right?"

Jake whistles. "How *hot* must she be?"

"You're the worst."

"I'll stop calling him Easter," Jake says.

"Wait," I say. "Why would you do that?"

He nods. "I mean, you do really like him, so if he's endgame, I should make it easier on you to keep me around."

Endgame.

It's a weird word to use, but I'm worried at how much I like the sound of it.

16

EASTON

The board wants to change our meeting plans, and I understand why, but I'm not about to give on that. Then it'll be one thing after another.

I decide to call my parents' bluff.

And the board's.

They all show up at the Red Horse. That's a step on the right path. I'm a little shocked and a little relieved that Bea's there as well. It would be harder to convince the board that she's the woman I know she is if she chickened out on facing them.

But Bea is here, eyes bright, head high.

After everyone has found a seat, I stand. "You all made it. I'm delighted." I force a smile, but I hope it doesn't show. "Today, I've taken the liberty of ordering the exact same meal for every one of you. It's the Japanese A5 Wagyu filet mignon. It's been wet aged, and it's the single most expensive steak you can order. It's not even on the menu, generally speaking, but I wanted to make sure my board got *the very best*."

It starts right away, of course. "But I don't eat red

meat," someone says. Someone else sounds pretty grumpy when he says, "I only like my steak paired with red wine, and we're not doing wine because it's a working lunch." The complaints grow from there.

I hold up my hand. "Don't worry. I've also ordered two sides for the table, the Hipster fries which are covered in bacon, parmesan cheese, and these amazing shishito peppers, and the Brussels sprouts, which the chef assured me is a healthy option. And each of you will have the same appetizer as well—the tuna and salmon tartare." As the complaints grow, my smile becomes less forced. "It's fine," I say, raising my voice so that they can hear me. "Those are the most expensive things on the menu. You're sure to like them."

"But I *don't* like Brussels sprouts," Mr. Dressel says. "Not when I was a kid, not with bacon, not ever."

I slam my hands down on the table. "You know, this is exactly what you wanted to do for my women's line."

Everyone falls silent.

"For *my* company, which I built from the ground up practically alone, you wanted to slap a women's line on from the moment you joined the team. And you hounded me to just come up with something, anything, as long as it was *top of the line*. My name, Sacrifice Nothing, would sell whatever it was, you insisted."

Out of the corner of my eye, I notice that the dozen plates of tuna and salmon tartare have arrived. I nod at Bea, and she starts setting them in front of people.

"You may be seeing now that for wealthy people, for a luxury brand, having something be top of the line isn't enough. The kind of people who pay top dollar want something that's just right *for them*. So when I pitched a better idea, the *best* idea, that we should meet with a curated list of designers and as part of our label, offer a service in which we find them the very best items *for them*, and offer it only for someone related to our existing customers, you leapt at the idea." I make eye contact with each one of them, slowly. "But I was inspired to do that right here, by this woman." I point at Bea.

She freezes.

"You wanted everyone to be offered only salmon tartare, which would have been a terrible idea. A lot of this fine food is going to go to waste today, unnecessarily. Bea gave me a better idea, and now you want me to dump her because she's *honest*."

"That's not why," Mr. Dressel says, poking at his salmon tartare with a sour face. "It's because, while at a party with you, she slandered your company and its customers."

"Slander is saying something false." I arch one eyebrow. "She gave her opinion, which stung because it was mostly true."

"You should be as upset as we are," Mr. Jimenez says. "She said people who buy from your brand have holes in their soul. You'll look pretty stupid if you keep dating her."

"I think I'd look pretty stupid for dumping someone I really like just because she disagreed with me." I frown. "If one of you made an error, should I just eliminate you immediately?"

"You can't fire us," Mrs. Yaltzinger says. "We're the board."

I roll my eyes. "What if an employee makes a mistake? Is that your only solution? Elimination?"

"But she isn't an employee, and you didn't even know her three weeks ago," Mr. Dressel says.

I wish I could fire him. He'd already be gone. "I'm

going to recommend we table further discussion of this until you've told me how our plans are going for the women's line."

That gets them moving, at least. My design team came up with a list of labels we should talk to about joining our new initiative. I've talked to a few on the phone—broad strokes—but it takes the better part of an hour to work out which ones we think we should work with and why.

"You'll be pretty busy meeting with all of them," Mrs. Yaltzinger says. "I doubt you'll even have time to date."

"You'd be surprised how good I am at multitasking." I glare at her.

By the end of the meal, they still seem pretty upset, but it's only been two days. "I think we should all do our work this week," I say. "We can revisit this issue next week."

"You're hoping it'll blow over and then it won't be an issue," Mr. Dressel says.

"It would be nice."

"I guess," Mr. Jimenez says. "We can see whether it blows over, but if this worsens, or worse, lingers." He shakes his head.

"I agree," Mrs. Yaltzinger says. "We can postpone this conversation for a week if you insist. But the conversation must be had unless this miraculously disappears."

I'm sure it will disappear. It's not as if anyone has any reason to focus on a tiny little blip like this. This time, when I pay, Bea's nowhere to be found. Surely she heard enough of our conversation to be convinced that I don't mean to give up.

"Looking for someone?" The manager raises one eyebrow. "Someone small with dark hair, maybe?"

"Where did she go?"

"I did tell her she can wait on this table and be done for the day each Tuesday," he says. "But last time. . ."

"Last time?"

"Doesn't matter," he says. "I'm sure she'll pop up."

Only, I don't see her on my way out, either. I'm just fishing my phone out to call her in the parking lot when I see her, peering at a grey SUV. "Bea?"

She jumps like she's been caught picking her nose at a fancy dinner. "Easton?"

"What are you doing?"

"I didn't want to meet any of them out here, so I thought I'd wait by your car," she says. "Only. . .is this it? I thought it was lighter than this."

I laugh. "That's an Acura. I have a Volvo."

She blinks. "But I don't see—"

"I didn't drive the XC90 today." I can't help my smile. "There may still be a few things about me for you to learn."

"Then. . .which one is yours?" She looks around. "I didn't see a 4Runner either."

"If you guess correctly, I'll take you to dinner anywhere you want." I gesture around. "Which do you think?"

She spins slowly, narrowing her eyes, and that's when I realize I have her. If she was going to insist on dumping me for the good of my company, she would have left already. She wouldn't be searching for my car.

I toss her my keys.

They nearly hit her in the face, but at the last minute she pops her hand up and catches them. "Easton!" In that moment, for the first and hopefully last time, she actually reminds me of my mother. Then she glances at the keys. "A *Porsche*?" She laughs. "That's more like it."

"More like it?"

"I was surprised you had such weird-old-married-man-in-the-suburbs kind of cars," she admits. "I figured you'd be more like Jake."

"His car's ghastly," I say. "Mine's a very nice black."

"A black Porsche." Now she's searching in earnest, and it only takes her half a dozen seconds before she points triumphantly and pumps her fist. "And I want dinner at *Per Se*."

"Where?"

"It's the place your horrible date was bragging about having been." She folds her arms. "A place that I've never been."

"Great," I say. "If I can get a reservation, we'll go."

Her shoulders sag. "It's always booked out."

"Lemme call Ace real quick," I say. "He's better with stuff like this, and he owes me."

"More like he owes me," she mutters, which is cute. She did land in hot water thanks to the favor he asked me to do.

Two minutes later, we have a reservation. "We're on. Hop in." I wave at the car, which currently only she can unlock.

"But what about my car?" She asks. "And I can't go in this." She looks down at her white button down and black pants. "And it's barely two in the afternoon. No proper date starts at three. Surely you have work to do?"

"Fine. I'll tell Ace to set it for seven. Is that a more proper start time for you?"

"Come pick me up at the house at six, then?" She looks up at me with the biggest, most beautiful eyes.

"Done," I say. "But don't back out."

"I wouldn't dare," she says. Just as my heart is doing a little flippy flop, she adds, "Because their goats' milk cheese is legendary."

"Way to make a guy feel special."

She goes up on her tiptoes and brushes a kiss against my cheek. "You were pretty close to legendary earlier, too."

Then she spins on her heel and marches off, like she wasn't just as spectacular herself.

When I get back to the office, my assistant practically clubs me over the head with a list of brands and various dates for meetings. After I dig my way through that, I head home straight away.

On our first date, the first time I ever picked Bea up to take her out, I knew just what to wear. I had, in fact, chosen the place. But tonight, I flounder a bit. Without a theme—western wear—or a stylist to tell me what to wear, I'm a little unsure. I do look up *Per Se* to verify that it's a three Michelin star restaurant in Manhattan, and that means I should probably dress up, but I change my pants and shoes so many times that I realize I'm in danger of being late myself to pick her up.

Which is why I speed.

And that's how I get a ticket.

The night may not be off to the best start, but when I knock on Bea's door, and she answers, I forget all about every other thing that led up to this moment. Beatrice Cipriani, in a floor length gown, is absolutely show-stopping.

"You—"

She wipes her mouth. "Is my lipstick smudged?" Her eyes widen. "Or did I get something on the dress?" She looks down.

I shake my head dumbly. "No, nothing like that. But you look. . ."

She winces. "Is it dumb? I bought it on clearance three years ago, and I've never had anywhere to wear it." She tugs on the bodice, trying to pull it up, I think, which is a *huge* mistake. "I almost wore it to Emerson's wedding, but then your sister asked me to be a bridesmaid. I was actually a little relieved, because it's a little too daring in the front."

I snag her wrist and lower her hand, interlacing our fingers. "It's perfect. Even the Devil who wears Prada wouldn't be able to find fault with this."

She rolls her eyes. "That was kind of the point of that movie, you know—she found fault with absolutely everything."

I shrug. "I didn't really see the movie. My sister was nattering on about. . ." I pause. "You know what? Doesn't matter. The point is that you couldn't look more beautiful, but thanks to some stuff at work, we're cutting it close. We should go."

"What's the stuff with work?" she asks.

Sometimes people ask about work—my parents, usually—and it's obvious they don't really want to know. But the way she asked, it feels like she actually cares. "Well, we're launching a new. . .service? We're branching out into women's style."

"That's huge," she says.

I open her door, and she pauses to raise one eyebrow. "I know it's a corny thing to do these days, but with you in that dress. . ." I shake my head. "You look like you're headed for a red carpet event. What was I supposed to do?"

"It's nice," she says softly.

She has this way of being small, of being so quiet,

that if she wasn't so stunning, she'd almost disappear. I love it, how demure and understated she can be—and I hate it. Because I'm not sure where it came from, her desire to shrink, to make herself smaller. She was clearly born to shine, not to hide. I mean to draw her out. I mean for the world to see what a rockstar she really is.

Once I'm seated and buckled and ready to go, I continue. "I have to make the calls to set up the meetings with the other brands myself." I explain the idea to her.

"Wow," she says. "That's. . .ambitious."

"I mean, it is and it isn't," I say.

"But won't all the other brands be able to steal your idea if you call and tell them about it?"

"Every other brand we're contacting already has a women's line," I say. "So they wouldn't be able to do this, because they'd be in direct competition with all the vendors they'd reach out to about it."

"What if they specialize in shoes?" I ask. "They could still reach out to other perfume, jewelry, or clothing vendors."

I shrug. "We currently provide nearly everything in the luxury world. . .for men. None of the other brands have the depth we have without having a corollary for women."

"So you knew you had a weakness, of sorts."

"I always focus on my strengths," I say, "and until recently, my sister and mother were my only connection to or insight into women."

"I don't hate hearing that." She's doing it again, being small, but I can't help it. I kind of like it, too. It kicks my protective instincts into overdrive.

"There really wasn't anyone before you, Bea."

She's smiling as we make our way into the City.

Once we reach the restaurant, though, she shuts down a little bit. "Are you alright?" I ask as they seat us.

She nods.

"Something's bothering you."

There's no menu—not at places like this. They have a dozen or so courses and everyone gets them. It's a special kind of arrogance to assume that your food is so good that everyone will like all of it, but that's part of the whole ambiance at the triple Michelin starred places.

"Come on," I press. "What's wrong?" She went from excitedly telling me about the song she's been working on to shutting up like a clam.

She waits for the waitress to disappear, and then she looks both ways like we're planning some kind of covert operation. "It's not that I'm upset—it just feels strange, sitting here as a customer."

She's stinking adorable. "Well, get used to it."

Her eyes narrow. "Why?"

"I plan to take you out every single chance I get, to places like this as often as you want."

She rolls her eyes.

"I mean it," I say. "And once your songs are famous, you'll be the one taking me."

"Famous?" She snorts. "I'd have been delighted with jingles."

"Your song launched Jake's career. True or false?"

She shakes her head. "Jake's face launched Jake's career. His physique. His timing and his expressions. That song. . ." She shrugs. "It was a step stool."

"But that's all you need, really," I say. "You need one break, and you have to be smart enough to take it when it comes." I brace my arms on the table and lean a little closer. "So tell me you're entering that contest with the song you've been working on."

She sits back. "I don't know."

"What's holding you back?"

"I looked it up—if I make it to the finals, I have to perform my own song. . .not just a jingle. An actual performance, and it's going to be live-streamed."

That's a hard one. I even get some of her reticence now. I haven't pressed to know more about her grandfather, but clearly there's some baggage there. I just can't tell how much of her concerns are because she has never been taught to believe in herself and how much is just because she doesn't enjoy things like this.

"I can do it," she says. "I mean, I can probably do it, but the problem is that the further I go, the more they'll want me to do it. And that's not even the only. . ."

The waitress brings our first course.

I'm happy, because Bea looks delighted. Even if it's barely more than a single bite of some kind of fruit tart, artfully shaped like a butterfly, she loves it.

So I love it.

But I also want to know what she was going to say.

"You said that's not the only reason. . . you were worried about the contest?" I feel like an interrogator, but I doubt she'd come back to it. I can't help her if I don't know what's standing in her way.

"Writing jingles may seem meaningless," she whispers, "but it's also safe."

Safe? "You mean. . .legally safe?"

She smiles.

And the waitress brings our second course—some kind of foamy green soup that tastes like summer. It's really pretty good for foam in a mushroom-shaped cup.

"The cup is edible," the waitress says with a smirk.

"Wonderful." I pop it into my mouth. "How many courses did you say there were?"

"Fourteen."

I'm going to kill her.

Bea's giggling. "You didn't look impressed. You looked irritated."

"She has terrible timing."

That sobers her. "Jingles promote a product, and all I have to do is come up with some catchy words and a solid melody. But with a real song, I'm sharing a message. Something personal. People can read into it, and they always do."

"Sure," I say. "That's true. We all like singing the songs musicians share, because they resonate with us. That's kind of the human experience."

"I don't want people to know how I feel," Bea says. "That feels. . .like a violation."

"Why?"

"You want everyone to know how you're feeling?" Her eyebrows rise.

"I mean, they usually do." I can't help smiling. "You knew how I felt when I showed up at the Opus Westchester, right? So did my miserable date, Shelly."

"Was that Miss Collagen USA's name?" she asks.

"Like I remember."

She's giving me her irritated smile. "I grew up trying to make sure no one ever found out how I felt."

"Why?"

"Are you a therapist?" She scowls. "It was just easier that way."

"Were you angry a lot?"

When the waitress shows up, I contemplate telling her to lay off for twenty minutes, but Bea's relief holds me off. I should stop pressing—she'll open up when she's ready. I hope. So for the rest of the meal, I don't ask any questions. I don't push about the song. I just make jokes. We chat about the food.

And then, just as dessert is coming out, she says, "Now the real test."

"The real test?"

"My mom's a great cook," she says.

"Your mom?"

She smacks her forehead. "Seren." She sighs. "I could call her Mom now, I guess. There's no one who can do anything about it, but Grandfather had a rule. I could only stay with Dave and Seren as long as I never called them that. He was worried that people might find out his granddaughter was in a foster home."

"And what does that have to do with this?" I point at the profiteroles. "They look pretty decent to me, although they aren't exactly large."

She pats her stomach and groans. "Thank goodness."

The portions were small, but there were a lot of courses of them. "But?"

"Seren's a pastry chef," she says. "Her desserts are to die for, and after years and years of listening to her tell me how various places fall short, I'll be curious how these rate."

"And what should the perfect cream puff be like?"

"Well, it should be crisp on the outside—a little chewy, and filled with a light, brilliant burst of flavor."

I pluck one from the center of the plate.

"You're using your hands?" Tiny lines appear between her eyebrows.

"They're the size of a grape. If I speared it with a fork, I'd be afraid it would roll off the plate and go flying across the floor."

"Like a meatball?"

"*On top of spaghetti*," I say with a smile. "Did your mom sing that song?"

"Seren did." She pops a profiterole into her mouth as well.

And then I wait for the verdict.

"Well?" she asks.

"I liked it." I shrug. "But I'm not the critic here."

She grabs another one.

"I'll take the consumption of more as high praise."

"I mean, shouldn't it be good, though?" She pops the second one in her mouth. "I don't even want to think about what these cost per bite."

"I think I need to come try something made by this famous Seren, if this place can barely compare."

"Maybe you should," she says. "She's actually instituting this new thing, Sunday dinners. If you can behave, I might take you along some time."

I hold up both my hands. "I'll be on my best behavior, I swear."

Once I've paid the check and we've walked out to the car, I ask, "So? What was it like being on the other side for a night?"

She rolls her eyes. "The Red Horse doesn't even have one Michelin star."

I walk toward her, and she backs up against my car. "Having been a customer of both," I say, "I think the Red Horse is definitely better."

"You do?" She looks up at me, her chin lifting a hair more. "Really?"

I drop one hand to her left, my palm flattening against the top of my car. "The food's more to my liking," I whisper. Then I drop my other hand on the right side of her. "But the service at the Red Horse?" I shake my head slowly. "Not even comparable."

"Really."

I nod slowly. "In fact, there's this one waitress I just cannot get enough of. I actually forced my entire board to relocate our weekly meetings to her restaurant just so I'd have an excuse to see her."

She arches one eyebrow. "You didn't."

I lean closer still, until our faces are less than two inches apart. "Don't tell her, but I'd eat cardboard if she brought it to me, and I'd pay top dollar for the privilege."

She presses one hand against my chest. "Easton."

"Again," I whisper.

"What?" Her eyes widen.

"Say it again."

The slow smile that curls the corners of her mouth upward is delicious. "Easton."

I drop my lips against hers, and thankfully, they're a far cry from cardboard. They may be the softest thing I've ever felt. I can still taste a hint of cream puff, and I can't help sucking her bottom lip into my mouth just a little.

She moans.

I pull her against me, flipping around to lean against the car myself, but it's short. Way too short. I'm basically sitting on it, which is distracting. Why don't I have a taller car? I'm buying nothing but SUVs, starting tomorrow.

Even the failures of my sportscar can't distract me from Bea's mouth—her little soft sigh, her hand, fisting around my shirt. "You—yes," I hiss.

"You're better than that meal," Bea says.

That makes me smile.

Kissing someone while smiling is strange and beautiful. I could do it all day. "Thank you," I say.

She pulls back.

"No, don't do that."

Her hand flattens, this time, keeping me away. "What did you just thank me for?" Her lips are compressed, but they're twitching. With excitement? Merriment? Curiosity?

I sigh. "For not getting a restraining order when I kept showing up? For being the most beautiful woman I've ever met? For bringing light and joy into my life?"

She cocks her head sideways. "Easton."

"Now you're just spoiling me."

"We should go home."

"Yes." I nod. "My place or yours?"

She slaps my arm, and I love that she knew me well enough to know it was a joke. At least, it was *mostly* a joke.

I've barely pulled out of the parking lot when my phone rings—and it's an old friend. "I need to take this," I warn her.

She nods, her expression earnest. "Oh, go ahead."

I tap the green button to pick up Laurent's call. "Hello?"

"You picked up!" His French accent always seems more pronounced when we haven't spoken in a while.

"Isn't it the middle of the night in Paris?" I ask.

"I'm in Shanghai," Laurent says.

"What are you doing there?"

"I have another meeting soon—no time to get into all that." Laurent clears his throat. "But Dad called me about your new proposal. He forwarded the whole thing to me."

"That's not promising," I say. "To be totally honest, we need Barbier, or I'm not sure it will work."

"We're like your opposite—all the best women's

luxury goods, and all with a twist." Laurent's laugh comes out more like a bark. "Dad said the same."

"Look, just tell me what I need to do—"

"Dad loved the idea, but I should warn you. He loved you enough that he wants to buy your company."

"*Buy us?*" Now I'm the one laughing. "You couldn't afford to."

"Dad and I can't, but Grandfather could," Laurent says, "and think about what a good fit it would be."

"That's not why I sent you the proposal," I say.

"Fine." He huffs. "Fine. Dad said you'd say no, but we at least wanted to ask. It would be a far-cry simpler than the service you're setting up."

"Simpler was never my forte," I say.

"I suppose not," Laurent says. "Not during school, and not now. But look, Dad has a few demands you're not going to like."

"Email them to me," I say. "We'll see what we can do."

"What other brands are on board?" Laurent asks.

"You know I can't tell you that. Not without a much more firm commitment."

"Let me get with legal and we'll send you something."

We're nearly to Bea's place. "I'm so sorry I wasted our whole drive home," I say.

"Wasted?" Bea's frowning. "It sounded like an encouraging call."

"It was," I say. "We need Barbier—the board's flipping out about it."

"Well, it sounds like you have a good shot of bringing them in."

I park. "As encouraging as that was, it was a long way from the best part of my day." I lean toward her and brush another kiss against her perfectly shaped mouth.

She's smiling when she hops out of the car and jogs to her apartment door. All in all, even if my date ran away at the end, I think things went pretty well.

My phone bings, and I whip it out. It's from Bea, which makes me grin.

I TALKED TO LEGAL. HERE ARE MY DEMANDS—IF YOU WANT TO COME FOR SUNDAY DINNER.

She's such a frigging delight. I DO, I text back immediately.

1. NO MORE DROP-INS WHILE I'M AT WORK

DONE, I text back.

2. YOU WILL DRIVE THE XC90 OR 4RUNNER

I smile. I THOUGHT YOU DIDN'T LIKE IT

DAVE AND SEREN ALWAYS MOCK JAKE FOR HIS CAR

DONE, THEN, I text.

WAIT, HOW MANY CARS DO YOU HAVE?

I PLEAD THE FIFTH.

THE FIFTH ONLY APPLIES IN A COURT OF LAW.

I DON'T THINK THAT'S TRUE. Or at least, whether it is or not, the last thing I need to do is confess that I have five. Three are parked at my parents' house anyway, so there's no need for her to know.

FINE. She sends an eye-roll emoji, and I can imagine her doing it in person. 3. YOU WILL NOT SAY A WORD ABOUT SEREN'S FAMOUS GRANDMOTHER

BUT I ALREADY KNOW ALL ABOUT HER— ELIZABETH TOLD US

OH, FINE. I'M FLEXIBLE ON NUMBER THREE

I THINK WE HAVE AN AGREEMENT, I text.

BUT I NEED TO SEE YOU BEFORE SUNDAY. I CAN'T WAIT THAT LONG. HOW ABOUT TOMORROW?

I'M WORKING

WHAT ABOUT BEFORE WORK?

I'M GOING FOR A RUN TO WORK OFF THE 9,000 CALORIES I JUST ATE

I'LL COME

I never run. I'm going to die, but if it has to happen someday, it may as well be with Bea.

17

BEA

I'm flying high from my recent date and the flurry of cute texts we just shared.

That's the only explanation.

Regular Bea would never have sat down to write a song, gotten upset about how Octavia had been so cavalier about making me lose the contest, and then sent an email to her, demanding she meet me for lunch. By the time I brush my teeth, put on my pajamas, and hop into bed, she's already replied. My hands are trembling when I click on her reply.

Great. Name the place. My treat. Noon.
-Octavia.

Between the twinges of a new song taking form inside my head, and my nerves about tomorrow's jog and lunch, I can't sleep. I toss. I turn. And finally, I wake up and drag myself into the family room. With a pencil in my mouth, I start working through what I've got.

No words.

Not a single one.

I have no idea what it's about yet, but the song—it's bright. Sharp. Clear. It's equal parts anger and joy. It's beautiful and furious. It's a tumult, like how I feel inside. It's a combination of my rage at my family and my joy in meeting Dave and Seren and Jake and Emerson. It's the relief that I'm loved and the fury that I was abandoned.

I've never written a song that's bright and dark in equal measure.

Actually, I'm not sure I've ever heard one close enough to compare this to. I scrawl one word across the top of the music once the gist of it is out—BIPOLAR. I finally collapse into bed and pass out.

That's probably why I struggle so much to wake up—that, and the fact that I usually roll out of bed around noon. Of course, as I down a glass of orange juice, which is about all I can tolerate before I go for a jog, the stupid song comes back. This is how it works for me. Until I can get the song finished, it'll yell at me in waves.

I'm pulled out of the fiddling of my brain when Jake comes banging out of his room, bleary-eyed and cranky. "That's my toothbrush."

I pull it out of my mouth slowly and stare. "It's not."

"It is." He holds out his hand, glaring.

"Jake, I bought this a week ago, and I have several more just like it right here." I open the top drawer and show him the package.

He swears under his breath. "Well, sorry."

"Sorry?" I arch one eyebrow.

"I've definitely been using it."

I spit and rinse my mouth. "Really?" I huff.

"I said sorry." He shrugs. "But, like, didn't you say you had a few more?"

I toss the toothbrush at him and shoot out the door.

"Where are you going in such a hurry?"

"Easton's coming over to go for a run with me."

"Of course he is. Is he bringing his golden retriever?"

I ignore the jab. He may be jealous, but Easton *is* the perfect guy. A golden dog would fit. "Do you want me to make you some coffee before I go?"

I hear him rinse his mouth. "Why would you do that?" His face, when he emerges from the bathroom, is suspicious.

"So I can spit in it." I lean over to tie my shoes.

Jake disappears.

"Hey, where'd you go?"

"If you think I'm going to let him steal my only running buddy, you've lost your mind."

"You don't even like to run," I say. "You only do it to bother me."

"You hate it as much as I do. That's why we run so well together."

"Mutual hatred?" I'm shaking my head, but it feels a little like sibling bonding. "I suppose that's better than nothing."

"What is?" Jake's slipping his feet into sneakers.

"Those shoes can't be helpful if you don't even have to tie them."

Jake stands up. "I have such perfect feet, it doesn't matter what I wear."

"You're insufferable."

"What's better than nothing? You never answered me. Is this a new thing, because I don't like it."

"Our trauma bond," I say. "That's what is better than nothing."

"It's not really trauma," Jake says. "Running is. . .miserable, but not traumatic."

"Misery bonding just sounds dumb." I reach for my air pods, but then I stop. "I can't even listen to music, can I?"

"Not when you're going to be watching two alpha males vying for your attention."

"Alpha males?" That makes me laugh. "Just stay home."

"Why?" Jake puffs out his chest. "Worried Easton will act dumb and I'll have to beat him down, ruining any admiration you had for him?"

"Hardly," I say. "I'm worried my alpha male will make you feel even more insecure, and you'll posture the entire run. That would be terribly sad and tiring for all of us."

Jake's frowning when there's a knock at the door.

"Right on time, as usual," I say. "Now tie your shoes tighter, or we'll leave you here."

The second he bends over and unties them, I jog to the door and run right through it. "You ready?"

Easton's mouth is dangling open, but his shoes are on, and he's wearing a water bottle on a belt.

"Great." I start jogging and he catches up quickly.

"What are we doing?" Easton's glancing behind me at the door I just slammed shut.

"We're trying to ditch Jake." I can't help my smile.

"Are we really?" He speeds up a bit.

"It's my favorite morning pastime."

"I can't tell if this is a joke or not." Easton keeps glancing behind us.

"I mean, it is for sure, but also, I really do ditch him

every time I can. I told him to tie his shoes and then took off."

Easton's able to keep up admirably well, though it should be pretty easy. With as short as I am, most guys could sort of saunter at my jogging pace.

"Why do you like ditching him?" Easton asks. "We could just go earlier next time, before he's even awake."

"He hears me getting ready," I say. "That's why it's funny. Jake's not even a runner. He just has such a horrible case of FOMO that he cannot help himself. When he's home, if I go running, he has to come along. It's like he's a tiny dog—not really interested in running, but he can't help but long to go."

"So ditching him?"

As if on cue, Jake comes huffing up behind us. "Really? You shouldn't do this with guests." He's wheezing.

"I thought movie stars were all in amazing shape," Easton says, speaking easily. "But you seem. . .remarkably unfit."

Predictably, Jake whips his shirt off, knotting it around a belt loop on his shorts. "Six pack and perfectly sculpted abdomen." He's wheezing like a smoker running the mile at school, but he looks like a Greek statue.

"You're a remarkable combination of bizarrely conflicting values, Jacob Priest," I say.

"Shut up, Hornet," he rasps. "Or I'll saran wrap the toilet again."

How he ever thought he was in love with me, I will never know. "Do it," I say. "You had to clean it up."

Easton's eyes are traveling back and forth between us like a tennis spectator. "You two are. . .a lot."

"Don't worry," I say. "He's leaving soon. He has a

movie—actually, will you be gone before Sunday? Because I'm taking Easton home with me. It would be nice to have a friendly face cheering for us."

"I mean, you'll have Elizabeth," Jake says. "But I'll be gone by the first family dinner."

"Will you really? When do you leave?" I ask.

"Next Wednesday," Jake says.

"I'm confused," Easton says. "The dinner's Sunday, right? And today's Wednesday."

"But this Sunday's Uncle Bentley and Aunt Barbara's wedding," Jake says.

"No way," I say. "They're doing a fall wedding theme —it's not until. . ." I freeze, swearing under my breath. "Wait." I stop running. "It's *this* Sunday? How self-centered am I?"

Jake jogs in a circle around me, grinning. "This is a fine moment for me. You're always so on the ball."

"I don't even have a gift yet," I say. "And I never took my dress to get it taken in."

"Your dress?" Easton asks.

"I'm a bridesmaid." I groan. "Shoot. How could I lose track of when the wedding is?"

"Too self-centered, I guess." Jake's smiling, probably because he's the most selfish person I know, and yet he remembered. What does that say about me?

The next mile or so, I come up with several ideas for gifts, but Jake shoots them all down.

"You could try their registry," Easton says. "Isn't that what people usually do?"

"Like Bentley would register," Jake says.

But I'm already poking around on my phone, desperately checking the usual places. "Nothing at Target."

"Multi-millionaires don't register at Target," Jake says.

I shove him. Hard.

He doesn't even stumble, the jerk.

"Aunt Barbara and Uncle Bentley have given us the best presents of anyone we know for our whole lives," I wail. "I have to give them something decent."

"I got them a *Greatest Showman* Broadway poster, signed by Hugh himself." Jake has never looked more smug. "Aunt Barbara loved that show."

"I really, really hate you."

"Love you, too." Jake's in front of me, keeping his distance thanks to my recent violence, and he spins around to blow me a kiss.

"What about a song?" Easton asks. "I know there's not much time, but I can't think of much that would be better than their own custom song."

"Oh my gosh," I wheeze. "Yes!" I'm not sure whether it's exhaustion, my anxiety over this wedding, or being generally out of shape, but I'm not sure I can go much farther. "We should turn around."

"Panicking much?" Jake jogs another annoying little circle around me, his gloating at maximum level. "Don't forget the dress modifications." He jogs back toward the apartment before I can even try to kick him.

Easton stayed with me. He's my new rock. "What's wrong with the dress?"

"In case you haven't noticed, I'm four feet tall. Every dress I buy off the rack has to be hemmed."

"Four feet?" Easton's smirking. "That might be a bit of an exaggeration."

"But not by much." I'm huffing and puffing, but at least we're headed home again. "I'm barely five feet tall, so the knee-length dress Aunt Barbara chose hits me a few inches above my ankle."

"Ouch," he says.

"If I had started sooner, I'd have had them take in the bodice too. It's always a little too long when they don't have a petite option."

"For my little China doll."

"Dude." I glare at him on principal. I've never met my dad, but he must have been from some Asian country, because my eyes are clearly not like those of my Italian mother.

"Not because—like, the Asian thing."

"Uh-huh."

"No, I meant *doll* for small, you know, petite. China doll is just a kind of doll."

I arch my eyebrow, but I let it go. I don't really care. It's just fun to mess with him.

"Speaking of alterations, if you don't mind coming by my office, we have a whole design team I'm sure I could put to work getting your dress fixed up."

"You have—what?"

"I mean, they mostly do men's clothing design, but they could definitely hem a dress. They could probably take up the bodice, too."

"You're suggesting that your *designers* could modify my bridesmaid dress?"

"I mean, if I were going to be the plus one for someone's wedding, it would only be right for my date to look her very best," Easton says. "It makes business sense." He is *so* stinking cute when he smiles.

"Alright," I say.

"Wait, does that mean I will be your plus one?" He looks nervous. "Because I had already blocked off Sunday for Bea."

"If you don't mind coming to a family wedding, then sure." It'll be really nice not to go alone for once.

"Maybe I can come by the office with the dress tomorrow morning," I say.

"What time do you have to be at work?" he presses. "If you came today, they'd have more time to get it done."

"I know, but I've already wasted most of my morning with you, and I'm meeting Octavia for lunch." I glance at my watch. "Really soon, actually."

"Octavia?" His brow furrows.

"Octavia? Why does that name sound familiar?" Jake has slowed down enough for us to catch up. "Wait, isn't that the snooty singer who voted your song down?"

"Someone voted it down?" Easton's frowning. "OH!" He nods. "With the burned face."

Jake glares at him.

"What?" Easton looks confused. "Is that who you mean?"

"That's who I mean." Like Jake, it bothers me that people would identify her that way, but I can't quite figure out why. I mean, it's probably her most distinguishing characteristic, but it's sad that it is. It makes her whole persona about something traumatic that happened. That's probably why it bothers me.

"Why are you going to lunch?" Jake asks.

"I have an idea I want to run past her," I say.

"About the song contest?" Easton asks.

"You and Octavia sent me information for the exact same contest," I say. "But I wonder whether either of you noticed that it requires us to perform the song, and that part of the prize is cash, but it's also a record deal."

"That's kind of awesome," Jake says. "So is she on the team that makes that decision too?" He snorts. "You should make sure she'll be on your side this time."

"She's not affiliated with this contest," I say. "She

works for the agency that put together the jingle thing for Jello."

Jake has always been doggedly fixed on anything he doesn't understand. "Then what are you going to ask her—"

"Jake, after our lunch, if my idea works out, I'll let you know. Okay?"

Easton and Jake exchange a glance, which is kind of cute and a little irritating. I'm not some high-strung diva who's hard to manage. "I have to shower quick. I'm low on time."

I take off as fast as my stubby legs will carry me.

"Wait, I could join you? It'll be time economical and save water." Easton's smiling, at least. "I'm all about saving the dolphins."

"Nice try, lover boy." Jake grunts. "But I really don't think you're there yet."

I should just be happy that Jake gave up on his idiotic insistence that I belonged to him. He's like a Golden Retriever dropping his slobbery ball, only I'm the ball. As it turns out, the dog's even more annoying after it lets go of the ball.

It takes me forever to blow dry my hair, and when I race out the door, I check the clock. I should have *just* enough time to get to Toss't and Press't. Thanks to lights, I'm a few minutes late, and when I get there, Octavia's already sitting in the corner with a jacket over the seat next to her. I can't help noticing that she's turned so that the non-burned side of her face is toward the window.

"Octavia," I say.

She turns, a half-smile on her face. "You made it."

I nod. "Parking's always a challenge, but thanks for meeting me here. I've been craving their oxtail tacos."

"I ordered a salmon taco already."

"Just one?" I arch one eyebrow. "I'll order you a second. You'll want it—trust me."

A moment later, I sit down next to her.

"I bet you're wondering why I asked to meet with you."

"You're angry," Octavia says. "And I think it's probably justified. I've wondered several times whether I did the right thing. I'm not someone who usually meddles in other people's lives."

"Why did you?" I ask. "Why me?"

"You—" She sighs. "You have a lot to offer, and you shouldn't get stuck doing jingles."

"Yes, you said."

"And I know that's not really my decision to make."

"You should have chosen the best song," I say. "For Jello and for me."

"I've thought about that a lot."

"Mhmm."

Her name's called, but since I'm in her way, I go grab it.

"You didn't have to do that." Her expression's pained.

"Do what?" I frown. "You'd have had to walk around me."

"Oh." She nods.

"Look, I asked to meet with you, because I think you owe me."

"I'm not sure what I could possibly—"

"I want a job at your agency, or at least, I want you to recommend my portfolio. Jingles are what I want to do."

"No way," she says. "That can't be true. No little kid's dream is writing jingles."

"Why not?" I arch my eyebrow. "Why can't that be my dream?"

"People want to write songs that touch others. Songs that stick with them. Songs that resonate."

"I can't perform my own songs," I say.

"You could." She takes a bite, and I wait. "Wow, this is really good."

"I don't *want* to perform my songs," I say. "It's not that I'm afraid or I have to get over it. It just sounds like torture to me. I can't think of anything that I would want to do less than sing my own songs. And besides, there are plenty of people who could do them better than I can."

"Plenty of people play piano better than you?" She sounds skeptical.

"Well, no, not that part, but the singing, yes. Including you."

"But your voice—"

"Is fine," I say. "I've been told. But you're not listening. I love writing songs. I don't like singing them. I don't want to perform them. I just don't. I'm not the gorgeous yet reserved girl who just needs to come out of her shell."

Octavia laughs, and even her laugh sounds like bells.

"Look," I say. "You were born to sing. I'm not sure whether you noticed, but the contest you sent me—the prize is a record deal. I don't even want that. I want someone else to sing my songs." I lean closer, but before I can say anything else, my stupid tacos come. "That one is for her." I point.

"You could negotiate all that with the label," Octavia says. "My agency could even represent you once you have a deal on the table."

"I'm negotiating now," I say. "With you."

"But I'm not the person at our agency who does this sort of thing."

"Not your agency," I say. "With *you*. I want *you* to sing my song."

"But the rules say—"

"Yes." I nod. "The rules say that the person or *persons* who are submitting the song will perform it. I will play the piano, and *you* will sing it."

Octavia freezes. "You don't know what you're asking."

"I sure do," I say. "In fact, I'm crystal clear on what I'm asking. You're the reason I lost the jingle contest, and you suggested this one as an alternative. I have not one, but three songs already in the works, and I'd like *you* to come over and work on them with me. Then I'd like the *two* of us to submit one of them. The best one. And with your voice? We'll make it to the finals. I'm sure of it."

She stares at me for a moment, and then another. Her hand is trembling where it's hovering above her taco. "You really don't understand. The second we walk on that stage, you'll lose, no matter what your song is."

"Why?" I want her to say it.

"Why?" Her eyes widen, but the one on her burned side widens slightly more. "Are you really asking?"

I nod.

"Because of my face. No one will ever risk having someone like me recording an album. Ever."

"You're beautiful."

"That makes exactly one person who thinks so." She folds her arms.

"Octavia."

She shakes her head. "No. Look, I don't know if you're trying to punish me or whatever, but I will not do this. Never."

"You said I can get up and sing my songs," I say. "I

have zero desire to do it, but I heard you that day. You love performing. Your voice—it's like an angel's. I know that's corny, but I have no idea how else to describe it. I could listen to you for—"

She crumples the end of her second taco into a ball and shoves the basket into the corner. "You could *listen* to me all day. You could listen to me all year. But Beatrice, no one wants to *look* at me. Not you, not the record label, not even *me*. I avoid mirrors. I try to spare people whenever I can. If you partner with me, not a single person will vote for us. Do you understand me?"

"I think you're wrong," I say. In that moment, something happens that has never happened. Something that may never happen again. It's *miraculous*. That's the only way I can describe it. The song that was bugging me, the song that I was up half the night writing, the melody without a message. . .distills.

The words are just *there*.

"I have *the* song already," I say. "I wrote it for you—for us. And if you follow me back to my place, and if you listen to it, and if you still don't want to submit it with me, I'll never bother you about it again. You'll recommend your agency consider my jingle portfolio, and we'll never speak."

"Beatrice."

"No." I shake my head. "I'm only asking you to listen to my song—to *our* song. And if you have no faith in me then, fine. *Fine*. I'll walk away. But at least listen."

"Our recording studio has a practice room," she says. "It's two blocks from here."

I don't have my music with me—the sketch from last night. But the notes are clear in my brain. "Sure." I nod. "Let's go."

She says exactly nothing as she cleans up her area. I

scarf down the end of my second taco, and then I drop some cash in the tip jar on my way out. I have another thirty-four minutes on my parking meter, so I should hopefully be fine. I follow her around the corner and down the street—two and a half blocks away, just as she said. I walk behind her into the studio.

She checks in with some woman at the front, who looks surprised to see us, but then we're waved through. And suddenly, I'm sitting in front of an unfamiliar piano. I sit, close my eyes, and inhale and exhale a few times. Then my fingers start to move.

The song starts out soft, lovely, wistful. The opening bars are harmonious and almost ethereal.

The world is full of beauty.
The world is full of peace.
The world is full of light and joy,
that almost never cease.
You made me lots of promises.
You made them all come true.
I can hardly imagine living in,
a world devoid of you.

B ut then it segues. The run becomes progressively more discordant until the chorus hits full force, and it's harsh. It's angry. It's full of rage and fury.

But the world is dark and terrifying.
    The promises were a lie.
The same ones who talked of beauty,
Were the first to decry.
The face that once was gorgeous
You say now is horrifying
The world has made it ugly,
A gorgeous monstrosity.

***

The transition to beauty again is seamless, like my fingers know what my heart wants to say as long as I stay out of their way.

***

You told me I was gorgeous.
    You told me I was beloved.
You said you would be faithful.
No matter what the world did.
All the joy inside of me,
All the hope for a brighter day,
The monster consumed it all,
I became beast and also prey.

***

The chorus stays the same—angry, all my rage and fury transformed into discordant notes and staccato rhythms, but then there's one last transition. The entire thing moves up a step, and the melodies from the two parts—angry and ethereal—combine.

The world is dark and terrifying.
*   That much, at least, was true.*
But those who spoke of beauty,
Were the villains, not me and you.
It's not the face at fault here
It's those glaring and jeering
The real beast is inside them,
They get back what they give.

So stop looking for monsters,
*   And start cleaning out yourself.*
The gorgeous monstrosity to fear
Is the one staring back in the mirror.

The only part of the song that fails me is what to do at the very end. As my notes trail off, I turn around. Most people look terrible when they cry. In fact, I'm not sure I've ever seen someone look beautiful when they're crying. Your face gets blotchy. Your eyes scrunch up, and your nose too, usually, but Octavia's the exception. Her face is nearly smooth, her eyes simply full of unshed tears.

One rolls down her face on the right—her unburned side. Then another slides down her face on the left, slipping over the ridges and curves made by the fire. As I look at her, I *feel* the words of my song.

I wrote it for me.

But I also wrote it for her.

"My mother neglected me." I've never said the words out loud. "She left me anywhere and everywhere. She was too busy getting high to care much where I was or what I was doing."

Octavia swipes at her tears.

"I wrote that song for myself—I spent the first eleven years of my life feeling like a monster every single day. The lies people told upset me. My mom and my grandfather would tell me that she would change. They would tell me that tomorrow would be different. But the biggest lie they told was that they loved me, when every action betrayed them."

She's still crying, but the tears are coming faster.

"I know you probably thought the song was about you, and it is. You're the most gorgeous woman I've ever met, and you have the most amazing voice. But I bet some people are too stupid to see it."

Now she's sobbing.

"That's not because of you. I want to show the world and make them face their own ugliness. It's all theirs. Not yours."

Octavia pulls me against herself for a hug. "Fine." Her whisper's barely audible. "I'll do it. But you'll regret it."

"Not for a single day," I say. "If the world has any real beauty in it, we'll win. And if they don't, they're the ugly ones. Not us."

It might not have been the best day to come in late.

"You said it would blow over." Mrs. Yaltzinger's quickly becoming one of my least favorite people.

I don't slap her hand away as she shoves a newspaper in my face. I do, however, duck around her and keep walking toward my office. "Who even reads newspapers these days?"

"This is the *New York Times*," Mrs. Yaltzinger says, doggedly trailing my steps. "But the *Post* ran it too, and they're also several hundred thousand in circulation."

I roll my eyes. "It was a rhetorical question. I don't really care. My point was—"

But Mr. Dressel's waiting with Mr. Jimenez to attack together in my office. In my shock, I pull up short and nearly fall, dropping my briefcase, which is fine. I mostly carry it because it's one of ours and it looks fancy. It has a few folders in it and my snacks, but nothing important. "How nice to see all of you."

"I wish I could say the same," Mr. Dressel says. "But we said we'd give you time, and you said this whole thing would die down."

"It's not," Mr. Jimenez says. "Look." He shoves his phone in my face, which is at least more relevant.

I sigh slowly as I read what they're all so bent on showing me. Apparently there was a photo of Bea and me taken while we were in the lobby at *Per Se,* and it's a great one. "I wonder if they'd send me a high res image of that." The caption says, "*Sacrifice Nothing* owner dines with its biggest critic."

"Mister Moorland," Mr. Jimenez says. "Please be serious."

I scan the text, which is predictably a criticism of our brand that implies I must agree with Ms. Cipriani's assessment, as we're clearly still dating. Then it links to the video, which at least the *New York Times* can't do.

Although, I suppose the online version can.

"Look, the point is that it's still only been a few days. Clearly they were slow news days, but if you just give it a bit more time, I'm sure—"

"You said we were right on track with the women's select launch," Mrs. Yaltzinger says. "If that's the case, around the time this dies down, that should kick it back to life." She arches one imperious eyebrow.

"What do you want me to do?" I ask. "Stop dating the first woman I've liked because—"

"Because it's bad for business?" Mr. Dressel asks. "Because if that's what you're asking, then yes. That's exactly what we want you to do. If our stock price drops again, or if the news outlets keep sharing her video and ill-advised quote, we're going to move for a vote of no confidence. On Friday."

"Tomorrow," I say. "You're going to move for a vote of no confidence over the person who created this brand, the person who has shown consistent profits, even through this public transition, because I'm dating a perfectly wonderful woman? She's not a crackhead. She's not a miscreant. She said 'sacrifice is good,' which anyone with half a brain will know is true. Our brand may be called Sacrifice Nothing, but we don't *really* mean that. Everyone knows that to succeed, you make sacrifices."

"It is strange," Mr. Jimenez says. "It's almost like someone is fanning the flames, but who would do that?"

"I mean, why would they?" Mr. Dressel asks.

But when I finally shoo them out, having made no progress on calming them down, I can't help thinking about what he said. *Who would* fan the flames of the dinky little nothing story of Bea spouting off her thoughts on my company's name?

Who?

I mean, her grandfather comes to mind, since they didn't seem to love each other, and she does have his last name. Cipriani. I type it into the search box, and stories on Beatrice Cipriani, granddaughter of New York's governor, pop up at the top of every search.

All the media outlets are describing her as a woman of the people—down-to-earth and sensible, a real champion of integrity and frugality. They're all asking why on earth she would date me. Apparently, without knowing it, I've become a symbol of all that's wrong with America. Overpriced shoes for the wealthy. Overpriced wristwatches for people who are out of touch with reality. Jewelry for men who don't care about human rights.

Which is ridiculous.

All our diamonds are cruelty free.

All our clothing is sustainable.

We donate five percent of our proceeds from several of our lines to various charities. My stupid luxury brand company gives back. We do our part.

Not that anyone is posting anything about that.

The real question is. . .why? Because the more I look into it, the stranger I find it. Sure, they did an article on me a few months ago that made my face a little more recognizable. It happened right after the company went public and my total worth became easier for people to ballpark. But the coverage at the time was largely very positive. So why the smear campaign now?

I have two in-person meetings and four calls set up today to line up our Women's Select vendors, and then several interviews for possible Dream-Makers, which is what the board thinks we should call the team who will be choosing clothing, shoes, jewelry, and makeup for women who opt in. But in between a call and a meeting, I have an idea.

I've never been someone who sits around, waiting for things to happen to me. All the success I've found, I've created. I decide to gamble a bit, and I call the Governor's office.

"Governor Cipriani's office," a perky woman says.

"Hello, there. My name is Easton Moorland, the CEO of Sacrifice Nothing. I'm dating Governor Cipriani's granddaughter, and I thought he might spare a minute to talk to me."

"Oh," the woman says. "I've seen your photos online." She giggles.

Giggles.

I sigh. "Yes, well, is there any chance I could chat with the governor sometime today?"

"He's very busy, but I'll check with his assistant and let you know. Would you like to leave a number?"

I'm suddenly a smidge uneasy giving Miss Giggles my phone number, but I do it. Shortly after, I'm drowning in pitches again, but I'm halfway through an interview when my assistant pokes her head into the conference room. "Mr. Moorland?"

The guy we're interviewing freezes.

"The governor's on the phone for you?" She looks a little shocked.

"The governor?" The interviewee has wide eyes.

It does feel a little strange. The owner of every designer label could call here, sure, but the governor? It's surreal. "I'll be right there." I stand. "Do you mind waiting?"

The poor guy shakes his head slowly. "Take your time."

I brace myself as I pick up the phone. I did make the governor wait, and he didn't seem the most pleasant to begin with. "Hello? This is Easton Moorland."

"Mr. Moorland." His voice sounds just like it does on the news. Strong. Sure. A high-pitched voice, but a confident one. "You called me."

"Yes, yes I did. The thing is—"

"I'm actually glad you called. If you could possibly break up with my granddaughter in a public place, that would be very helpful."

"Break up?" I can't help spluttering. "I have no intention of breaking up with Bea. I adore her."

"Adore?" He harrumphs. "At least you didn't say love. Listen, with everything that's going on right now, I really can't have her dating the CEO of some kind of luxury brand. I've worked hard to make people see that I'm a family man, and that our family values hard work and sensible choices. My constituents know that I buy my shoes at H&M, same as them."

"H and—" I sigh. "Governor Cipriani, I understand that for a politician, your image is important, but surely that doesn't extend to telling your granddaughter who she can and cannot date. I'm an upstanding person, with no skeletons hiding in my closet. I—"

"Listen carefully," he says. "In about two hours, my candidacy for the open Senate seat in New York is going to be announced. People will speculate that taking this position will put me in line to run for President, and those people would be right. I've waited decades for my turn, and it's finally here. My useless daughter is finally clean, or at least, she has been for more than six months, and her lovely daughter is going to have to stand up next to me at every campaign event for the next few years. Right now, people love her. They like her honesty, her charm, and her willingness to say things like they are. If, however, she keeps dating the rich man who sells shoes for a thousand dollars, their admiration for her morals will quickly wane."

"But America was built on capitalist values," I say. "I think that most people admire a self-made man."

"You're a silver-spoon trust baby," Governor Cipriani says. "I'm sure you think that, but you're out of touch. I'm not sure how I could be any more clear. Dump her somewhere public, and do it before the weekend, or you will run into all sorts of issues at work. That's not a threat. It's a promise." He hangs up.

Why would he go from Governor to Senate if he wants to make a Presidential run? Federal experience? Some kind of favor for the party? I shake my head to clear my thoughts, because none of that matters. What does matter is. . .Bea might be upset, and she might even want to dump me. But my board definitely will, because there *is* someone fanning the flames of that dumb video.

Bea's grandfather.

That's a lot of pressure—on my company, but also on Bea. Pressure can make diamonds, sure, but it can also collapse buildings. A few years ago, I would've told you that owning my company would make me strong. It would keep me safe.

I thought it was the only way to keep my family safe —to protect what mattered.

But now, even with a public company, even with strong revenues, even with good ideas and ongoing progress, I'm being pushed around. My parents still don't have my back, even now that they have money that *I* gave them.

In that moment, I realize something.

I thought money would give me power. I thought my company would make me strong. I put all my effort and all my work into this, because I thought that I would finally be free of the ups and downs Mom and Dad were constantly dealing with. I thought I could work hard enough and make enough money to be invulnerable.

But in this moment, the only thing I'm really afraid of losing is Bea.

I don't go back to the interview. I tell my assistant to reschedule my next call as well. All of that can wait. None of it really matters. Not if it will make Bea want to dump me. Not if it'll put more pressure on her.

I think about her smile.

The way she teases me and her family.

Her soft vulnerability. Her shocking talent. Her brave demands.

I didn't tell her grandfather that I love her, but I realize that I do. I love Beatrice Cipriani, and that's why I call my friend.

I spent over a decade of my life working to get where I am, building up a company that turns a profit every quarter. Developing a business model that is sustainable. Creating a brand people will pay top dollar to buy, to wear, and to show off. I gave my parents a large part of it so that they, too, could rest easy.

They didn't have my back when I needed them.

Maybe they never have.

"Easton?" Laurent sounds groggy. "Is everything alright?"

"You're asleep at eleven p.m.? How the mighty have fallen."

"You're so dumb," Laurent says. "I'm in *Shanghai*, remember? It may be eleven in Paris, but it's five a.m. here."

"I thought you were back," I say. "Sorry. But listen, I know I said I would never sell, but. . ."

"Sell?" Laurent clears his throat. "Wait. Are you saying—you might sell your company after all?"

"It's complicated," I say.

"Is something wrong?" he asks. "Are your sales down?"

I snort. "Hardly. It's about a girl."

Laurent whistles. "It's about time, my man. It's about time."

"Do you think your dad really meant it? Would your grandpa really put up enough money to make it worth my while?"

"Dad meant it, and Grandfather's passing things off to him," he says. "In fact, when we talked about this last night, he asked me again if you might sell."

"It's his lucky day then," I say.

"He'll want a controlling interest. Can you provide that?"

"Yes," I lie. Because somehow, I'll force my parents to sell to him, too. "Send me a decent offer. Send it quick."

I can hear him yawning on the other end of the phone. "Gardez votre sang-froid, s'il vous plaît."

"I told you—it's about a girl. And after what I did for you and Min Min, I'd think—"

"I knew you'd bring that up."

"Only because you're telling me to hold my horses."

"Your French sucks. I'm impressed you even understood me."

I passed French thanks to Laurent's help, but barely. "Talk to your dad and call me back."

After work, I drive out to my parents' house. Mom has a friend over, and Dad's on the phone, but I wait. When they're finally free, I drag them into the kitchen.

"What's this about?" Mom asks.

"You didn't even tell us you were coming," Dad says.

"I have voluntarily loaned you money on fourteen occasions. Money you have never repaid me, in spite of there being a formal accounting and instrument documenting the debt in each instance." I drop a sheet of paper in front of them. "This lists the amounts and the dates."

"Easton." Dad's brow furrows.

"You have also stolen my money on at least seven more occasions that I can prove." I drop another paper on the table.

"Are you in trouble?" Mom asks. "What's going on?"

"And I voluntarily gifted you shares of my company before it went public. I had a valuation done at the time, so that the shares would be all yours when they appreciated in value."

"We know, son," Dad says. "Believe me, we appreciate all you've done."

"When I called Mom and told her I needed her to vote with me, she told me to break up with Bea."

Mom exhales loudly, throwing her hands up in the air. "Easton. Don't tell me all this is about that little foster kid."

"Emerson Duplessis is a foster kid."

"Emerson *Richmond*," Mom clarifies, "is the grandchild of a very powerful woman, and he's inheriting her entire fortune."

I think about telling them that Bea's grandfather is the governor. I think about telling them that it gives us yet another tie to Emerson. I think about mentioning that her brother is a very famous actor.

But I don't.

None of that matters. It's not why I love her.

I didn't want to have to do this, but for Bea, I'll do whatever it takes. Arguing with them about Bea's worth is just making me angry. "I gave you funds on all those dates." I point. "Because at each point, you were on the verge of being totally ruined. The first time, I gave you half my trust fund, the money left by Grandpa. This time—" I jam my finger down on the other paper. "You stole money from my college fund, also from Grandpa, and I had to drop out of school. I lied to cover for you."

"We know that," Dad says, "and you have no idea how much we appreciate—"

"Oh, on the contrary, I think I know exactly how much you *appreciate* me." I shake my head. "I think that I've enabled you, and that's on me. But if you don't agree to sell your shares, the shares *I gave you*, to a friend of mine when he makes a very fair proposal to buy my company, I'll take these lists with the dates and all the supporting evidence to the *New York Times*, and I'll tell them how I created my company in spite of having a silver-spoon-shaped millstone hanging around my neck. I'm sure the Richmonds will be very impressed."

Mom's mouth dangles open.

Dad's entire face turns bright red.

"I wonder how many business partners you'll find who want to work with you after that." I stand up. "The offer for purchase of the company will probably be a good one, but even if it's not, see that you approve it."

I don't stay to argue with them. I don't listen to their complaints and their frustration. I walk through the front door and get in my car, and then I drive away.

19

BEA

When I check my phone after my shift, my grandfather has called me eight times. The last time he bothered trying to reach me that much, my mom had coded and been dead for four and a half minutes. Mom's supposed to be clean, so this should be interesting.

A feeling of dread claws its way into my stomach as I call him back.

"Hello?" He doesn't sound upset, so hopefully Mom's fine.

"I was at work," I say. "I can't chat while I'm at work, and I work Tuesday through Saturday every week, like I have for the last five years."

"I've emailed you some talking points," he says.

"Excuse me?"

"Surely you heard the news," he says.

"About?"

"I'm running for the empty Senate seat."

"Okay." I'm not sure how the Senate is really very different than being governor. "Is that a demotion? Did you do something wrong?"

"Beatrice Emmeline Cipriani, please tell me you're kidding."

"I'm guessing that's not covered in the talking points."

"The kind of publicity this will generate—a governor stepping down from a well-run state to step *into* the fray and protect citizens where they need it most—will help me."

"Help you with what? Are you in trouble?"

His sigh weighs fifty pounds. "Help in my bid for the presidency."

This is literally a scene from one of my nightmares. "Oh, goodie."

"With the wedding coming up this weekend, I want to make sure our message is coordinated."

"Our message?" I can't help laughing. "*We* do not have a message. I have no message. I'm confused about why you might think we did."

"I need you to read the talking points, and if you could have Bentley seat us together, I can do all the talking for both of us. That would make things much easier all around."

"Grandma can't make it?" I ask.

"Your grandmother will be there," he says, "obviously."

"Then why would you want to sit by me?"

"Since you won't have a plus one—"

"Grandpa, Easton's coming as my plus one."

"He hasn't spoken to you yet?"

A pit opens up in my stomach. "Spoken to me?"

"You will have to break up," he says. "You set that in motion yourself. One thing Ciprianis can never be accused of is wishy-washiness. You made a clear point about the brand Easton Moorland runs, and it was a good one. It resonated."

"That was an offhand comment at a party," I say. "I didn't mean—"

"It was perfectly timed and exactly on message. For once in my life, one of my family members was pulling their weight. I spoke to the young man today, and he understood, probably better than you seem to, so it would be great if you could have Bentley seat us together."

"Until I hear from Easton himself that he's not going, I will not be doing that. In fact, especially if he's not going, I don't want to be anywhere near you."

"Why?"

"Do you even hear yourself? When's the last time you heard that I was dating someone?"

"Beatrice," he says.

"No." I park on the side of the road. I'm too upset to be driving. "No, you don't get to tell my boyfriend to break up with me. And you don't get to make me part of your checklist of managed assets, either. I'm not even related to you. Seren and Dave are my parents, and I'm done ignoring that."

"Not related—"

"Yes, not related. My real grandfather wouldn't have ever surrendered me back to Mom, but I'm glad you did, because staying at your stupid mansion was even worse than being ignored by her."

After I hang up, it takes me at least five minutes of sobbing to calm down enough to drive. And then, of course, I have a mild panic attack. In my entire life, I've never really stood up to Grandfather. Not when push comes to shove. I've always backed down.

Mom calls me five minutes later.

Her dad's clearly yanking her leash. He's probably threatening to stop paying for her posh rehab center if she can't get me in line.

Good luck, Mom.

I delete her voicemail too, for good measure.

But then it occurs to me to wonder why Grandfather would be so sure that Easton would dump me. He should be worried that Easton might be crazy about me. He should be nervous that his plan to break us up will fail.

Unless. . . Could he have threatened him? Or his business?

ARE YOU AWAKE?

It's after midnight and Easton has a real, respectable job. He should be asleep, and I should not be bothering him right now. But by the time I wake up, he'll probably already be at work. Ugh.

INSOMNIAC.

That makes me smile. Not because I'm happy he's an insomniac, but because he could send one word as a reply, and I know he's telling me it's fine to ding him. MY GRANDFATHER CALLED ME AND IT WAS A WEIRD CALL. That's actually a redundant thing for me to say, but he probably doesn't know yet that a call from my grandfather is always strange or bad or both.

AND?

DID HE TALK TO YOU TODAY, BY CHANCE?

Please say no. Please say no. Please say no.

I CALLED HIM. I HAD A SUSPICION, AND IT WAS CONFIRMED.

He's been pushing that stupid video, because people are rallying behind it for some reason. I should have thought of that. I know him well enough to have realized that already. I'M SORRY.

In that moment, I'm so sorry that I feel it in my toes. My nose. My eyes. My entire body is just throbbing with misery. What do I bring to the table? Other than being cute in a very girl-next-door-who-is-not-at-all-glamourous way?

Nothing.

I'm a waitress.

My grandfather's a disaster.

My mom's even worse.

My foster brother-roommate is a rabid dog.

I honestly can't think of any reason why Easton even likes me, much less a reason why he should put up with all the trash that has been hailed down on him since we met. I THINK WE SHOULD BREAK UP.

I'M COMING OVER.

NO, DON'T.

He calls.

My finger hovers over the talk button for a second. Then another, but before it can go to voicemail, I swipe to answer. "I'm not trying to be melodramatic."

"It feels like you are," Easton says. "Because there's no way we're going to break up because your politician grandfather is a megalomaniac. All politicians are like that, and it's hardly your fault."

"What did he say to you?"

"He threatened to make things hard for my company if I didn't dump you," Easton says.

I want to cry. Not a lovely, sophisticated cry like Octavia earlier. No, I want to wad my fists up and press them against my eyes and cry long, and terrible, and ugly. "That's why you should dump me," I manage to say. "Exactly that. It's too much. I'm like the taco you're not sure if you want, and then it gives you food poisoning and you really, really regret eating it in the first place."

Easton laughs.

He *laughs*.

"I love tacos. I've never once regretted eating a taco. Not ever."

I find myself laughing too, even though I don't think any of this is funny. "Easton, you're not listening to me."

"Oh, I am listening. You're not listening to *me*."

"You haven't said anything."

"I don't mean right now. I mean to everything I've said since we met. The only reason you'd liken yourself to a taco you think I don't even want is if you weren't *listening*. You are the first and only girl I've *ever* really wanted. You're kind, funny, brilliant, and unbelievably talented. As I sat in the audience at that jingle thing, I remember thinking *mine*, not once, but several times. Every time you spoke, played, or sang." He grunts. "You're impressive anywhere you're put, with anything you do, and in everything you say. Even now, your first inclination when your grandfather tries to take a dump on you is to try and keep me safe from it. But his crap isn't your fault. It's his."

"But it's really not your fault, and it'll become yours," I say. "That's the problem. I'm not worth the misery."

"*Au contraire*," he says. "You are nothing but joy to me, and if misery tags along, you're still worth it. Do you know what *I* did today?"

"No."

"My parents have been sponging off me as long as I've been alive. First, they stole from the trust fund my grandparents gave me. Then they borrowed from my college fund—not one they had created in the first place. And then, once I started making money, they took every dime of it they could."

"Emerson hasn't been overly impressed with them either," I confess.

"And he doesn't know the half of it, believe me. But I've enabled them all along, and thanks to you, I realized that was the wrong move. Today, I cut them off."

"Whoa," I say. "I'm not sure how that's my fault, but I certainly didn't—"

"Oh, I'm not blaming you. I'm crediting you. You told me it was enabling. You said that you had to stop doing it with your mom, and at first I got mad. My parents aren't junkies. But I realized that they're even worse, in their own way. Elizabeth has told me for years not to help them, but you were the first person who really told me that I'd be helping them by cutting them off."

"That's not—"

"Bea, you have made my life better in every way."

"But now my grandfather is trying to wreck it, and if you just—"

"Don't say break up with me."

"But if you—"

"La la la la la."

"What are you doing?"

"If it sounds like you're going to suggest we break up again, I'm going to sing."

"That wasn't even a real song."

"I never claimed to be musical," he says. "In fact, if I recall correctly, I told you that I sound like Sebastian the Crab in the *Little Mermaid*."

He has me chuckling. "Actually, Sebastian could sing. You said you sounded like Scuttle."

"Wait, who's Scuttle?"

"The seagull."

"Oh, right, that's the one."

Which he knew. He said it was the seagull himself, so he's just trying to distract me from the point. "Easton."

"Bea, I don't know how else to say this. That's a no to breaking up—a firm no," he says. "I have a plan, and my plan will work. So just trust in the plan."

"This is a plan for us to survive my grandfather the governor who wants to break us up?"

"Yes. And listen, if your resolve starts to crumble, I have a suggestion. My sister Elizabeth has gotten super into K-dramas, and she was just telling me how in a lot of them, the parents try to break up the couple, but they don't succeed."

"Easton."

"I know one of them was called *Boys over Flowers*, and I think another one was *Secret Garden,* or maybe it was called *Heirs*. Or that could be a whole different one. But I can have her text you a list if you need some inspiration."

"Easton."

"I love hearing you say my name, but maybe in the future, don't use that weird, kind of motherly tone?"

"Well, our breakup didn't go as I expected."

"Stop saying that word," he says. "In fact, I forbid you to use it at all from now on."

"What if my socks get stuck together and I need to break them up?"

"You can say that you need to pull them apart."

"Alright," I say. "What if I need to break up a fight?"

"You need to get the idiots to cool down," he says. "I could do this all day."

"You're a real wordsmith."

"How's this one?" he says. "I didn't want to say it

over the phone, but since you're going to see me next at the office, I figure it's better tonight than tomorrow."

"Wait, why will I see you at the office?"

"Aren't you coming in with your bridesmaid's dress tomorrow?"

I'd forgotten that he would be my wedding date—in my brain, that was off. "My grandfather will be at the wedding," I say. "I'm not sure whether it's a great plan to egg him on. Maybe we lie low for a bit, not breaking up, but not flaunting it, and then—"

"I can't wait to see him. Did you know that he might be a senator soon?"

"I've heard," I say. "Yes."

"Well, I think it's great. And I'm delighted to see him again on Sunday."

"Are you?" He must be deranged. Or he's kidding.

"Honestly, I love you so much, I don't care who else is there as long as you are."

I nearly drop the phone. "You—that's what you didn't want to say at work tomorrow?"

"I told your grandfather that I adored you, and it felt wrong. I mean, I *do* adore you, but I felt like it just wasn't enough. I needed a stronger word, and that's when I realized why adore wasn't the right word. I've never told any woman, other than my mom and my sister, that I love them. Until right now." He pauses.

I have no idea what to say.

Clearly he's not similarly afflicted. "Beatrice Cipriani, I love you."

I should say it back. I know that. It's the etiquette, but I can't help thinking that he might be making a mistake. We really should be breaking up, not professing our love. And if he realizes, soon probably, that the price of dating me is too high. . .it'll hurt more if I've admitted that I love him.

So I just say, "I'll see you tomorrow, Easton."

"That you will."

And then I hang up.

20

BEA

After telling me he loves me, I don't hear from Easton for an entire day. When I go by his office, he's not even there. His assistant says he's meeting with lawyers, which sounds ominous, but when you do what he does, it's probably just a typical day.

And it's fine.

I'm busy, too.

His people really do get my dress altered—while I wait. It's insane. This one woman does 90% of it in front of me, with this sewing machine that whizzes and whirs. By the time they're done, they've taken the deep ochre dress, turned the excess hem into a sash around the waist, and shortened the bodice so that it hits me just above my waist instead of below.

The buttons that were straight up the middle are now offset, and the skirt is asymmetrical in a way that makes me look like a Barbie doll. I would be majorly stressing, but Barbara got us all different styles from the same line, with colors that coordinate on some palette she chose with her wedding planner.

"You're a wizard," I tell the woman. "Thank you."

"I was excited when I thought they were adding a women's line," she says. "I'm better with women's clothing. More scope."

"Maybe they'll add one yet," I say.

She shrugs, not getting too excited, clearly.

Once I get home, the dress taken care of, I have to start working on my wedding gift. But before I can focus, I need to get the details of the song I wrote and plan to submit down on paper. I arranged to meet with Octavia tomorrow morning to record it for the contest. Once I get it reduced to notes and words on a page, I sit back and sigh with relief.

But then I stare at the piano, completely devoid of any ideas.

I'm going to show up at their wedding entirely emptyhanded, and probably emptyheaded, too. I whip out my phone and start googling wedding gift ideas, but within ten minutes I'm right back where I started. Bentley makes so much money that they can already buy whatever they want. After all the thoughtful gifts they've given me over the years, I have *got* to come up with something good.

But by the time I have to change for work, I still have zero.

HEY. SO. CAN YOU PUT MY NAME ON THE POSTER?

Jake sends me a whole line of laughing emojis.

YOU SUCK.

More laughing faces. This time, with tears.

Bizarrely, work is slow, so I have plenty of time to fret over what I ought to give Aunt Barbara and Uncle Bentley. I mean, I know I should give them a song, but my brain's just not engaging. Three songs in a week is a lot, and I probably shouldn't be annoyed that there's not another one waiting in the wings, but here we are.

In between tables, I pull up my phone browser and manage to find an account on Etsy that paints portraits from photos. I shoot her a message and ask if she could do an expedited one. . .Since the image is digitally painted, I could probably have it printed before the wedding, if she did it quick. Thankfully, she replies. The cost is a little painful, but that's on me for needing it done in days.

All in all, it's not a terrible day at work. I'm changing for bed when a message comes through from Easton. SORRY—SLAMMED ALL DAY TODAY. SEE YOU IN THE MORNING?

CAN'T. MEETING OCTAVIA TO WORK ON OUR SONG.

OUR SONG?

I haven't really talked to anyone about it. I HATE PERFORMING. I'M WRITING A SONG, AND SHE'S HELPING. WE'LL PERFORM IT TOGETHER IF IT ADVANCES TO FINALS.

THAT'S A BRILLIANT IDEA. SHE HAD A NICE VOICE.

That's like calling the David a 'nice' statue. Or saying the Mona Lisa was a 'nice' portrait, but I let it slide. For someone who's not in the music world, 'nice' is probably a perfectly acceptable word. YES. YES, SHE DOES.

I MISSED YOU TODAY.

YOUR PEOPLE WERE GREAT. THAT LADY WAS LIKE WILLY WONKA, BUT INSTEAD OF CANDY, SHE MAKES MAGIC WITH CLOTH.

I ASSEMBLED A GOOD TEAM.

He did. I hadn't really thought about it like that, but probably every person at that place was hired by him, or at least, hired by someone who was hired by him. The whole company is literally a thing that he built. It's his song equivalent, only he's not entering contests and hoping. He's already won.

Again, I wonder why he likes me.

MAYBE I CAN BRING LUNCH BY FOR YOU TWO WHILE YOU WORK.

I do want to see his face. I'm just a little worried that the more time he spends with me, the more likely it becomes that he'll realize I'm a loser and give up. I need to get over myself. If that's going to happen, it's going to happen. Even so, I wave him off this time. WHAT A NICE OFFER, BUT I DON'T THINK WE'LL HAVE TIME.

IN THE FUTURE, IF I DID BRING FOOD BY, WHAT WOULD YOU LIKE? THAI? SUSHI? PIZZA?

YES.

He sends me laughing emojis next.

I'M NOT SUPER PICKY, ESPECIALLY WHEN IT'S FREE.

PEANUT BUTTER AND JELLY IT IS.

The next morning, I wake up way too early, because the Gorgeous Monstrosity song keeps repeating over and over in my head. Before Octavia arrives, I've cleaned up the messy transition, added a harmonic uplift, and made all the changes on paper.

Which means, once we record, we'll be ready to submit.

I'm not sure why that's so scary, but it really and truly is. I was nervous about the jingle, but this might give me an ulcer. When Octavia knocks at the door, I'm relieved Jake's not home. He left to meet his trainer twenty minutes ago. He makes most things harder.

I open the door slowly, but Octavia looks even more nervous than I do. Her eyes are darting around like she's afraid she'll be attacked. "Come on in," I say.

"This isn't what I expected."

"What did you expect?" I raise my eyebrows.

She shrugs. "It's just really. . .normal."

"I'm a pretty normal person," I say.

"But isn't Jake your roommate?"

I laugh. "You know, Jake's high profile, and he makes a lot of money, and he drives a flashy car, but down deep, he feels way happier here than he would anywhere else."

"Because it's normal."

I nod slowly. "Jake doesn't welcome people easily, but yes. He's with family here, and I'm comfortable in this place, so he is, too." I point at his door and Emerson's. "Even so, I'd recommend you stay out of those two rooms. One is his room, and one is now his closet, and both of them are disastrously messy. He pays for a cleaning lady to come once a week, and I swear, she spends half her time in there washing, folding, and putting things away. The man is a pig."

"I wonder how many views a video of Jake Priest's messy room would get me on TikTok."

"Quite a lot, I'm sure," I say.

Thankfully, Octavia doesn't seem like the kind of person who has a salacious TikTok account. I should keep an eye on Uncle Bentley and Aunt Barbara's girls, Ricki and Nikki, though. I could totally see them posting something like that on theirs to boost their engagement.

After doing a few vocal runs to help her warm up, we actually try the song. She has a few suggestions, which are all good, and it's more fun than I anticipated working with someone on a song instead of doing it myself. My piano teacher sometimes works with me, but more often than not, I'm either writing it myself or just cleaning up her messes. This is more collaborative, even more so than when Jake helps me with words, and I love it.

"Alright, so with those word shifts, and with the change to the harmony here—"

"You need to sing the melody, though." Octavia's smiling now.

"I told you. I'll play, but I don't want to sing."

"It's the only way it works. It needs the complexity to elevate that line."

I wish she was wrong. "Fine." People rarely really listen to the alto line. It'll mostly just blend in underneath hers, so it should be fine. "If we make it to the finals, I can sing from the back, in front of the piano."

She doesn't argue with me about that, thankfully, but it makes me think.

"Are you dreading it?" I ask. "Having all the eyes on you?"

She shrugs. "I used to spend half my life on a stage. I've been performing since I was a child."

"But?"

She inhales slowly. "The shock and horror from every person who looks at me, it wears on me. I have to kind of prepare myself for it."

"Shock and horror?" I can barely believe what she's saying. "Who's shocked and horrified?"

"Who isn't?" She shrugs. "I get it. The first time I saw myself after it happened. . ." She shakes her head. "It's not comfortable to look at something like my burn. People cringe. I think it makes them realize that all of us are vulnerable, fragile even. Our lives are not guaranteed."

Holy wow, she's right.

I *did* cringe a little inside when I saw her. Not because I didn't want to see her. Not because I thought she looked awful, but because I thought about how much it must have hurt, and how glad I was that I'd never had to endure something like that. "I'm really sorry." I don't know what else to say.

"Thanks for caring, and for being honest." Her half smile feels like forgiveness. It must be tiring having to forgive people all the time for their own inadequacies.

"Alright, I think we may be ready to record it," I say. "Feel up to it? Submissions are due this Saturday at midnight."

"Sure," she says. "Let's go."

But when we try to start, the batteries on my mic are dead. I groan. When I rummage around in the battery drawer, none of the ones in there seem to work either. "Jake puts old ones back in sometimes, the idiot."

"He sounds like a real joy to live with."

"His strengths outweigh his weaknesses. If I messaged him, he'd stop and pick up anything I needed, but he's not great with the organization." I glance at the clock. "I can just run to Balducci's around the corner and grab some. It'll take two minutes."

"Maybe not literally." Octavia smirks.

"Probably not literally," I agree.

"I'll come with. I need to get some tape. I'm all out at home."

She hops in my car—one of the best things about Scarsdale over New York City is that stores have actual parking spots, and I can drive right over to them. "Tape, huh?"

"And chapstick," she says. "I wear lipstick for work—need every little boost I can get—but I'm a chapstick addict otherwise."

"Me too," I say. "To both. I look super washed out without lipstick, but I hate bothering with it unless I'm working."

"We're basically twins," she says.

"Other than the angelic voice, and the height, and the amazing physique."

"And the unburned, perfect skin on your face and shoulder." But she's smiling. It feels like, somehow, we've passed most of the awkwardness.

"Do you mind me asking what happened?"

"I was eleven. I was in *My Fair Lady*—like always—and I had to wear this wig for it."

"What role were you playing at age eleven?"

"It was through the community theater, and they cast me as Eliza."

"Because of your voice."

She shrugs. "Most of the actors were children, actually. It was going to be all children, but they wound up filling Hugh Pickering's role with an adult. There were a few more."

"And the wig?" It's easy to get sidetracked when the topic's one you'd rather avoid. We're already at the store, so I wait for her to climb out and lock the door.

"Well, it kept coming off during rehearsals, so Mom and I were trying things to get it to stay on. We braided parts of it into my hair, and it was staying much, much better. I'd been dancing all around, wearing it from morning til night."

This isn't going anywhere good.

"Anyway, Mom was making my favorite food—french fries. But we didn't have a frier, so she was making them in a wok over the stove. She asked me to check on them, the oil popped and hit the burner, the fire caught the edge of the wig, and then." She swallows. "We couldn't get it off."

We've just walked into the store, but she stops for a moment and I wait. She's staring off at nothing, almost like she's remembering it.

"It only got my face and my shoulder, which was lucky. It could have been much, much worse."

"This may be a bad thing to ask, but don't they do skin grafts? Could that help?"

She nods slowly. "We did a lot of grafts on my shoulder, which was ironically the worst part of it. For some people, they work great. For me. . .they didn't heal well." She shudders. "It was painful. And at the end, instead of a burn, my shoulder, well." She shakes her head. "I could show you sometime, maybe. It looks like, I don't know, like Frankenstein. I've thought about trying more a few times, but when I turned fourteen, I just stopped. I was done." She shrugs. "No one has even been able to promise that they would make things better, and I'm used to my face like this. It's almost artistic."

She's right. There are no strange ridges. It's smooth ripples from her forehead down around her lips. Her neck's mostly clear, and then the rest is covered by her shirt.

It takes me two minutes to grab the batteries, which are annoyingly at the very back, but I see her looking over the nine million lip glosses on the toiletry aisle on my way back to the front. "Ready?"

"What do you think will look better with my hair color?" She purses her lips, which are entirely unburned. I hadn't really noticed that before. "Rose Frappe." She holds up a gloss. "Or Champagne Honey?" She holds up another.

Before I can even answer, a little girl pops around the end of the row and starts to cry. "Mom!"

Her mother's right behind her, thankfully. "What's wrong, sweetie?"

"Look," she says. "It's a monster. A *monster*."

I'm horrified. The little girl's pointing right at Octavia.

"Don't look at her, sweetheart. Mom won't let her hurt you." The woman grabs her little girl's shoulder and starts to steer her away.

"Excuse me," I say. "How dare you—"

But Octavia's hand drops on my forearm, and she shakes her head. It's small. It's tight. But her eyes don't even look distressed. They look *resigned.* "Kids say stuff. It's fine."

"But that mother should not have told her—"

"Bea, I love that you care, but really. It's fine."

My heart's racing so fast that I can hear a ringing in my ears. "It's not fine." And then, like a big, fat baby, I'm crying in the middle of the store. "How could she say that?"

Octavia tilts her head, her eyes welling with tears, probably in response to my own. "It happens a lot. It's really okay."

But it's not.

It's really, really not.

The world is such an ugly place, but not because of Octavia.

Because of mothers who say the wrong thing. Because of children who are taught the wrong things. Because of people who only look at the superficial. Because of beauty standards that don't recognize anything but the ideal.

Then I remember what I said to Easton when those

women made fun of my pajamas. Maybe, like I felt then, she's just too *tired* to address it. Why should it be her job to fix all these ugly people?

But I feel the need to make sure she knows it's not her fault. I have to make sure she knows that she's not the problem. "I love your face," I say. "I love it so much, I could marry it."

A single tear rolls down Octavia's cheek, but she swipes it away so fast, it's almost like it was never there. "Thank you, Bea."

Then we walk to the register, pay for our batteries, and leave. We're all the way to the car when I realize that she didn't buy her lip gloss. I almost suggest we go back in, but I think that maybe, just maybe, she had lost her interest in it.

What kind of person rubs salt in that wound?

I leave it be.

When we get back, the microphone works just fine, thankfully. If it had been some other kind of problem, it could have derailed everything. When Octavia sings the words—

❦

All the joy inside of me,
All the hope for a brighter day,
The monster consumed it all,
I became beast and also prey.

❦

I start to cry all over again. Luckily, it's not time for my part yet. And when that time comes, I've gotten myself together enough to do my lines. Octavia's voice singing the harmony rises, higher, higher, higher, so high in parts that I'm not sure how she can sound so gorgeous at such a high pitch, but the words ring truer to me than ever before after one tiny moment in what must be the entirety of her life.

*T*he world is dark and terrifying.
     That much, at least, was true.
But those who spoke of beauty,
Were the villains, not me and you.
It's not my face at fault here
It's those who glare and jeer
The real beast lives inside of them,
They get back what they give.

*S*o stop looking to slay monsters,
     And start working on yourself.

*T*he gorgeous monstrosity you should fear
     Is the one staring back at you in the mirror.
Work on the beast you have some hope to tame,
And when you see the ugliness,
Call it out by name. Oh, call it out by name.

"I thought we'd need to do this over and over," I say, shutting off the machine.

"That was. . ." Octavia shakes her head.

"I'm sure we could probably improve it," I say.

"But I have no idea how." Her smile is light and joy and peace. Five minutes later, we've made the changes to the sheet music, scanned it, and hit 'submit.'

"Thank you." Octavia inhales sharply, and I realize she's trying not to cry again. "Thank you for wanting to do this." She swallows again. "With me." She stands up abruptly and grabs her purse. "I should let you get ready for work."

Two seconds later, she's ducking out the door.

I don't try to call her back, in part because I do need to get ready for work, and in part because it looked like she needed some time to process.

If Dave and Seren have taught me anything, it's that the world around us may be ugly. It may be dark. It may be full of yuckiness and misery. But the only way to make the world into what we want it to be is to change it, one small thing, and one small person at a time. I like to think that working with Octavia is in some small part like their work with me. With Emerson. With Jake.

She has some damage, just like we did, but good people can heal that damage better than any graft ever could. She just needs to know that we all see the beauty inside of her, just like Dave and Seren saw it in me when I didn't see it in myself.

When Seren calls me on the way to work, I pick up with a happy heart. "Hey, you."

"Hey, Mom."

She pauses for a second, and I wonder how many times she's heard me call her mom. Not many, I imagine.

That's a darkness I intend to change. "I just wanted to make sure you and Jake are coming to Barbara and Bentley's wedding a little early. They want to go over placement and whatnot."

"I'm bringing someone," I say.

"Is it Elizabeth's brother?"

"How do you know everything?"

"Emerson and Elizabeth came by yesterday, and she mentioned you were dating."

"He is. . ."

"Handsome?"

I laugh.

"Brilliant?"

"Mom."

"Super, duper rich?"

"I was going to say he's amazing. I think it kind of encompasses all of that."

"I'm happy for you," Seren says. "I'm not a huge fan of Elizabeth's parents, all cards on the table, but if she came from them, there's hope for Easton too."

"Yeah, what are the odds that two such greedy, selfish people would wind up with two amazing children?"

"Luck plays a role, but I imagine those two kids helped one another to be good," Seren says. "Synergy works like that sometimes."

"I guess."

"And how long has this been going on?"

"Not long," I say. "But I think it's real."

"Sometimes you know pretty fast," Seren says. "And sometimes people know each other twenty years and are too stupid to see it."

"Uncle Bentley and Aunt Barbara."

"If we're laying blame, I put it on him," Seren says.

"I'm sure you do." I pull into the work parking lot. "But, Mom."

"Your grandfather's coming," she says. "I just wanted to warn you. We put him clear on the other side of the ballroom, but he takes up a lot of space."

"Why did Bentley have to invite him?"

"Well, back when we were planning this, we didn't realize it was a problem, and he's been helpful to Bentley in a few business deals."

"It's fine," I say. "It'll be just fine."

"If it's not, let us know. We'll figure out a way to keep him out."

Grandfather? I really doubt it. I feel like he could break into Fort Knox if he had to. "I appreciate it."

"I'll see you soon, beautiful Bea."

"And hey, Mom?" I inhale and exhale slowly. Even saying it out loud is daunting for some reason. "I entered a song contest today with a friend. If we make the final round, I'll have to perform the song live."

"Oh, that's amazing. When will you hear back?"

"Not sure," I say. "They didn't have that posted."

"Well, win or lose, I'm so proud of you for trying." Seren would be proud of me for dancing terribly in a flash mob while wearing a trash bag, but it's still nice to hear.

"Thanks."

"You're one in a billion," Seren says. "Never forget it."

I'm certainly not one in a billion, but I do feel pretty good as I walk into work, like I'm on top of the world for once.

It's a nice feeling, which is why it probably can't last.

The last wedding I attended was my sister's, and it had a lot of the same people as this one. I'm not entirely sure what to expect with this one. I know that to Bea, Bentley Harrison is like an uncle. But in the business world, the man's a terrifying shark.

Everyone's afraid of him.

Everyone.

Even Catherine Richmond gives him a wide berth. It doesn't hurt that, on top of having family money and wealth of his own, Bentley's also got a father *and* an uncle who are judges. There have been rumors lately that his uncle might be next in line when a certain Supreme Court Justice retires.

I can't imagine Bea's grandfather would try to make a scene at the wedding, but just in case, I'm going into it prepared. It took me forty hours a day for the past several days, but I've got a signed letter of intent from Laurent's father, and the deal will be closed by some time next week. If good old grandpa gets rude or feisty, I'm ready for it.

Bring it, old man.

The problem with people like Bea, people who are so good that it practically oozes out of them, is that bad people can smell their vulnerability. They latch on and never let go, milking the poor givers for every last drop. If I have anything to say about it, this particular leech has pushed Bea around for the last time.

When I reach Bea's house, I'm already in my tux. It's gotten cool enough in New York that I'm not sweating, which is nice. I know that's when things get irritating for the ladies, though, because they usually wear dramatically less clothing for formal events.

Something really ought to be done about that. If I wasn't selling off my company, I'd make a note of it. Either more revealing clothing for the men, or more full coverage for the women. . . Given how hard it was to get designers to start putting pockets in women's clothing, I'm not sure it will be an easy thing to address. But that's a problem for another day.

Today, I only really care about Bea.

When I knock, the door opens almost immediately. Jake's already wearing his penguin suit, too. He tosses his head in the universal sign for *what's up?*

"Not ready to go?" I lift my eyebrows.

Jake drags one finger across his throat and then presses the same finger to his mouth.

"Who is it?" Bea pokes her head out the door, her hair tied up on the top of her head like a big, poofy bow. "It's *Easton* already?" She's shrieking. "Why didn't you tell me how late it was?"

"He's early," Jake says in a calm, measured voice. When he turns around to face me, he hisses. "Dude, you *never* come early. You have a sister."

That makes me laugh. "Elizabeth's more of a 'throw on whatever and schlep your way over' kind of girl."

Jake grimaces and shakes his head. "Bea's not."

I point at the TV. "Giants game?"

He frowns. "Not this early. Maybe Knicks?"

"Dude." I snort. "Not for two weeks."

He shrugs. "I used to keep up better, but when I start filming, I really lose track."

"Maybe there's some hockey on?"

Jake drops into the corner of the sofa. "Eh. It's fine. She's probably just got ten or fifteen minutes left."

"Did you see her hair?"

"That's what threw you off. Putting on her dress takes thirty seconds," Jake says. "The reason her hair looked so weird is she's done the whole bottom half. Doing just the top is quick, and her makeup is done. She spent *way* too long on that earlier."

"*Jacob Priest.*"

He cringes. "Shoot. She heard me." He stands, mouthing the words "Save yourself."

"Get in here right now."

He sighs and pivots, heading for her door.

His time estimate is about right, though. About ten minutes later, they both come out, and her hair. . .It falls around her shoulders like a tumultuous waterfall of shining deep brown curls. Something in it sparkles from several places, but I can't tell what. Her dress is the perfect color for her skin and eyes, a golden russet that makes her look both tan and glowing at the same time. Her eyes pop—probably thanks in some part to her makeup—in contrast to the fabric color as well.

"Oh, no," I say.

"What?" She freezes.

Jake's eyes widen and he shakes his head behind her.

"I'm not sure you can go like that." I exhale. "The bride won't let you in if you upstage her. It *is* supposed to be her day."

Bea rolls her eyes and bites her lip.

It's absolutely adorable.

"You two are gross," Jake says. "I'm taking my car."

"You could have left half an hour ago and spared me the misery." Bea's shaking her head. "Why didn't you? You're so annoying."

"I was trying to keep Easter here alive." He glares. "She'd eat you alive when she's stressed about getting ready, little boy. Learning to survive this part takes some training."

She shoves him.

It's actually pretty nice of him to drive himself. Clearly he could insist on driving, and that would leave me crammed into the back of his Porsche. No thanks.

Or if Bea drove, she'd have had to pick one of us for the front seat, and that might have been awkward too. I expected him to be more of a problem, actually, but he seems to be better than I anticipated. Honestly, at the beginning, right after I met Bea, I kind of thought he liked her.

I was actually almost positive.

Clearly I'm not always right, and this time, it's a relief.

Jake grabs his keys and disappears.

"You ready?"

"Yeah," Bea says. "I just need to grab my gift."

"How are you going to grab a song?" I look around to see if maybe there's a CD or something sitting around. Though who listens to CDs anymore, I'm not sure.

Her cheeks turn pink.

"What?" Did I say something stupid?

"I didn't really have time," she says. "So instead, I got them a portrait of their family."

"Oh." I nod. "That still sounds really cool."

She picks up a two by three foot gift that was leaning against the side wall in the kitchen. I should have noticed it. My powers of observation are clearly offline after my long week. "The artist even added their names with this really pretty calligraphy under each of them."

"I'm sure they'll love it," I say.

She shrugs. "It's hard to shop for rich people." She bumps me with her hip as she passes. "I'm not looking forward to your birthday." Then she frowns. "When is it, anyway?"

"You lucked out. It was the week before I came into your restaurant."

Her eyes widen. "I'm sorry I missed it."

"When's yours?"

She groans. "Day after Christmas." She shakes her head. "I drew the short straw."

"I guess so."

"It's fine," she says. "I'm used to it by now, and Seren always turned it into a big production."

"At least you never go to school on your birthday. Mine was the first day of school twice."

Bea laughs. "I suppose everything has its trade-offs."

I take the gift from her and gesture for the door. "Let's go, or we'll be late."

"Can't have that," she says. "I have someone to show off." Her grin lifts my heart.

When we get into the car, I start tapping the address in. "Oh, you can just go," Bea says. "I'll tell you how to get there."

"You know how to get there by heart?"

"It's at my parent's inn," she says. "It's home."

"Oh." I hadn't noticed that when she sent me the address before. "That's kind of cool. Is it big enough for the Harrison wedding?"

"Barbara wanted a small wedding," Bea says. "Not sure she'll be getting that, but they really did try to contain the guest list. No more than three hundred guests."

"So four hundred?"

Bea laughs. "Probably. One of the problems with being fancy is that you have a lot of work contacts you don't want to offend."

"And a lot of them probably come in sets," I say. "Like, if I were to invite Jean-François to our wedding, I'd have to invite Sabato as well, or I swear, Gucci would blackball me."

"Gucci?" Her smile is so cute. "Really?"

I shrug. "It happened once. I thought Sabato was still in France, so I only called Jean-François about this kind of last-minute gathering."

"How did you fix it?"

"It's a long story that involves me wearing a women's swimsuit for an entire round of golf."

Bea's laughter's loud and long. "I'm afraid I need evidence of that."

"There better not be any," I say. "Because if there is, I'm going to have to murder someone."

"Yes, well, most of my stories involve people that no one has ever heard of."

"Says the granddaughter of Audrey Colburn—"

"Foster *great* granddaughter. I never even met her."

"And the granddaughter of the Governor."

She rolls her eyes.

"Roommate of Jake Priest."

"He's a pain in the pattoo."

"Can't argue that one. But your other brother is the heir to the Richmond fortune, and you're family to Bentley Harrison." I shrug. "I'm just saying, you're not exactly one to talk about having no connections."

She grunts.

It feels kind of nice to win a round.

"Alright, how's this for a story? The first time I met Uncle Bentley, I threatened to stab him."

"You're kidding."

She shakes her head. "Nope. I had been at Dave and Seren's for three days, and he came flying through the door with a gun in his hand." She's smiling. "He had found some kind of old gun from the war or something, and Dave knew he was looking for it. Maybe Seren did, too, but to me, he was some strange man barging in with a gun."

"And you threatened him with a knife?"

"I think what I said was something like, 'you might shoot me, but I'm a blade master, and I'll slice your throat before I die.' Dave and Seren were in the back room, and the way they laughed, you'd think they'd never been amused before in their lives."

"After that, you're still invited to the wedding?" I can't help imagining it, tiny Bea, brandishing a knife when most girls would be screaming and huddling on the floor. It doesn't even surprise me. She seems small. She seems slight. She hates being the center of attention, but if she's shoved against a wall, she comes back swinging.

Bea shrugs. "I think they have to invite me."

"Oh?"

She leans a little closer and drops her voice. "I know all the dirt on them."

That makes me laugh. But with just one more turn, we're there, which makes sense. I doubt any of Dave and Seren's foster kids live too far from them. They may not always call them mom or dad, but they clearly all orient around them like electrons in orbit.

As we pull up outside, a valet's waiting to take the car. I hate handing off the keys, but I can't really wrestle them to the ground and insist on parking my own car. I grit my teeth and pass the fob to the twenty-year-old.

I have insurance. I have insurance. This is why I have insurance.

"You okay?"

"Did you do anything stupid when you were twenty?"

"You may need to be more specific," Bea says. "Most of what I did when I was twenty was stupid."

"Oh?" I feel like I need to know more about that. "But I mean, when you were driving."

"Oh." She frowns. "I mean, maybe. I think I was twenty when I kind of backed into a dumpster." She scrunches up her nose. "Insurance covered the repairs, but my bumper has been a little crooked ever since."

"I just handed a twenty-year-old my hundred thousand dollar car. That's all."

She bobs her head. "That's why you shouldn't ever spend more than twenty grand on a car."

"I think I'll take my chances," I say. "I can't think of a single car for twenty grand that I would want to drive."

"Snob."

But now we're walking through the front gate, and Dave and Seren are there. Before I can even re-introduce myself, Seren's hugging me. "Easton." She releases me, her smile bright. "Welcome. So happy to see you again."

"Oh." Before I can really process how *nice* she is, Dave's hugging me too.

"I didn't use to be a hugger," he's saying, "but after long enough with someone, they start to rub off on you, so here we are."

"It's fine," I say. "I don't mind."

"I hear our girl Bea is smiling more these days, thanks to you." Dave bobs his head. "That's what I like to hear."

"Me too," I say.

"Jake doesn't praise people very often, so that's a pretty strong recommendation from him." Dave gestures. "Wedding party's waiting at our house until they're ready for us."

"Oh. Right." Bea's already walking that way, but when I start to follow her, Dave grabs my elbow.

"And son?"

I turn back. "Yes?"

"If you make her cry?" He's still beaming like he's telling me a joke or something. "This inn sits on acres and acres of gardens. No one would ever even find where I put your body, because I'd spread it into pieces so small even a cadaver dog couldn't find it." He lifts both eyebrows. "We clear?"

I blink.

"Bea has been through enough misery for three lifetimes. I won't tolerate *any* nonsense."

Yeah, she basically has no connections at all. I force a smile and nod. "Right, I hear you, sir."

He pats my shoulder. "No need to call me sir. Mister's fine."

I can't tell if he's kidding, but I can feel a bead of sweat roll down between my shoulder blades. I knew to prepare for a confrontation with the grandfather, but I had no idea her dad would be this scary. "No reason to worry on my account," I say. "I love her to the moon and back."

Dave's smile widens. "That's the right answer, son."

Jake jogs over. "Did he give you the 'my gardens are really big' speech?" He slugs Dave on the shoulder. "That is *so* not as scary as you think it is. You need to rework it or something. You're going to put poor Easton to sleep." Jake bumps my arm and starts walking, dragging me along in his wake.

"It was actually terrifying," I confess as we pull closer to the small cottage house.

"Oh, believe me, I know. When they brought me into the family, he gave me the same one, but about all the girls." Jake's eyes are dancing. "But you don't exactly get a Doberman to stand down by telling him his growling is super effective, do you?"

Bea's family is very strange.

She's worth it, though.

When I follow her through the door, there's already a full house inside. I know the youngest is her other foster brother, Killian, and I'm guessing the stoic one wearing chunky glasses is Ardath. She's a doctor, and she stitched up Catherine Richmond at Elizabeth's wedding, but that's as much as I know about either of them.

"Easton, right?" Killian stands. "Good to meet you."

"We met at Elizabeth and Emerson's wedding," I say.

Killian shrugs. "I mean, probably, but you were just another suit then." He grins. "Now you're knocking boots with my sister." He pulls a face.

Bea squeals. "Killian McGregor, you apologize right now." She spins around. "I'm so sorry—he's at that stage where he's constantly trying to horrify people."

"He's pretty good at it." Jake high fives Killian.

"Jake." Bea's eyes are flashing, but neither of the boys looks concerned. "If you two don't both apologize to Easton right now—we are taking things slow, and we're being respectful." She glares. "I'll tell everyone about the funnel."

Jake's jaw drops.

Killian coughs.

"I'm sorry," Killian blurts, and then he looks at Bea.

She frowns.

Killian continues. "Like, really sorry for being rude, dude. We chill?"

I nod.

He shoots a sideways glare at Bea, and then he darts down the hall.

"Me too," Jake says.

"No way." Bea folds her arms. "Actors can certainly use their words better than that. I'll even give you your line. 'Oh, Easton, I'm so sorry I encouraged my goofy little brother who worships me to be rude.'" She tosses her head, like she's nudging a recalcitrant toddler to return the M&Ms he stole.

He huffs. "I'm sorry that I laughed when Killian was being a jerk." He turns his head. "We good?"

She holds his gaze for a moment, and then she nods. "Fine."

"I have to know about this funnel," I say.

"No way," Bea says at the same time Jake says, "I'll actually kill you."

It's not very long before they have us lining up to head over to the outdoor arbor where the ceremony will be. There are mums everywhere. I can't even begin to guess how much money in flowers I'm looking at, but Dave was right about one thing. They have a prodigious amount of garden space, especially this close to the City.

We only have time to run through the details once before guests begin arriving, and then we're all on tap to help greet people and get them to their proper seats. I should've known I'd be right here on the front lines—between my sister being married to Bea's brother, and them being Bentley and Barbara's family, I'm basically family already.

I don't hate that idea.

In fact, when my parents arrive, they lie shamelessly. I hear them telling everyone how utterly delighted they were to discover that Bea and I were dating. I glare at them once, just so they know I see their lie, and then I let it go. After all, I do want them to support us.

But within a few moments, I'm finding my seat as well, and then the orchestra starts to play. I should probably have expected it, but Barbara and Bentley's two girls walk up the aisle first. One of them's wearing a cute little pine green dress and spreading rose petals, and the other's wearing a pair of black slacks and a golden blouse, being dragged up the aisle by a border collie—I think it's the same dog that flipped out and almost ruined Elizabeth and Emerson's wedding. At least this time, it just runs to the front and jumps up on Bentley.

He seems ready for it, smiling broadly and crouching a little to let it lick his face. When the wedding march starts, I turn around and watch with everyone else.

Barbara has been married before. I knew that much.

Still, I didn't expect her to wear a blood red dress that looks a little like a salsa dancer's costume and the queen's coronation dress had a one night stand. It's got flouncy ruffles all along the asymmetrical skirt, which is slit up the right side. Matching asymmetrical ruffles, going the other direction, rise up the one-shoulder bodice.

It's absolutely stunning.

For a fall wedding, where all the accent colors are shades of brown, gold, russet, and mahogany? It's unexpectedly stand-out and glamorous in a way a white gown never could be. I'm dying to know who designed the dress. It really, really looks like Laurent's work. If he didn't do it, I bet someone who copies him did.

It's totally not what I should be fixating on, so I let it go and enjoy the show.

The two little girls are dancing back and forth a little from one foot to the other, but everyone else is smiling calmly as Barbara finally reaches the front. Bea winks at me from where she's standing next to Seren. The ceremony goes on a little too long, and my mind starts to wander, but the man with the white hat finally does pronounce them husband and wife.

And then they both share their vows.

"You took long enough to notice me," Barbara says. "I figured, after more than a decade of knowing you, that you had no interest in me. I think that was a reasonable assumption."

Everyone laughs.

"But I suppose men sometimes just don't know their minds."

"Often." Dave clears his throat.

"Luckily, you did figure out that you liked me."

"I love you." Bentley takes her hands in his. "And I promise that from now on, I will never ever take you for granted again."

"You better keep that promise," Barbara says, "because if you don't, I get all of them in the divorce." She waves at the audience. "Even if they're all horrified that I'm saying the word divorce at our wedding." She's smiling as she shakes her head. "I used to be superstitious, but after doing everything right the first time and having everything go wrong, we've done everything backward, and I've never felt better about anything in my life."

She releases Bentley's hands and opens her arms.

Before the girls can reach her side, the border collie jumps up, trying to lick her face.

"No, Lucky," Bentley says. "Down."

But the girls are giggling as they hug their mother.

"We got the kids first," Barbara says. "I knew that night, when you came to help me without any reason, I knew I wanted you by my side, whatever came. And I promise you that, no matter how strange things are in our lives, no matter how backward, no matter how slow or how fast, I will be here. I will keep loving you through it all. The dog licks. The crazy family. The business ups and downs. I'll be here for everything."

Bentley drops to his knees. "And my first promise is to you girls."

This is a little weird.

"I promise that I will love your mother every single day, every single minute, from now until forever. You don't need to worry that we'll get in an argument and things will change. We fight plenty, but it never changes how much I love her."

The girls are smiling.

He stands up. "And I promise that I will listen to the excellent advice of Dave and Seren." He mock whispers, "But when they disagree, I'll go with Seren."

Everyone laughs at that.

"I finally got this one tied down," Barbara says.

And everyone cheers.

It's a really lovely wedding—no rain, no strange

outbursts. No bizarre displays or awkward interchanges. Just a little boring, and really, really cute.

Of course, the wedding dinner, which is inside in the ballroom, is when the alcohol comes out. I'm as surprised as everyone else when, after moving into the ballroom with Bea at my side, the bride unties something around her waist and the bottom half of her dress just drops to the ground in a bright red puddle.

"Now it's time to have a little fun." Barbara waves at the band in the corner and they start to play. "And you should probably brace yourselves. Apparently some of the family's planning to toast us."

"In spite of our best efforts." Bentley groans. "They're a gregarious bunch."

There's some jeering and laughter, but most everyone starts looking for their seat. There are little placards, but they're small. Bea's waving me over, presumably having found ours, when someone taps my shoulder.

When I turn around, it's the man I've been preparing to see, the future senator of New York, more than likely. "Easton." He purses his lips. "I'm not happy to see you here."

"No?"

His nostrils flare. "I think I was pretty clear. You should've broken up with my granddaughter as I asked."

"And yet, I have no intention to."

"You think I'm being a tyrant," he says. "I understand that from your perspective, it feels that way. But trust me when I say that I know better than you what she needs in her life, and you're all wrong for Bea. It's not just about my campaign."

"How am I wrong for her?" I spread my arms. "I'm not deformed. I'm not a pervert. I hold down a job." I shrug. "I'm educated, and polite, and I love her."

He scowls. "Yes, you've said, but Bea needs someone who puts her needs first. She needs someone who's solid. A family man."

Before I can even tell him exactly how I've put her first, Bea steps next to me. "Grandfather."

He sighs. "Beatrice. I'm just having a word with—"

"No." She folds her arms. "I forbid it."

❧ 22 ❧

BEA

When I saw my grandfather moving toward Easton, I knew what I needed to do. I nearly dropped our nameplates and then scrambled across the room, waving people off rudely.

When I draw near, I hear my grandfather, spewing nonsense as usual. "Bea needs someone who puts her needs first. She needs someone who's solid. A family man."

As if he has any idea what I need. Or even more ridiculous, as if he cares. Before poor Easton has to take one more second of abuse, I take his arm. "Grandfather."

My grandfather sighs. "Beatrice. I'm just having a word with—"

"No." I fold my arms. "I forbid it."

"Pardon me?" He's always saying that. It's his polite way of saying 'I reject your premise. Try again.' Only, I'm done trying to please him. Done for good.

"I said, you're not allowed to talk to *my boyfriend*. I'm worried about what you might say, and I don't want you talking to the man I love."

Easton freezes beside me. In hindsight, it might not have been the best time or place to tell him that I love him, too.

"You don't want *me* talking to him?"

But I can't back down now. "You have a track record of saying all the wrong things."

"I have a record of saying—" Grandfather splutters. "That's rich, coming from you."

"I'm sure you threatened him already," I say. "I'm not sure quite what you're willing to do, but I'm guessing whatever it was would constitute a massive violation of due process." I step closer. "And you should think very carefully about all the things I know that might harm you before you threaten anyone in my life again."

"Before I threaten. . ." His eyes are wide, his lips open.

"Mom is the tip of the iceberg. I could tell them about how you always left me in her care. I could tell the media how you threatened my foster parents. I could tell them so many things that you don't even know I know, from the mess with that oil company, to the things I heard you doing with the much-too-young woman I saw leaving your house six years ago. It was the week Grandmother was out of town with her friends. Florida, I think you said she was?"

Chew on that, old man.

"Beatrice Cipriani—"

"From now on, I'm going to be called Beatrice Fansee," I say. "They may not be able to adopt me, but Dave and Seren have been my parents for a very long time now. You can either get on board, or I'll throw you right under the bus with a smile on my face."

He swallows, straightens, glances around at the

people watching us quietly, and nods. "I can see that tonight is not the right time to discuss this."

I lean closer, drop my voice, and say, "And if I get even the smallest whiff that you're bullying a local New York business to get your way, you had better believe that would be shared far and wide. A governor persecuting a New York business to further his own agenda would be an impeachable offense, and I'd be the first in line to testify."

Grandfather's completely unable to disguise his fury as he stomps away, and when he reaches my cardboard-cutout grandmother's side, Grandmother grabs her bag without so much as a complaint and they head for the door.

Good riddance.

"I'm sorry," I say. "I know that seemed nasty, but if you had any idea what a terrible person he is, you'd know it was a long time in coming."

Easton shakes his head. "It was glorious."

"I hope he didn't threaten you with anything too horrible."

His smile's broad. "You know, he tried, but I actually might owe him a thank you for that."

"Why?"

"It was the incentive I needed to stand up to my own personal Goliath."

"Oh?"

"I signed an agreement this morning obligating me to sell my shares of Sacrifice Nothing—and my parents to sell their shares—to a friend of mine and his father. You heard us talking the other day."

"Wait." I grab his hand. "You didn't."

"I got the idea when your grandfather tried to bully me, but honestly." He shakes his head. "It's very freeing.

I'm going to start over, and this time, I'm not going to take the company public. I'm going to find another latency, and I'm going to make that company exactly what I want."

"But Easton, your whole life has been that company."

"Not anymore it's not." He's looking into my eyes. "It never should have been, and believe me. I'm getting a very, *very* large pile of money to ease any anxiety I have about it."

"I can't even remember when I met the groom." Dave's voice from the front of the room washes over us, and I realize I should *not* be up here, chatting while Aunt Barbara and Uncle Bentley's wedding is underway. I've had my moment, but the rest of the moments are for them.

Easton and I find our seats pretty quickly.

I still feel a little bad about Easton selling his company, but surely it's not too late to stop that from happening. Then I'm able to watch, eating the amazing salads the waitstaff keep bringing out, first a strawberry salad, and then a pasta salad, while our family members stand up and talk about Uncle Bentley and Aunt Barbara.

As I listen, something strange happens.

I can hear it, the similarity between what everyone says about them.

The stories kind of converge in my brain, and a melody emerges. A melody that *is* Bentley and Barbara. It's their devotion. It's their patience. It's their enduring kindness. Their frustration and weariness with the world, and then their joy in turning toward one another.

It's how individually, they're all less, but as a family, they're *enough*.

I stand up, patting Easton's arm, and cross the edge

of the room to where the band's playing softly. Luckily, there's a keyboard. "Can I borrow this?"

The poor player blinks, and then nods. He stands up and steps back toward the wall. When Killian stops talking, which frankly is a relief, I step into the gap. "I'm Beatrice," I say into the microphone. "And I wasn't sure whether I'd get an invite, since the first time I met Uncle Bentley, I threatened to cut his throat."

That gets everyone's attention.

"When I first came to live with Mom and Dad, I didn't think I belonged there. I figured it was just a matter of time before I packed up my junk and found a new place to stay, with new people to annoy. The idea that I might have found my family." I choke up, but I forge ahead. "It hadn't even occurred to me."

Jake catches my eye, and he's not smiling. He looks sad.

"But you know, that never happened. No matter what dumb things I said, no matter what idiotic things I did, like threatening Uncle Bentley, Mom and Dad kept right on loving me. And Uncle Bentley, not three weeks after I threatened his life, came to my very first birthday party."

I drop my fingers on the keys of the keyboard.

"I'm not sure either of you will remember what you gave me for my birthday." This time, my eyes well with tears. "But Uncle Bentley, you had heard I liked music, so you bought me a keyboard, not unlike this one." I place my hands on the keys.

"It was one of the best gifts I ever gave," Uncle Bentley says.

"And Aunt Barbara, you gave me a pair of headphones to connect to the keyboard. That's probably the only reason no one took the thing away, because I had no idea what I was doing at first."

Everyone laughs.

"For a long time, I didn't want to play in front of anyone. I'll be honest, I still don't really enjoy this part. I like to make up songs, and I like to play them—but I do it in the peace and quiet of my own family room. For a long time, that's where my songs stayed."

I point at the wall.

"Over there, in that pile, you'll find the panic-gift I bought you. I think you might like it, but who knows? The gift I wanted to give you, a song, just didn't come to me. Not until I watched you. Not until I heard all your guests talking about the love you share and about the family you've built."

I play the opening chord. It's hopeful. It's bright. And then it segues into something mournful. Something tragic. I don't have words yet, but I think some songs are better without words. It's pure emotion.

Like me, Uncle Bentley and Aunt Barbara had some rough times. They felt alone, they felt unloved, and they felt unworthy. I could tell in the way they joked. I could tell in the way they smiled as Dad kissed Mom. I play that sorrow into the beginning.

But then the hope comes back. The chords progress into something lighter. Something tentative, something new.

And then comes the real transition. The key signature from the tragic and the key signature from the hopeful combine, and the harmony meets the melody. The sorrow and the joy combine to form something more. Strength.

That's what I'll call this song.

Strength.

When I play the final chords, I stand up. "My mom and dad were there for me, lending me their strength, lending me their faith when I didn't have any of my own. And you two—I can feel it. Together, you're just as strong as Mom and Dad. You're better together than you were apart, and you'll only grow stronger." I shift to look at Ricki and Nikki. "You may have times you doubt, moments of fear, but I promise you that eventually, you'll realize that their strength is also yours."

I turn back toward Aunt Barbara and Uncle Bentley. "I'm so happy for all of you. I'm delighted that I'll be around to watch as you only grow stronger. Congratulations and best wishes for the years ahead of you."

When I walk back to my seat, Uncle Bentley starts clapping, and then everyone else joins in. It's the first, and probably the last, time that I've ever been happy to perform.

But when we finish eating, I notice that Octavia has tried to call me four times. I'm not sure she's ever called me before. She's always just texted. When I slide to my texts, I read hers. CHECK YOUR EMAIL.

So I do.

And buried between something from Tractor Supply Company—how I got on their list I will never know— and Ann Taylor Loft is an email that says ***Finalist: Sony Music Record Competition.***

I don't squeal. I'm proud of that.

I do, however, drop my phone.

Luckily, the screen doesn't even crack. The rest of the night is a complete wash, though. I can't think about the wedding, not anymore. All I can think about is going up on that stage in front of who knows how many, being live-streamed to many more, and playing my own song, with lyrics I wrote, in the hopes of getting an album of my own.

Things in my life have been going so well, this is sure to nosedive.

I start trying to brace for it.

23

BEA

There are sixteen days between the wedding and the finals performance.

Each and every day is an agony.

"Do you feel ready?" Easton's face is bright and happy in the lights from the stage. I know he's here to support me. I know he's trying to be helpful.

I might punch him on the nose.

"Is that the wrong thing to ask?" He cringes. "Sorry. This is the first time my girlfriend has ever been preparing to perform in the hopes of winning a record deal."

Octavia laughs.

I scowl at her. "How are you not more nervous?"

She shrugs. "I've been on stage a lot, and also, I'm not harboring any of the false hope you are."

"It's not false hope," Easton says. "Your song is *amazing*."

"And you're not biased at all." Octavia rolls her eyes.

"I'm not," Easton says, insistent in his delusion.

"I'm ready," I say. "Or at least, as ready as I'm going to be."

"You've had it memorized since, well. All along," Octavia says. "It would help if you'd stop changing things, though."

"It's just a tweak," I say. "Because that one spot where the C goes into—"

"Has always bugged you," Octavia says. "You said."

I sigh. "I'm being annoying. I know."

"I just don't want to sing the wrong note," she says. "When you look like me, you don't need to give them any excuse to vote against you."

I step closer. I run my hand over the shoulder of her dress. Like the first time I ever saw her, she's wearing an asymmetrical dress that covers her left shoulder. She has shown her shoulder to me, and I understand her desire. The seams of the grafts are. . .unsettling. "You look absolutely gorgeous." And it's true. Her dress is a pale blue chiffon, and it exactly matches her eyes. Her hair's a rich, faceted brown that makes her eyes pop even more.

She wanted to wear a mask over the left side of her face, but I have consistently refused.

"I still think," she says, "that the mask would be a good idea. I could take it off at the end if you insist, but then the song would be the focus."

I shake my head. "You should be the focus. Your voice is what makes the song. I haven't met another single person who could sing those notes—no, not sing them. *Nail them*. This song was literally written for you. So go out there as you, all of you, and own it. You're spectacular, Octavia."

As if there's someone directing this for us, they call our number. "Number eight, you're on deck."

Unlike the jingle contest, with its two hundred entries, this had literally thousands of hopefuls. They've narrowed it down to a top forty, but the competition is fierce.

"How does anyone ever break out?" Easton's shaking his head as he follows us to the edge of the stage. "The pressure. The numbers. The odds aren't great."

"Thanks, honey." I start to walk past him, and he grabs me, circles my waist with his hands, and dips me. My heart is pounding when he presses a kiss against my lips.

"You, Beatrice Fansee, are the most talented woman I've ever met. Now go show all them what I already know. The other performers should just go home."

It helps.

Having someone watching on the side stage, having Jake and Emerson, Elizabeth, Ardath, Dave, Seren, and even Killian in the audience, it all helps. Even if we mess up, even if we come in dead last, they'll still be cheering for us.

I squeeze Octavia's hand.

The music for the band in front of us is so loud, I can barely hear that she's running through one of her vocal warm-ups. It's like she can't help herself. She's been flawless in every practice, in every warm-up. Her voice alone would make a heavenly chorus jealous, and she's still nervous.

Something about that calms me.

"Alright, you gorgeous monster," I whisper. "Let's go show those beasts out there what they came here to experience. Let's open their eyes."

Her smile's tentative, but it's genuine.

When the music cuts, we take our first steps onto the stage.

As the applause for the song in front of us fades, I'm seated at the piano. Just like we discussed, Octavia's standing sideways so the audience can only see her 'good' side.

I keep the notes light. Sharp and haunting, but bright. When Octavia's voice joins me, it hits like a cool stroke along my spine.

⁂

The world is full of beauty.
    The world is full of peace.
The world is full of light and joy,
That almost never cease.
You made me lots of promises.
You made them all come true.
I can hardly imagine living in
A world devoid of you.

⁂

But when the music segues, when the chords shift, she turns too. She looks out at the audience, and their gasp is a palpable thing. I keep playing, but something inside me curls up as her voice shifts, too. It's sharp, it's dark, and it sounds dangerous.

⁂

The world is dark and terrifying.
    All your promises were lies.
The ones who talked of beauty,
Were the first to avert their eyes.
The face you said was gorgeous,
You now cringe and turn away.
The world has made it ugly,

Your gorgeous monstrosity.

⚜

The transition back into beauty is smooth. It's clear. It's strong. I can see out of the corner of my eye that Octavia has shifted again. We didn't discuss this, but she turns so that only her good side is facing the audience.

She once told me that it's hard for people to look at her. Seeing her face, her injury, pains them. In this moment, that statement pains me, truly. I play through the misery, but it hurts.

When she reenters the song, her tone cuts like a blade. This time, instead of just bringing beauty, the words condemn.

You told me I was gorgeous.
You told me I was beloved.
You said you would be faithful.
No matter what the world did.
All the joy inside me,
My hope for a brighter day,
The monster consumed it all,
And I became both beast and prey.

⚜

I've boosted this second to last transition. I do layer the angry and the lovely, but I also add a few twinges of accusation. Octavia's right—this music evolves as we play it together. I suppose when it's played by the creator, it's the way it should be.

294

This is by far the best version we've ever had. Her voice, when it returns, feels like a gut punch.

❧

The world is dark and terrifying.
* That much, at least, was true.*
But those who spoke of beauty,
Were the villains, not me and you.
It's not my face at fault here
It's those who glare and jeer
The real beast lives inside of them,
They get back what they give.

❧

I extend the transition a little, and I glance out at the audience. They're all watching, attention rapt. Not a single word. No murmurs. They're invested. My heart soars at the sight. Maybe the world is more beautiful than we knew. Maybe it's lovelier than we dared hope.

I finally play it, the call to action at the end, the final rise. Octavia spreads her arms wide, lifts her chin, and she belts it.

Stop looking to slay monsters,
* And start working on yourself.*
The gorgeous monstrosity you should fear
Is the one staring back at you in the mirror.
Work on the creature only you can tame,
And when you see the ugliness,
Call it by name, oh, call it out by name.

W hen Octavia sings the final line, she doesn't turn back. Not this time. She stares out at the audience, holding their gaze. Only when the last note plays does she relax her shoulders and incline her head. When I walk away from the piano, she doesn't walk with me to the edge of the stage. She grabs my hand and holds it high.

The audience cheers, maybe louder than I've ever heard. People stand, like they do at the end of a play. It's a good moment. It gives me hope—more hope than I thought I'd really have that we might win. Like the jingle contest, the audience votes count for something, thirty percent in this case.

To be honest, the audience votes are really the only ones I care about.

I think they're the thing Octavia needs most. The knowledge that she was wrong about the world we live in. She may have endured pain most of us can't comprehend. She may have watched as her dreams slithered down the drain, but it's not over. The world sees her beauty, real beauty. Beauty she wasn't gifted, beauty she created.

The next two and a half hours are the longest of my life.

Longer than when I sat in Serendipity Inn waiting for my mom.

Longer than the weeks I prepared myself to be taken away from there, dragged back to Grandfather's.

Longer, even, than the days and days I waited for Jake to trust me in school.

But finally, it's time. The fortieth song has been sung. The audience is exhausted—I can see it. It's late. Nearly ten o'clock on a Tuesday. Why they chose a Tuesday for this, I will never understand.

It does come though, the moment when the announcer stands up. He smooths his hair back from his face, and he grabs the mic. "Well, folks, as you know, the audience votes count for thirty percent of each song's score. The judges over there have scored the songs as well, and they're each worth a ten-percent total. They're Sony executives and talent, and they're better than anyone else I can imagine at picking rising stars from a pile of talent." The guy beams. "They chose me not two years ago, so they clearly have good taste."

His new album just dropped, so I should know who he is, but all I can think is what on earth he must be thinking, wearing sneakers to something like this.

"Nikes with a suit?" Easton feels me. He shakes his head at my side. "Bad call."

"Without further ado, I'm going to announce our winner for tonight."

Someone from the judges' table waves and shakes his head.

"My bad. Apparently first, I'm announcing the runner up." He grins, and I can see a little more why they chose him. I wish it was all talent, but clearly it's not always talent or intelligence. "Okay, so our first runner up will get a two thousand dollar prize, as well as an article written about them." He smiles again. "And for tonight, I'm pretty pleased to announce that our runner up of the Sony Music Breakout Album Contest is Gorgeous Monstrosity by Beatrice Cipriani and Octavia Rothschild." He spreads his arms wide. "Where are you two? I can't be the only person in this room who had chills when they performed."

The audience is cheering, but my heart is broken.

Runners up? Again?

I know there are forty finalists. I know runner up is good, but *how?* Were they in a different auditorium? Easton shepherds the two of us toward the edge of the stage and then sort of shoves us out on the platform. The entire time we're standing there, I just keep thinking how unfair it is.

And when they call the group who had the most insipid, most *boring*, most predictable song I've ever heard, but with a frontman with shiny hair and horse teeth, I'm done.

The world might have seen our beauty, but our flaws matter more.

After it's over, when I'm stumbling trying to walk down the stairs, a man with white hair catches my elbow. "Philip Owens," he says. "Executive with Sony."

"Okay," I say.

"I just wanted to say congratulations to you on that very moving song. I hear you're the one who wrote it— that you brought in the other lady because of her voice."

I want to rip my arm away from him, but I settle for simply shaking him off.

"Listen. I wanted to catch you now that you're alone for a moment." He smiles in what I'm guessing he thinks is a fatherly way.

It's not a good start.

"Is it true that Octavia's just the vocal talent. Is that right?"

I frown. "It's not. She helped me quite a lot."

"Still, you wrote the song, right?"

I shrug.

"We'd be very interested in talking to you about a record deal."

"I don't understand. I thought it was the grand prize winner only who got a deal."

"We're not interested in signing Gorgeous Monstrosity," he says. "We are interested in signing you, Beatrice Cipriani, as a solo artist." He tilts his head. "Any relation to the Governor, by the way?"

I don't even dignify that with a response. "You want to talk to *me* about a record deal, just not Octavia?"

He swallows.

"She has the most incredible, the most unparalleled voice I have ever heard in my entire life, and her feedback was critical to me in fine-tuning the song."

"Yes, well." He shakes his head. "It's complicated."

"Because of her face?" I want to slap him, or better yet, burn his face. "Is that why?"

He shrugs. "So much of what we do is controlled by optics. Music videos, social media, all of it. I hate it, but it is what it is."

"No." I turn so I'm facing him directly. "In case you couldn't tell what I was saying, because I'm looking right at you, I want to be clear on my optics. Not only no, but *hell no* to your suggestion that I sign without Octavia. Was that clear enough for you?" I shake my head in disgust and spin around to leave.

I nearly slam into Octavia where she was standing off-stage in the dark.

I feel sick. Like, I might actually puke.

"Octavia." Oh, no. I'm going to bawl right here, on stage right. "I—I didn't know you were here."

She just hugs me. "You should've said yes." She's crying when she shoots past me and out the door.

24

EASTON

I almost backed out of the sale of Sacrifice Nothing. After all, Beatrice threatened her grandfather, and it worked. The video died, the board calmed down. Things could've gone back to how they were.

Sometimes, though, the change that's forced on us is precisely the one we need. I decide to go through with it. Rid myself of my parents' involvement. Eliminate the misery of answering to a board, and start over.

It's a pretty clean break.

With the way our companies align, I have confidence that the acquisition will be a relatively seamless integration, even if they're mostly located in France and we're mostly headquartered here. I'm stuck doing as much as twenty hours a week of consulting for a full year, but I'll be paid well enough that I hope they won't need me too often.

I haven't found my next market latency yet, though I'm looking, but I have found an interim project I deem worthy of my time and investment. Shortly after the catastrophic miscarriage of justice they called an album contest—that song gave every single person in the entire auditorium chills in the best way—Jake came to me with a proposal.

"I'm going to take this to Bea, but my producer's worried that our investors might object. He won't let me ask for it unless I have a fallback plan."

"Take what to Bea?"

"The movie I'm filming is about a kid who wound up in the mob at an early age. He's struggling now that he's grown. He meets a woman who's totally good, and he's falling for her, but he thinks he's too broken to be with her." He pauses. "I want their song to be the title track. I'd like to have the two of them do the music for the whole movie, if I'm being honest, because I think they'd nail it, but at least for the opening and closing, I want their song."

"Why would the investors back out?"

"Because I want the movie to find a label to put it out, at least as a single, and have the release coincide with the movie release. I think it could be synergistic, right? Like, as the movie does well, people will listen to the song, and as it trends. . ."

"That leads people to the movie."

He nods.

"You're not as dumb as you look," I say.

Jake beams. "I knew I'd grow on you."

"You have, actually," I say. "I hated you at first, and just last night, I handed you that popcorn bowl, and I didn't even want to spit in it first."

"You know, right after you started dating, I tried to break you up."

I did not expect him to say that.

"Bea's the smartest person I know. She just laughed, and she told me something I was too dumb to have realized. She told me that I'm her family, and that I wasn't ever in love with her—I just didn't want to lose her."

That's a lot of information to process.

"She was right, as always, and I just wanted to mention that I'm not going anywhere. Ever. Bea and me, we're a package deal."

"I know the entire Fansee family's pretty close."

Jake shakes his head. "I mean, yeah, they are, but no. It's not the same. Bea and me, she's probably my only *real* family in the whole world. I'd murder for her. I'd die for her. And what's more, I will live for her—anything she needs, I'll do it."

"Did she tell you that the label offered her a deal?"

Jake frowns. "What? Why would she turn it down?"

"They offered *her* a deal—not Octavia."

Jake's entire face darkens. "You're kidding."

I shake my head. "It wasn't a good moment, and for almost a week, Octavia wouldn't answer Bea's calls, because she heard them make the offer."

Jake swears under his breath. "That's messed up."

He's right. It is. "The two of them are talking again at least, and I think they even wrote a new song last week."

"That's good for me," Jake says. "Look, I have to go out of town again tomorrow, but I'm going to send you some paperwork for the movie. Investment stuff. Is that alright?"

"Whatever you need," I say. "But I am curious. I thought you might be upset she turned the offer down. That's why she didn't tell you. She thought you'd yell."

Jake's shoulders droop. "I've known Bea for a long time, and she's been a musical genius that entire time. But I have never, not *ever*, seen her this excited or this passionate. They may have just met, but she loves that

Octavia woman, and she's good for Bea. She really *saw* Bea that night, at the jingle thing. It made me angry at the time, but maybe we miss the things the people close to us really need. Nothing else would have fired her up to actually write the songs that consume her. Believe me —I've tried everything since that first song she wrote launched my career."

"You think she did the right thing, turning the label down?"

"I think she did the only thing Bea could ever have done." Jake shrugs. "It's who she is—she's just like her mother."

"How so?" I ask.

Jake frowns.

"I've never met her mother, so I don't really know what you mean, but I'd like to understand."

"You've met Seren," Jake says. "Above all else, she's loyal, and Bea got that from her."

I'm such an idiot. I was thinking her real mom, but Seren *is* her real mom, the mom of her heart, anyway. I see it now, what he means. They're both fierce, and they're both happier surrounded by loved ones but not in the spotlight themselves.

I think about the story with the knife. When push comes to shove, Bea pushes back. Always.

"You didn't say 'our' mom," I finally realize. "I thought you meant her birth mom, because you said Bea is like *her* mom."

"I don't have a mom." Jake's words are simple. Unemotional, like he really believes it.

"No?" I think he's wrong, but he's the only one who can come to grips with that.

"Look, I've got to get ready to go, but I'll be in touch, alright?"

"Will you tell Bea?"

"I'd rather not tell her you're even involved if I can help it," Jake says.

"No?"

He shrugs. "She'll see it as a pity thing, if we do. She'll feel like her boyfriend has to come in and pay for her dreams, and that'll ruin it."

"But I actually think it would be a good investment."

Jake's expression is pained. "You're an optimist, then."

"How so?"

"In your heart of hearts, you believe in people. You think they'll look past their fear, beyond their own baggage, and see something beautiful."

"I guess I am an optimist," I say. "Is that bad?"

"It's cute," Jake says. "Probably misguided, but cute."

"So do you think I'm throwing my money away if I invest in this?"

"I told them I'd take half my fee," Jake says. "And they can use the other half to produce the record."

"So you're as stupidly optimistic as I am."

He shrugs. "They're the chumps. I'd have given them all of it. For Bea? Gladly."

"Why?" I ask. "Because she's your family?"

His brow furrows. "It's more than that. That song— it's right. If we want the world to change, if we want it to be better, that's on us. We have to change it. No one else is going to do it."

Jake's not the person I thought he was when we first met, and he's not even quite the person I thought he was when we really started talking the first time. I understand a little more about why Bea puts up with him.

"Hey, I have a question for you."

"Oh, man." Jake runs a hand through his hair. "You're going to propose, aren't you?"

I stare.

"Look, I'm not the best guy, but I'm pretty good at reading people, and you seem like the kind of guy who has been carrying around a ring in his pocket since the first date."

He's rude. "I still don't have a ring, but you're right that I've known for a while."

"You've been holding off because you don't want to scare her?"

"Maybe."

"Well, I can't help you. Bea's a hard read on that. You know her birth mom has had like a zillion boyfriends, and none of them have been more important than getting high. Certainly Bea has never been more important to her than either a boyfriend *or* getting high."

"Does she not want to get married, then?"

Jake shrugs. "I really have no idea."

"You've never talked about it?"

"That's not the kind of thing we talk about. Maybe with Ardath?"

Ardath and I have never said more than three words to each other, even at family dinners. She's not the most talkative. Honestly, I've never seen her talk to Bea either, or heard them chatting on the phone. "That would be. . ."

"Weird," Jake says.

I nod. "Yeah, Ardath kind of scares me."

He chuckles. "Me too."

"I'll have to go in blind."

Jake nods. "I know she cares a lot about you, and I think that, even if she isn't ready, it's got to be nice to know you are."

"She told you I said I love you first."

His smirk confirms it.

"I'm not chill," I say. "I have no coolness, not anywhere inside of me."

"I mean, you're a cool guy, but yeah, you're pretty tightly wound."

"I don't even know what kind of ring to get her."

"Now, there, you have a secret weapon, right?"

I have no idea what he means.

"You have a sister."

"But not all girls like the same things."

Jake groans. "This stuff is too hard."

But I do have an idea, so I decide to run with it. "You said you'd rather I not be involved in the initial presentation, right?"

Jake narrows his eyes. "This is going somewhere interesting, I can tell."

I hope he's right.

But most of all, I hope that Bea's real mom was able to repair the damage her birth mom did. I really hope Bea doesn't just turn me down flat. I'm not one hundred percent positive that's something I can recover from—a complete rejection. Which means that proposing carries a real risk, because in my entire life, I've never wanted someone to say yes more.

25

BEA

It takes three days for her to pick up my calls, and more than two weeks for Octavia to finally come over and meet me before work to try a new song. When she walked through the door, she acted like nothing had ever happened. I almost insisted that we talk through things, but then I decided I'd let her lead this part. It's not my wound.

"You know, some people can go weeks or even months without having a new song idea," she says.

"People can, I guess," I say. "But not me."

"So you're saying your whole life. . ."

"I've had songs rolling around in my head."

"What did you do with them?"

I take three steps and kick a box in the corner.

"Wait," she says. "Are all of those. . ." Her eyebrows rise.

"Mom and Dad have a few more boxes in the attic. A lot of them aren't very good."

She tries to bend over and lift the lid.

"Focus." I shove the box with my foot, sliding it under the edge of the piano. "I said I had a *new* song."

"Right, but I want to see what those look like."

"They're crap compared to the song I just wrote, I promise."

She drops her hands on her hips. "I will sing this song with you if you agree to let me rummage around in that box for half an hour."

"Ten minutes."

She arches one eyebrow. "Half an hour, or I walk."

I roll my eyes. "Fine. Half an hour."

She beams, and it's totally worth it. We're just finishing the initial run through when Jake breezes through the door. It's strange, because he's supposed to be filming. But even stranger than Jake being where he shouldn't is Jake bringing *a friend*.

"Who's that?" I ask.

"Adam Forrest, this is my sister, Bea, and this is their lead vocal, Octavia Rothschild."

"I've heard a lot about you," Adam says, extending his hand.

"Wait, Adam Forrest, as in the producer?" Octavia looks like someone just slapped her. Her eyes are round and her good cheek is bright red. I wonder whether the burned side doesn't flush as well. It makes sense, I suppose.

"The very same," Adam says. "We had to come to the City for a scene in Central Park, and this joker convinced me I had to meet you."

"Me?" I ask.

"Both of you," he says. "He's pretty persuasive when he wants to be."

I stand. "Why did you need to meet us?"

Adam shoots a pretty crusty look at Jake. "You didn't tell them?"

"Tell us?"

"You do a better job at all that," Jake says.

Adam looks ready to spit nails. "Look, he says you're talented songwriters and musicians, and he wants you to do the music for the movie. On top of that, he wants us to push our production company a little—we have an affiliated record label."

I blink.

Octavia exhales in a large whoosh.

"Just sing your song," Jake says.

"Which one?"

He scowls.

"It's way better on a stage," I excuse. "It's not the same in the middle of a living room."

"Make do," Jake says, widening his eyes and mouthing something I can't quite get.

"Fine," I say. "Whatever."

I whip the sheet music out, but Octavia's looking at me like I'm speaking Swahili. "Right here?" she hisses. "I haven't even warmed up."

I shrug and start to play. I'm banking on her training kicking in to override her shock and dismay.

It works, mostly. She misses the first cue, but that's fine. I do a little doodle and swing back around. She catches it this time, and we're off. All in all, the dynamics and showmanship can't compare, but it sounds alright.

"Do you have anything else?"

"We just tried a new song for the first time today," I say.

Octavia's shaking her head. "I've sung it exactly one time. You have whole sections with no lyrics yet."

"What about those two you wrote the week before the contest?" Jake tosses his head at the box.

I sigh. "Fine. We could do those."

In the end, Adam Forrest is very persistent. We perform at least a dozen songs for him before he plops down on the couch, staring at his hands. "He wasn't kidding."

"About what?" I ask.

"The face. The songs. The voice." He shakes his head. "Exactly like you said."

Jake shrugs. "I don't exaggerate that stuff."

"He exaggerates *everything* else," Adam says. "So I'm sure you can excuse my incredulity."

"Not everything," Jake mutters.

"Look." Adam stands up suddenly. "You two need to come do what you just did for me, but for the label. I can get you a meeting tomorrow."

"*Tomorrow?*" I ask. "I have work tomorrow."

"So do I," Octavia says.

Adam stares at us.

Jake's shaking his head vigorously behind him, like he's suffering from some kind of seizure.

"I can call in sick?" Octavia asks.

"I guess I can too."

"Good. So you'll be in Hollywood, at the studio tomorrow at two."

"They can just fly back with us," Jake says.

"How fun for us," Adam says.

And just like that, we're hopping a ride on the studio's jet to California. Octavia insists on hauling two-thirds of the stupid box with us, even though I told her most of the songs are junk. She sorts them into two piles on the flight over.

"What are you doing?" I ask.

"This pile is the ones that need to be reworked." It's got half a dozen sheets of paper in it.

"What's that one?" I point at the stack of almost a hundred pages.

"These are my favorites."

I roll my eyes. "Very funny."

"I'm not kidding." She sighs so heavily that it makes her hair blow back on her head. "You are now my favorite artist."

"Well, we're a package deal, girlfriend, so pat yourself on the back." I'm not going to lie to myself though. Hearing that from her feels pretty good. "Besides. You can't tell whether they're good by looking at them."

"Most people couldn't," she says. "But I can."

When I finish rolling my eyes, twenty minutes later, I start thinking about what's about to happen. "Do you really think we'll get an album?" I whisper. "Because that's wild."

"You should be thinking about what kind of people you'd be willing to work with," Jake says.

"Why would we work with anyone else?" I ask.

"Your sound is balanced, clear, and well articulated," Adam says. "But it's not full enough. They'll bring in a bass, a drummer, and probably a guitar to supplement the piano, at least, if you insist on keeping it?"

I nod vigorously. "I can strum a banjo, but if we nix the piano, I'm out."

"Keyboard, probably," Adam says.

I shake my head. "Piano."

"We'll talk about it," he says, which is not very promising. Isn't that what people say when they intend to totally ignore you?

I text Easton the second we land. Things were so hectic with the last-minute packing that I didn't even tell him I was leaving. JUST LANDED IN L.A. JAKE

GOT US A MEETING WITH A RECORD LABEL—
HE WANTS TO USE OUR SONG FOR HIS MOVIE.

THAT'S AMAZING, Easton texts back right away.
GOOD LUCK.

MEETING IS TOMORROW, I say, BUT WE ARE
EXCITED.

Jake offers to put us up at his L.A. apartment, which
he assures me is way nicer than ours, but Octavia and I
both refuse. "We'll share a hotel room," Octavia says.
"We have some work to do in case they want to hear
more than just a song or two."

"Where are you going to find a hotel with a piano?"
Jake asks.

"Does your apartment have a piano?"

He shakes his head.

We have to call nineteen places, but we finally find
one that has a piano in a conference room they say we
can use as late as we'd like. And we do. We don't go to
bed until almost two-thirty in the morning.

"At least I feel more prepared," Octavia says.

"Do you think we're only getting this meeting
because of Jake?" The idea makes me a little uncom-
fortable.

"We got the last meeting because of him," she says.
"The one where that Adam guy made us play a dozen
things. We're getting this meeting because the last one
went well. If you'd just been some kind of mediocre
scribbler, he'd have told Jake to shove it."

I guess so. "That makes me feel a little better."

I've brushed my teeth and climbed into bed—lights
are out—when Octavia whispers. "You would already
have an album if it weren't for me."

It's the first time she's talked about it.

"Not a good one," I say. "I wrote those songs for you."

"Yeah, but there are other singers," she says. "Loads and loads of them. Talented ones."

"There are," I say. "And there are loads and loads of songwriters, too. You think I'm special, so why can't I think the same thing about you?"

She doesn't ask anything else, but I know she's still thinking it. That she's the liability. That she's the weak link.

I know, because I've felt like that most of my life.

The next morning, Jake calls me three times while I'm in the shower. I finally answer, my hair dripping all over the bathroom counter and my phone. "What?"

"The meeting got moved," he says. "They want you here by nine-thirty."

"Shoot."

"With Orange County traffic, you need to leave in the next fifteen minutes. Can you do that?"

My hair's not even close to dry, and my makeup looks. . .amateur in the extreme, but we step into a cab fourteen minutes after I hang up. We make the meeting with two minutes to spare. Jake's waiting, tapping his foot like a husband waiting for the kids to be ready for Sunday morning church. "You're here."

"Why the change?" I'm panting.

"They want you to record some things first, like a sound test." Jake's smiling, but it's forced. Why's it forced?

"This was Adam's idea," Octavia says.

Jake's flinch is so infinitesimal that if I didn't know him extremely well, I might have missed it. "He thinks it's a good idea to sell them on the songs first."

"Fine," she says. "Let's do it."

The process of recording an album in an actual studio is almost surreal. It's rough, and we're not really doing *all* the things, but the way they put it down—I'm amazed.

"What if we increased that." I point at the stabilizer. "And toned this down." I point at the compression aspect. "Just a hair."

"You have a real knack for that," the guy who was showing me what the different knobs and buttons do says. "Have you done this before?"

I shake my head. "Don't laugh, but I have a PreSonus Audiobox."

He does laugh. "That's a respectable hobby setup. The M7 condenser mic isn't bad."

"Really?"

He shrugs. "I mean, I think it's better for people who are doing, like, podcasts, but you can learn the basics with it."

But an hour and a half later, once we have some decent recordings, it's time for us to clear out. After a rather awkward lunch with Adam, who doesn't seem that pleased to still be dealing with this, we head over for the real meeting.

"I sent them the rough cuts." Adam's staring at his phone. "Stu loved it."

"Really?" Jake's nodding. "He's the one who never likes anything."

"But now they're going to see my face," Octavia says.

"I told them about it," Jake says.

"Nothing quite prepares you, though, does it?" Adam's grimacing.

I'm going to punch him.

"Stand down," Jake hisses. "He's on our side."

Even so, I can tell that this time, Octavia and I are both preparing ourselves for rejection. It hurt too bad last time, when I thought we had it in the bag. So when we meet Stu, Frances, and Eddy, I try not to get my hopes up too high.

"We really want something a little edgier for this movie," Eddy says. "I know Stu and Frances just care about the marketability of the songs, but I have to find something that really fits the tone of the movie. I liked that first track, the beast one, but the others are too. . ." He waves his hand through the air. "Too frivolous. Too happy."

"I think we can do a little edgier," I say.

"Adding the guitar, drums, and bass will go a long way," Adam says. "Remember that."

"Do you know how to write their parts?" Frances asks. "Some pianists are. . .not the best at integrating other sounds."

"I'm good at guitar," Octavia says. "Played for more than ten years."

That's a surprise. "And I often wish I could add some drums and percussion," I say. "I think we can do it."

"Fine." Stu leans closer. "I'll talk to publicity and marketing, but I think we can work this angle." He frowns, staring rather rudely. "Is that considered a disability?"

I'm ready to start swinging again, but Octavia looks remarkably unruffled. "The Social Security Blue Book lists significant burn injuries as an impairment, but I'm not eligible for benefits because the location of my burns does not preclude me from manual labor, for the most part, at least with reasonable accommodations."

"Wait, what does that mean?" Frances asks.

"I have severe photosensitivity," Octavia says, "for

example, but sunblock and a hat could mitigate the impact."

"Can you film a music video outside?"

"Of course," Octavia says, "but depending on the length and sun intensity, I might need special makeup or regular reapplication of sunblock."

Stu nods. "We can work with that."

"I'd rather we not try to cover up her face," I say. "It's uniquely beautiful, and we do not want to change that."

Octavia winces, but she doesn't look angry. I realize what I'm seeing—she's bracing herself for them to change their minds.

"I think we just have the one last stipulation," Frances says. "There's one investor who wants to meet you two and see you himself."

Octavia's lips compress.

"He was possibly the most excited about your song, but he would like to introduce himself. He's put up quite a bit of capital through the Private Equity firm that's sharing the costs with the studio, and we thought one small meeting wasn't too much to ask."

Octavia squares her shoulders.

I nod. "Sure. Is he here now?"

The three of them stand, and so does Adam. "We'll invite him in."

"Oh, wait," Jake says. "Costuming had that question."

"Costuming?" I frown. "Isn't that a little premature?"

"They wanted you to give them some input on some jewelry. One of our sponsors is a pretty well-known jeweler, and we'll be pushing their stuff in the music video and the movie."

"Your job is so weird," I say.

"Your job too, now." Jake drops a box in front of me. "Both of you need to pick your favorite ring from the box. Once you have, I can take it to them and let them know."

"Rings?" Octavia flips the lid up.

Eight diamond rings that look like engagement rings are lying flat on black velvet inside the heavy box.

"Geez. These look really expensive," I say. "Who's the jeweler?"

"Doesn't matter," Jake says. "We're not paid to care about that stuff."

I lean forward to look closer.

"This one for sure." Octavia picks the wide yellow gold band, made of a delicate filigree that almost looks like lace. The large oval diamond is almost nestled against it. The combination of flat gold, hammered finishes, and the delicate shape makes it look like something they might have worn in the early nineteen hundreds, at least, to me.

It suits her.

She has a classic, elegant beauty that reminds me of Katherine Hepburn or Elizabeth Taylor—if either of them was burned, I guess. Even her curls fall in soft waves, like the women back then.

I glance at the rings that are left.

One is a simple platinum band with a massive diamond. Tacky.

The next is probably the most boring ring I've ever seen. One big round stone, framed on either side by two smaller circles. Snooze.

Then there's a very sharp-looking one with a marquis diamond and slice-looking diamonds framing it on either side. Next to those are small squares. I feel like I could scratch myself seven ways from Sunday while wearing it. The dagger diamonds. That's what I'd call that one.

There's a very nice blue-center-stone ring with white

cushion-cut diamonds on either side. It looks like something my new sister-in-law Elizabeth would choose.

But the last ring, the one kind of shoved over on the end, is by far the strangest. I pick it up. It has a massive champagne-colored diamond in the center, and it's a large emerald shape. The prongs holding the golden stone are yellow gold, but next to it, pressed seamlessly against it on either side are two more diamonds cut in triangles, with the point dripping down on either side toward the finger. They're both flawless to the naked eye.

"I like this one," I say. "It's stunning in its own, unique way."

"Are you picking it because of the song?" Jake asks. "Or because you like it?"

"I think I like it because it fits the song—a song I wrote. A song I love. A song that speaks to who I am." I shrug. "Does it matter? Won't that make the marketing easier?"

"Actually," Easton says, strolling through the door at the back of the room. "That diamond has a name. It's called the Verona diamond."

"The—what?"

"It's rare, a flawless champagne diamond, and it's brilliant—reflecting double the light that most diamonds would reflect. The second I saw it, I thought of you."

I blink. "What are you doing here?"

"Me?" Easton bites his lip. "You haven't guessed?"

"You're the investor," Octavia says.

He shrugs. "They didn't need me, in fact. Jake brought me in just in case the other investors wanted to back out."

"Because of my face," Octavia says.

"No," Jake says. "Because of their own idiocy."

She sighs.

"But they didn't," Easton says. "I had to badger them into cutting me in on the deal. Peachtree complained and harangued, but finally, they took some of my money so I could be a part of things."

"And so you could. . ." Jake snaps his mouth shut.

"So I could propose to the woman of my dreams," Easton says. "I know we've barely known each other for more than two months."

"Well, I knew you for a year and change before that," I say.

"But next week is Thanksgiving, and our first date was in September," Easton says. "Some people would say this is crazy."

"Not me," Octavia whispers. "I think it's beautiful."

It's nice to know that she approves, at least, and clearly Jake does.

"What did she say?" a small muffled voice asks. "I can't hear. Turn the screen."

"What was that?" I ask.

"Dude, I said you had to be *quiet,*" Jake says. "You guys never keep your promises." But when he swivels his phone around, Mom and Dad, Emerson and Elizabeth, Ardath, and even Killian are all on a zoom. They wave.

When I squint, I realize Grandma and Grandpa Fansee are also there, and so is Barbara. They're absurd.

"What did she say?" Seren asks again. "Can you guys speak up?"

"Did you send out an invite to your whole email list?" I ask. "Did everyone know?"

"I told you California was a bad idea," Elizabeth says. "You should have just done it here."

"Can you all shut up long enough for me to ask her

properly?" Easton drops down on one knee. "You're already holding the ring, but I knew the moment we met that you were just as unique—no, more unique than that Verona diamond. It's perfect for you, just like you're perfect for me. Please, *please,* say you'll marry me. Because the other rings, they'll take back as returns, but that one, well. It cost a bundle, and I'm stuck with it even if you say no."

"Is that really true?" I glance at Jake's phone.

Elizabeth's shaking her head.

"A marriage founded on lies isn't a good one." I frown.

"Fine," Easton says. "But clearly you like that one best, so just put it on."

"No." I step toward him and pull him to his feet. "I like you the best." I smile. "The ring's just frosting on an already amazing cake."

"Except the frosting's the best part," Killian says. "The cake's just an excuse to eat it."

"Hush," Seren says. "I can barely hear as it is."

"Oh, she's going to say yes," Octavia says. "Just kiss her already."

"How embarrassing would it be if I said no?"

But Easton's sliding the ring on my finger, and everyone's cheering, and when he's done, I look up at him and nod. "Yes, alright. I'll marry you, Easton Moorland. But only because this ring is one of a kind."

He kisses me then, and like everything else in our lives, it's pretty darn special. Even with all the jeers, hoots, and hollers from my ridiculous family.

Actually, I wouldn't have it any other way.

A moment later, when waiters come in with trays covered in strawberries and cream, I can't help laughing. I suppose this is my life now—joy and laughter.

"Please tell me these are the twenty-dollar variety," I whisper.

"Even if they aren't," Easton hisses. "You don't have to worry anymore." His smile is the most beautiful thing I've ever seen.

The first key to the success of any good con is choosing your mark wisely. I hadn't been enrolled for very long when I spotted Beatrice. She was kind, she was open, and she was almost unbearably naive.

She was also alone and desperate for a friend.

As the new kid in school, it was pathetically easy to convince her that I too had no friends, and that I too really wanted one. Dad said we were in a hurry, so I didn't waste a lot of time. I started with the small signs right away.

A minor but persistent cough.

Fatigue, which as a side benefit got me out of pointless running in gym class. A little bit of wheezing.

But the clincher was that Bea wanted me to join choir with her. Of course, the second I tried to sing, my symptoms worsened. It only took me a week to get her entirely vested. And that's when I confessed that I was sick—no, I was dying.

"You need to see another doctor," Bea says, her eyes

utterly sincere. "Get a second opinion. Your dad should take you right away."

"No." I shake my head and step back, lifting my chin. Strong men are always a little defiant. "I won't waste his money like that."

"But Jake, you have to—"

"No." I shake my head this time. "Just drop it, Bea."

"You know what's wrong." She stares at me, her sorrow very real. I've done my job perfectly.

I shrug and try to walk off, knowing she'll stop me.

"Jake. Just tell me."

"Look, I always had asthma, but with my dad's job. . . His crew smoked. They all did. And with my asthma." I sigh. "The only thing that can save me is a lung transplant, and it's too expensive."

"How much?"

It was enough for the day of the big reveal. I had planted the seed. I cut the conversation off and ran home on cue. But when I get home that night, I feel almost *sick* about it.

"What's wrong?" my dad asks.

"Nothing."

"Something," he insists. He can always read my moods. "You can't lie to your one person."

One of the first things Dad taught me was that all con men had one person, *one* person they really loved. One person they cared about. That one person was their true north. It was the one person they could never betray, never con.

He's my person.

And I'm his.

It's always been Dad and me against the world, and one day, I'll be as good as he is at tricking stupid people

out of money they don't need. For now, I'm learning.
"It's just that the girl at school—"

"Bea, right?"

I nod.

"What about her?'

I don't want to say it. "I mean, I'm not sure she really has money."

"You said her parents own that fancy hotel."

I shrug. "But they're not really her parents, and anyway, I'm not sure if she can get them to help."

"Not really her parents?" he asks. "What does that mean?"

"They're like, her foster parents, or something."

Dad smiles. "Foster parents? They're suckers for sure, then."

But my unease didn't go away. Every day I spend, Bea cares more. She becomes more and more vested, and by the third week, she's already told her parents, over my objections. Her stepmom or foster mom or whatever actually comes to talk to me at lunch.

"You must be Jake." When she smiles, I can't help staring. It's dopey, but she's just *so* pretty. I haven't really met anyone quite that pretty before. Ever.

I nod.

"Well, I'm Seren Colburn—er. Fansee."

"Fancy?" I ask. "That's a weird name." Then I cough a little for good measure.

"Oh, you sweet thing. I'm so sorry about that cough. Bea tells me it won't go away."

I shrug. "It's fine."

She doesn't argue, but she starts sending little snacks for me with Bea's lunch. I made an impression. Every-thing's right on track when Dad's con and mine cross.

If we had realized, we might have avoided the worst. Unfortunately, we didn't figure out the connection until it was too late. What threw us off was the stupid tiny town crap. We had no way of knowing that Bea's stupid dad knew the real estate guy Dad was working.

Or that the real estate guy had a few good friends he trusted implicitly who helped him. The whole thing was a mess, and Dad got caught with his hand in the cookie jar, or that's what he said.

I'm there on the day Dad's taken away. He's in cuffs when they shove him into a car. I would have been freaking out, but he's just chatting with some uniformed officer.

They call a social worker to deal with me, and Bea's crying. I'm not sure whether she's more angry with me or mad at herself. That's pretty common, I think, when saps realize they've been conned. This is a little different because our plan failed. But the idea's the same.

The worst thing I could imagine was being stuck here to deal with the people I'd almost duped, but that's exactly how it goes down. Only, when I knew they'd be coming to yell at me, they don't.

Bea throws her arms around me, tears running down her face. "Does that mean you're not really sick?" She's beaming. "Because that's amazing news."

Any sane person would have yelled at me. Any normal person would have given me a pounding. But Bea, the idiot, she's *happy*.

"My dad's going to jail, dummy." I shove her. "Leave me alone."

"But you're not sick, right?" The way she looks up at me from the dirt, it brings that feeling back, the uncom-fortable, twisty one I had the first time I was bragging about how well I'd set things up. She looks like she's more worried about my well-being than about how I tricked her.

I roll my eyes and walk away.

Before anyone can come running after me, Bea's foster mom crouches down on the ground and holds out her hands to stop me. "Hold on just a moment, Jake."

"What?" My dad's right behind her, glaring at the officer who's asking him things.

And there's nothing I can do about it.

My one person's about to go away for a long time.

It's all my fault. Dad wouldn't ever have screwed up like this—I messed it up.

"Your father may be unable to care for you for quite some time." She's amazing at stating the obvious.

"Yeah."

"Bea thinks the world of you."

Because she's a moron.

"She begged us to invite you to join our family."

I don't laugh, no matter how much I want to. "To join your family?" Dad taught me, whenever I'm having trouble with something a mark says that's so painfully stupid that I'm going to react badly, that I should just repeat it back to them.

It works.

"Exactly. It's just Dave, me, Emerson, and Bea. I think you'll like our house, even though it's small. It's comfortable, and no one smokes." She winks at me.

Does she get that it was a lie? I don't have asthma, and I don't need new lungs because of Dad's crew smoking. I'm totally lost about why she would even ask me to come live with them, and it's even stranger that Bea and her crazy mom aren't mad at me.

"Please say yes." Bea has brushed herself off and is standing behind her mom now, peering over her shoulder. "Please." She smiles, and it hurts. It makes my heart hurt really badly.

"It's real nice of you to offer," I say, "but—"

"Son." Dad's voice is curt when he lifts his hands and waves me over. It's painful to watch, because they're cuffed, but the officer next to him nods.

"Five minutes or less." His voice is gruff, but he moves a few dozen feet away.

"I'm not sure when you'll see me again," Dad says. "But you know the basics—the important stuff."

I nod, trying my best not to cry.

"We knew this was always a risk, and now it's happened, but don't worry. You got luckier than I thought possible."

Dad's not mad at me. He's not yelling that I ruined our lives with my stupid mistake. "Okay."

"That family over there." Dad whistles. "They're a special kind of stupid."

I frown. I know Dad's right, but for some reason, it still bothers me.

"Now you listen up. I don't have much time." Dad drops his voice. "There's a bird called a brown-head cowbird, you hear?"

I nod.

"That bird is smart. It figured out that laying eggs and sitting on them and then feeding the babies is a lot of work. It wants there to be more cowbirds, but it doesn't want to do the work, right? Because it's a smart bird."

I nod.

"That smart cowbird, it finds another bird that's

close to its size, one that's got a nice nest and is laying eggs. Then it goes and it shoves the dumb bird's eggs out when the mother bird's off finding food."

"Okay."

"And then it lays its eggs there. Then that dumb bird mom comes back and raises the cowbird babies for the smart bird." He grins. "That's a long con, son, but it pays off."

"I don't understand."

"I'm True North. You know that." He ruffles the hair on my head.

"But Dad—"

He shushes me. "Listen up, now. I'm almost out of time."

I sigh.

"You're about to play the longest con of all, my boy. I'd be worried, but I know you're ready."

"What?"

"Those dupes have a nice nest. They're already raising two chicks that ain't theirs. So we're going to drop you into their nest, let you win them over, and when I get out, we'll bleed them dry. Together." Dad grins. "I trust you. You know enough to do this. When I get out, it'll be the perfect way for us to start over. Alright?"

I nod, and it starts to really sink in that Dad's going away. "But it's their fault you're going to jail." I shake my head. "I don't want to live with them, with the people who got you locked up."

Dad presses his face against my cheek. "That's why you *have* to do it. We'll get our revenge, son. When I get out, you'll know everything you need to know about them, and we'll get them back, you and me. Just play the long con now, and sit in that nest, and Dad will come for you as soon as he can."

"But—"

"Never forget the number one rule."

"Dad."

"You cannot ever fall for the marks. You can't pity them. You can't care for them. You can never *ever* love them. You hear me, boy?" Dad ruffles my hair again. "Now, you go do what I taught you, you little cowbird."

To my great embarrassment, I'm crying when they close up the car and drive my dad away. But I do as he asked, and the next time Seren Colburn Fansee asks if I want to stay with them for a while, I say yes.

When Dad gets sentenced to twenty years and they ask if I want to stay with them more permanently, I grit my teeth, and I say yes again. Because Dad is True North for me, and that's what he wanted. It's hard to pretend that I like them; it's hard to disguise how angry I am that they sent Dad away.

But I do it.

And little by little, it gets easier.

But I never forget that I'm not a Fansee.

In my heart of hearts, I'm a cowbird. I'll always be a cowbird. Which is why I'll never really belong. At least, not until Dad's free.

I hope you liked this story, and I hope you're ready *** for JAKE AND OCTAVIA's STORY NEXT. Filthy Rich should be out by June of 2025 at the VERY latest. (There's a new women's fiction series I'd like to start, and I'm not sure which I will write first. With art, sometimes I have to write the story that's nagging me the most. Filthy Rich COULD be out this fall, if Jake and Octavia get annoying.)

In the meantime, if you can leave me a review, that would be amazing. <3 AND if you aren't sure what to read next, can I suggest you try my Finding Home Series, my Birch Creek Ranch Series? I've included a sample chapter of The Bequest after this, so if you want to give it a try, keep on scrolling.

SAMPLE CHAPTER THE
BEQUEST: ABIGAIL

In the week after my husband died, I said I was fine more than one hundred times. I didn't even start counting until the second day.

I was lying every single time, of course.

When Nate was first diagnosed with pancreatic cancer, I was not fine. During the next few weeks, while he underwent surgery and then every treatment they could throw at it, I was not fine. And even though I drew up every document that we might need and spent every possible moment with him before the end, after he died, I was not fine.

But now it's been a year, and with careful planning and a lot of hard work, I can actually tell the truth when someone asks how I'm doing.

"How's it going?" Robert Marwell's standing in my doorway, a half smile on his face. He's not a managing partner with Chase, Holden, and Park, but he probably will be in the next few years.

"I'm fine," I say. And I mean it.

He takes a few steps into my office and sits in one of the wingback chairs. One of the things I like best about

Robert is that even though I'm an associate and he's a partner, he doesn't summon me. He walks all the way down the hall to my office when he has something to discuss. "They're voting in early September," he says. "I know that feels like a long way off, but I think it's good timing."

In just four and a half months, they'll be voting on whether to add any new partners. "Why is it good?" It's not that I think it's bad, but I'd like to know his reasoning.

He glances back at the open doorway and drops his voice. "You've been at the firm for just as long as Nate and I, but other than your first two years, you've always been part time. If you were wanting to be Of Counsel or something, it would be a lock. But as it is. . ." He looks over his shoulder again.

Who's he worried might overhear?

His voice is barely a whisper now. "Lance isn't keen on adding you. Since you own Nate's share in a limited capacity, if we make you partner—"

"I'll be entitled to buy my own share when I'm voted in, and then I'd have double the ownership of anyone other than the named partners—which would give me twice the voting rights."

"I told them that didn't matter. How often do we disagree? When would your double share actually matter?" Robert shrugs. "You know Lance. It's less about what will really happen and more about his ego."

"But why is September good?" I press. "It's not like he gets happier and more easygoing over the summer." If anything, all the people taking vacation drives his blood pressure up.

Robert laughs. "No, but my other piece of news will help you understand."

I raise my eyebrows. "And?"

"The BenchMark case goes to trial in August." He leans forward. "I made sure you're on it, but when it comes time to try the case, I'll step back and let you take first chair."

A big win on something like that would go a long way toward reassuring the partners that I can perform when the stakes are high.

He crosses his arms. "If you win something like this, no one could justify voting against you, not even Lance."

I'm not even sure what to say. It's such a generous offer, and it's exactly the opportunity for which I've been hoping. With Robert in my corner, if this all goes as planned, my family will be back on track by the end of this year. "Thank you, so much."

He stands up and shakes his head. "Please. Nate would have done the same for me if our roles were reversed."

"Maybe not." I scrunch my nose. "I can't even imagine him handing a case to Maisie."

"You know what I mean," Robert says. "If I still had a wife and she needed his help, he would have given it." When he laughs, his eyes brighten and his perfect, white teeth flash. Even with a tiny streak of grey at his temples, Robert's a good-looking guy. "Nate certainly chose more wisely than I did. I'm just sorry that—" He swallows. "You know what I mean."

I do. Robert was nearly as upset as our family when Nate passed away. They'd been best friends since college. And I didn't meet the two of them until law school. I still remember the summer when the three of us had our first clerkship, together, at this very firm.

He pivots on his heel and walks to the doorway,

pausing just before he leaves. "Do you have plans for lunch?"

I haven't gone out for lunch since Nate died. He must know that—he's certainly never asked me before. A warning bell goes off in the back of my brain. Is Robert asking me out? Surely not. First of all, he's one of my oldest friends—and Nate's. That alone would make it strange, but secondly, Nate's only been gone a year. Surely no one could expect me to date again so soon.

"It would be nice to have a little time away from the office to discuss the plans for the case. I obviously can't mention my full plans too loudly here." He looks surreptitiously up and down the hall one last time, like we're spies or something. "I have a deposition this afternoon, so if you want to hammer out some rough plans, lunch is probably our best bet." He tilts his head sideways. "I promise not to bite."

The case, duh. I'm such an idiot sometimes. Hopefully he didn't notice my hesitation. "Oh, sure."

My cell phone rings. Only my kids or their school call me on it, as Robert knows. "Take your call. I'll circle back around in half an hour."

Tension I didn't realize I was holding in my back releases the second he's gone, and I swipe to answer. "Hello?"

"Hey Mom, it's me."

"Gosh, I'm so glad you clarified, Ethan. One of these days I might even figure out how this phone thing works, and when I see your name, I'll know who's calling."

"I'm not holding my breath, boomer," he says.

"That's rude. I'm Gen Y, okay?"

"Barely."

"Everything okay?" He rarely calls me when I'm at work. Text messages are so much easier.

"Yeah, I'm fine. But look, Mom—I know you're busy, and I know your gut instinct is going to be to shut me down, but can you just listen?"

I suppress the giant sigh that's trying to claw its way out. "Is this about Dave's speakers again? Because we—"

"Mom, no, it's not about the speakers."

"What, then?"

"Just listen, right? Before you freak out or say no, you'll just hear me out?"

"I am listening," I say. "And I never freak out."

"You do say no a lot."

"What do you want?"

"Look, Riley's dad's competing in the Baja 1000 and they need some extra cash, so he's selling his brand new RZR XP turbo."

"Didn't Riley wreck it last week?"

"I mean, it got a little banged up, but it's nothing I can't fix. Seriously, Mom. Once it's repaired, it'll be worth thirty grand, easy, but Riley said he'd sell it to me for nineteen!"

I don't laugh. Or at least, I try not to laugh. "You don't want me to say no, and yet, you don't have the money to buy that. Please help me out. What am I supposed to say right now?"

"Mom!"

"Ethan!" I know he's struggling with his dad being gone. Spending time with Riley and his dad has been helpful, I think. But I don't have the time, and we don't have the money with only my (currently much lower) income, to buy huge things like fancy side-by-sides.

"How can you say I don't have the money? I have like eighty grand!"

"Are you talking about your college fund?" He's got to be kidding. All my sympathy for his cause just disappeared if he's really trying to convince me to sacrifice his future on some fun weekend plans. "I know you're not talking about spending your college fund on something this frivolous. And may I remind you, we would then need a trailer and a truck in order to even use that thing."

"Mom—"

"Ethan, I don't have time—"

"You didn't even listen to me," he says. "With the money I'd save getting this one—"

"The money you would *save?*" I can't help laughing this time. "You sound like a spoiled housewife. You aren't saving a single dollar—you're buying something that costs, what? Twenty-five times the amount you have personally saved?"

"I have a job now, Mom. And—"

My office phone rings.

Even Ethan knows what that means. "I know, I know. You have to answer that. But don't hang up. Hear me out at least. I'll wait."

I often wonder what God was thinking when he planned out the teenage years. They're emotionally miswired, they rage against the people who are helping them (who have nothing to gain, incidentally), and they're never satisfied with anything. Maybe it's not about the kids. Maybe these years were created to expand parents' patience. "Fine." I set my cell phone on the desk and pick up my office line.

"Hello?"

"Mrs. Brooks? Mrs. Nathaniel Brooks?"

I haven't been called Mrs. Nathaniel Brooks in nearly

a year. It catches me by surprise and leaves me almost unable to speak.

"Hello?"

"Yes," I manage to say. "That's me." I clear my throat.

"Good." The man shuffles some papers. "My name is Karl Swift." Something about his voice, perhaps the wobbly timbre, makes me think that Karl is quite old.

"What can I help you with, Mr. Swift?"

"Er, well, it might be more correct for me to tell you what I think I can help you with."

He sounds like Bilbo Baggins at his birthday party. "Okay."

"I'm actually a lawyer as well—I found your name on your firm website from a simple search. I'm calling to notify you that last night, I read a will that had been posted in all the local papers and online."

"A will for whom?" I still have no idea why he called, and I'm beginning to think he was improperly named. Spit it out, Ol' Man River!

"Jedediah Brooks passed away almost two weeks ago."

Brooks. He's related to Nate, then. The name finally registers. "Nate's uncle?"

"Even so," Mr. Swift says.

"I'm very sorry to hear that he passed," I say, rotely. I didn't meet Nate's uncle more than a handful of times, and even then we barely exchanged a handful of words. He had a full head of white hair the first time we met, nearly twenty years ago at my wedding to Nate. He must have lived quite a long life.

"Thank you. His death was quite a shock, but at least it was quick. Jed always said he wanted it to be fast, not drawn out."

My hand trembles where it's holding the phone.

Nate's wasn't quick at all—and it was so fast I could barely think straight. "Is that why you called? To let me know that he'd passed?"

"Not precisely," Mr. Swift says. "You see, as I understand it, both of Mr. Brooks' nephews, Nathaniel and Paul, predeceased him."

I murmur my assent. They were both so young. It still sounds so wrong to agree that they're both dead, even now.

"In that case, there is quite a substantial bequest made to your children, Mrs. Brooks."

"Excuse me?"

"Jed has a three thousand, two hundred and eleven acre cattle ranch out here, on the northern side of Utah. It's one of only six properties in the state that date back to the original land grant. In fact, portions of the property are actually in Wyoming, but it's mostly in a place called Daggett County."

"Are you saying that my children's great-uncle left them a three-thousand acre ranch?"

"Not entirely."

I wish Mr. Swift would cut to the chase. For a lawyer, he certainly lacks in clarity. "What does the will say, then?"

"Specifically, it provides that the ranch and all its appurtenances, including the home, a guest house, two large barns, an outbuilding for storage, and some three hundred and fifty head of cattle should be left to your children and the children of Nathaniel's brother, Paul, per stirpes."

I wonder what something like that is worth. Maybe Ethan could get his Razor after all. "Well, that's unexpected."

"However." Mr. Swift rustles more papers. "In order for the bequest to vest, the heirs or, in the case that they're minors, their appointed guardians, must adequately and actively operate the Birch Creek Ranch for a period of one full year."

Whoa. "A year?"

"Yes, that's correct."

"And if I hire someone?"

"I will, of course, send you the actual document so that you can read it yourself, but it was drawn up by a rather hot-shot lawyer in California. I doubt it will have any surprising loopholes."

"Does that mean I can't hire someone to run it for us?"

"I'm afraid the bequest stipulates that the heirs or their guardian must operate the ranch themselves and live on site for the full year. It allows no more than three ten day runs away from the ranch during that period."

And the Razor is back off the table. "My email address is listed on the same firm website," I say. "I would appreciate if you sent me a copy of that will."

"Of course," Mr. Swift says. "And I'm sorry it's not a simpler bequest."

"That's alright," I say. "I'm no stranger to the phrase, 'easy come, easy go.' I certainly didn't expect anything from dear Uncle Jedediah, so I won't be disappointed that nothing has materialized. My condolences, again."

"So you anticipate that you'll be turning down the offer?"

"I'm quite positive," I say. "If you'd like to send over whatever paperwork your office would like to keep on file, I'm happy to sign it."

"If none of his nephew's children accept the bequest,

the ranch will be sold and the proceeds will be donated to the Institute of Research into Alien Life on Planet Earth."

The *what?* "That's certainly. . .interesting."

"The RALPE Institute received annual donations from Jed from the time he was doing well enough to make them. It's not everyone's thing, but that's what the will says. If that changes your mind, please do let me know."

"I wish them every bit of luck finding alien life." I'm proud of myself for keeping my voice steady.

"Do you happen to have a phone number on a Mrs. Paul Brooks?"

"Amanda?" I scroll through my contacts on Outlook. "Sure." I rattle off the phone number that I rarely use, and wish him a good day.

Robert pokes his head around the corner just as I hang up. "Ready?"

I'm about to stand when I remember that Ethan might still be on hold. "Almost."

"I'll go down and get the car. Meet you at the front?"

"Perfect, thanks." I press the phone to my ear. "Ethan? Are you still there?"

But he's not on the line anymore. I should have known. Teenagers aren't celebrated for their long attention spans. I'm sure he'll talk my ear off about all the reasons buying a wrecked Razor is the best idea he's ever had as soon as I get home from work.

Robert's waiting for me when I reach the ground level, his black BMW sleek and shiny. When he opens the door and stands up, my heart races. He can't possibly be planning to come around and open my door for me, right? That would be squarely in date territory.

I practically leap for the passenger door and open it myself, sliding inside as quickly as I can in four-inch heels and a fitted suit skirt.

"Where do you want to eat?" he asks.

I have no idea what's good around here. Before Nate died, I only came in for the morning, never staying for lunch, and since his death, I've been coming in at 7:15 after school drop off and leaving at 3:15, so I haven't had time to take a lunch and still work a full day.

"I'm fine with anything other than Chinese food," I say.

"You don't like Chinese?" He frowns. "Really?"

"I'll eat P.F. Changs or Pei Wei," I say. "Maybe it's the MSG, but all the other Chinese food I've tried gives me a headache."

"How about Thai food?"

"I like that."

"Great." He spends the rest of the drive and our entire meal discussing his plan for the case and my role in it.

I'm glad I brought a notepad along, because I fill two full pages with notes.

"You didn't have to write all of that down," he says. "I'd have been happy to clarify anything you forget."

"I don't like asking people to repeat themselves."

"Probably why everyone likes working with you."

When the waitress brings the check, Robert doesn't even glance at it. He just hands her his black American Express.

"You don't want to verify you were charged correctly?" I try not to let a note of censure enter my tone, but I'm not sure I succeed.

"You're such a lawyer." He laughs. "But the firm is

paying—we worked every second. We both drank water, and we each only ordered one entree. I'm not sure how badly they could possibly screw it up."

I look at my hands as I smooth the napkin over my lap. "I do tend to worry about every little detail."

"It's what makes you a top notch litigator."

"And a giant pain in the rear." I don't look up, because I know it's true. I don't need to see the confirmation in his eyes.

"Abigail."

I swallow.

"Abby."

I finally look up.

His expression is soft. "You work harder than anyone I know. No one thinks you're a pain."

I am, however, terrible at accepting compliments with grace. "Well, thanks."

"I mean it. Not everyone wants to add another partner, but one hundred percent of the partners acknowledge that you're the highest caliber associate." He sighs. "It actually may be part of the reason they don't want to promote you. You won't be available to make their lives easier if you're handling your own cases."

"I'm also the oldest associate." I didn't mind when Nate was earning money too, but I can't really catch up on the savings goals for our family on an associate's salary. I try not to think about the hit our savings took when we paid for the expensive treatments we threw at Nate's cancer, but I can't help it when I get the statements. It weighs on me.

"We aren't that old," Robert says.

"Bush was president when we were in law school," I say. "*Friends* was still on the air."

"You were so stunning in law school." He leans back in his chair, his head shaking slowly. "Everyone called you Elle, remember?"

"That pissed me off," I say.

"You did sort of decide to do law school on a whim," he says. "You didn't know the different types of law."

"I was nineteen years old. I didn't know gasoline came from crude oil and not natural gas." I laugh.

"You did."

"Fine, I was pretty smart for a teenager, but I still don't get it. It's not like that character started school young. She was just unmotivated and ditzy. She went for a guy. It was offensive."

"The women probably intended it as an insult, but none of the guys took it that way."

I huff. "I looked nothing like Reese Witherspoon in *Legally Blonde*."

He snorts. "Nothing like her? You were blonde, you were in great shape, and you dressed stylishly."

"I *was* blonde?" I pretend to be annoyed. "I pay a lot for this color."

"I'm so sorry," Robert says. "You were as blonde then as you are now. Is that better?" He rolls his eyes. "Lawyers are the worst."

"They really are," I agree.

"Law students may be the only thing worse, but you showed them—top of the class." Robert looks down at the table. "I was pretty stupid as a law student too."

"Whoa," I say. "Are you finally admitting that your Birkenstocks were a crime against fashion?"

He meets my eyes, his gaze as intense as I've ever seen it. "You had just broken up with your college boyfriend when we started, remember?"

For some reason, mentioning my breakup with Shawn makes my heart race, which is crazy. That guy was a major loser. "I do, yeah. I was kind of wrecked."

"Nate and I had been roommates at UCLA and we both met you at orientation—you were wearing that yellow sundress. But I'm not sure you ever knew that we were both interested."

What? I've never heard this, not once.

"Nate insisted he was going to go after you right away. My sister told me that was idiotic—if you really like a girl, you wait for her to rebound first." He swallows. "I thought it was wise to play the 'friend' angle. Once Nate struck out, I figured you'd be ready for something real." He sighs. "Then you married Nate."

"Robert—"

"I know it's probably a shock, but I just need to get it out there. That's still the biggest mistake I've ever made, but I never let myself regret it. I loved both of you, and you were really happy. But now. . ."

Robert liked me? I had no idea. "But you and Maisie—"

"You mean the girl who was the closest I could find to a facsimile of you?" He snorts. "She wasn't nearly close enough, clearly. You know how miserable we were better than anyone."

Is he implying that if she'd been more like me, they'd have been happy? "I'm not sure—"

"Fool me once, shame on you. Fool me twice, shame on me, right? That's how the saying goes?"

He's hopping around so fast I can't keep up.

"Earlier today, I *was* asking you on a date, or at least I was trying to ask you. Then you looked like I'd stabbed a puppy, so I pretended it was a work lunch. I almost let it be, but I can't do that, not again, Abby. Because if I miss my chance a second time, I'll never be able to live with myself."

That's the first chapter of The Bequest, so if you enjoyed it, you can grab it on any platform where you like to read.

ACKNOWLEDGMENTS

I am so grateful for my readers. You guys make this whole thing possible.

And for this book, I'm grateful that I have an epic cousin, Katie, who always taught me that true beauty goes far deeper than our skin.

I'm grateful for my husband and kids and their endless patience.

I am NOT grateful for my horses, who kept going lame and having issues that made it almost impossible for me to finish this book. Stop being stupid, horses. PLEASE. (Just for, like, two months??) :P

ABOUT THE AUTHOR

I have five kids, eight horses, three dogs, three cats, thirty chickens, and just the one husband. I'm a lawyer who gave up law to follow her passion, and thankfully, I've found readers who appreciate my books enough that I'm not a laughingstock... I LOVE my job, which you guys make possible. Thank you for loving my weird stories almost as much as I love writing them.

The Reboot

The Surprise

The Setback

The Lookback

Children's Picture Book

Yuck! What's for Dinner?

I also write Fantasy Romance under Bridget E. Baker.

The Dragon Captured Series: (dragon shifter romance!)

Ensnared

Entwined

Embroiled

Embattled

The Russian Witch's Curse: (horse shifter romance!)

My Queendom for a Horse

My Dark Horse Prince

My High Horse Czar

My Wild Horse King

My Trojan Horse Majesty

The Magical Misfits Series: (paranormal humor!)

My Pigeon Familiar

My Mongrel Pack

The Birthright Series:

Displaced (1)

unForgiven (2)

Disillusioned (3)

misUnderstood (4)